Praise for Sharan Newman and *Guinevere*

"Newman has the rare gift of creating characters as believable and alive as our own acquaintances.... With an exciting plot and a graceful, sparkling style, *Guinevere* is a real joy to read."
— *Denver Post*

"Sharan Newman writes with all the fierceness and magic the Arthurian legend deserves." — *Asbury Park Press*

"*Guinevere* is sensitive and imaginative.... Sharan Newman does for Arthur's queen what Mary Stewart did for Merlin and Arthur." — *Chattanooga Times*

"An uncloying fable with a strain of tangy humor and a lilt of lyrical fancy." — *Kirkus Reviews*

"Guinevere emerges as an intriguing, well-realized character ... a fresh and original addition to Arthurian romances."
— *Library Journal*

GUINEVERE

GUINEVERE

SHARAN NEWMAN

TOR®

A TOM DOHERTY ASSOCIATES BOOK
NEW YORK

GUINEVERE

Copyright © 1981, 1996 by Sharan Newman

The lines from Ovid's *Metamorphoses* (Book I, lines 102–112) were translated by Rolfe Humphries and originally published by the Indiana University Press, 1955. All rights reserved.

This book is printed on acid-free paper.

A Tor Book
Published by Tom Doherty Associates, Inc.
175 Fifth Avenue
New York, NY 10010

Tor Books on the World Wide Web.
http://www.tor.com

Tor® is a registered trademark of Tom Doherty Associates, Inc.

Design by Laura Hammond

Library of Congress Cataloging-in-Publication Data

Newman, Sharan.
    Guinevere / by Sharan Newman.
      p.   cm.
    "A Tom Doherty Associates book."
    ISBN 0–312–86233–4

    1. Guinevere, Queen (Legendary character)—Fiction.
2. Arthurian romances—Adaptations. 3. Queens—Great Britain—Fiction.
I. Title.
PS3564.E926G8   1996
813'.54—dc20   96–23853
                                    CIP

First Tor Edition: November 1996

Printed in the United States of America

0 9 8 7 6 5 4 3 2 1

For Lisa
Who has golden hair

GUINEVERE

CHAPTER ONE

There was a sound in the night. The child woke suddenly, clutching the blankets. Someone was calling her, she was sure. Was it coming, then, the time they never mentioned? Were the Saxon invaders even now crashing down the gates, crushing her mother's flowers with their ugly, studded boots? Why else would anyone wake her in the middle of the night? She held her breath, straining to hear. The still moonlight poured between the slats in her shuttered window. A shadow passed, blocking the light for an instant. She bit the rough blanket to keep from crying out. It was only the guard, steadily pacing his watch from house to wall and back. Slowly her body relaxed. If the guard were still on duty she had no cause for alarm. There were no screams, no clashing of sword and shield. Nothing but the moonlight and the muted slap of the guard's sandals as he passed the window. There was no surprise attack, no invasion. But then who had called her? It had been so insistent, so urgent.

Fear had made her thirsty. She slid from her bed and tiptoed over to the pitcher on her dressing table across the room. Her bare feet caught a little on the tiles of the mosaic on the floor. In the semi-dark the pattern was only a series of blobs, but by daylight it was a great floral wreath with animals playing in the center around a giant tree. She loved it and stopped to pat with her toe the blob she knew was a fat baby rabbit. The picture was somewhat childish for her now, since she was past twelve, but she had slept in that room since babyhood and the mosaic was as familiar and comforting to her as the face of her nurse. Though the spring night was chilly, the floor was warm from the hot water pipes that ran beneath it. She reached the table and fumbled about for her cup. Her hand brushed against a pot of herbs and it crashed to the floor. In the midnight quiet the sound of the breaking pot seemed to echo through the house. Before the child had time to recover, a shape appeared at the door, an old woman, wrapped in a blanket.

"Lady Guinevere!" The girl jumped guiltily. "What are you doing out of bed, startling the entire household from their sleep?"

"I woke up, Flora, and wanted some water."

"And look at this mess!" Flora stooped and gathered up the shards of the pot. "Dirt everywhere, and my poor rosemary plant!"

"I'm sorry." Guinevere felt on the floor for the pieces. She stepped on the plant and a pungent aroma filled the room. "I didn't see it in the dark."

"That's why you should stay in bed in the dark, instead of roaming around. There, we'll clean up the rest in the morning. Here's your water. Now hop! Right back to bed. I don't want to hear a peep out of you until well after sunrise."

So Guinevere sipped her water and climbed back into bed. Flora bustled about, pulling up the blanket and tucking it in with the strange soothing noises people make to quiet sleepy children. Then she slipped out and down the hallway to her own room. Guinevere lay awake for a while. Now she had two mysteries: What had wakened her, and why, under her blanket, was Flora dressed in gold and scarlet robes?

There were no answers. She listened for a time, but heard nothing more. Finally, she rolled on to her side, her hands crossed under her chin, fast asleep.

When she next awoke, the sun was sending bright ribbons of light into the room. Motes were dancing through them settling on her bed. She had only a vague memory of waking in the night, a subtle feeling of disquiet. The sense that someone had called her was still strong. Who or what could it have been? She lay in bed a few minutes, considering. The clatter of the household preparing for the day's work intruded on her thoughts and cleared away her uneasy feeling. It must have been only a dream. The morning was bright and she suddenly remembered that her father had promised her a special treat today—to take her riding, just the two of them. She got up quickly, the last vestige of her worry gone.

Guinevere's mother, Guenlian, sat at her dressing table. She was watching her husband, Leodegrance, put on his riding clothes. She shook her head with disapproval.

"You are spoiling the child, my dear," she told him. "You have too many other duties to waste an entire morning out riding with your daughter."

Leodegrance grimaced as he pulled the lacings more tightly on his boots. "I promised her we would go riding today. She is bored here, now that her brothers are gone. She needs the exercise and so do I."

"*You* are bored now that her brothers are gone," she retorted. "You won't admit how much you miss them. They say the Saxons have sent over a hundred boats this spring to bolster their forces here. And the Irish raids on the west are getting more frequent."

She wasn't thinking of Guinevere then, but of her three sons all fighting together against the Saxon incursions in the north.

"My cousin Cador is a fine general, Guenlian. We could not have entrusted our boys to anyone better. Would you rather we had run away like the others?"

"Don't taunt me with that," Guenlian said, annoyed. "I have never been one to counsel flight. We have stayed and built and rebuilt our home when everyone else fled. Did I ever suggest that we would be happier or safer in Armorica? Britain is our home and I will live to see it Roman again. What else have we fought all these years for? Why else have we raised our sons to be warriors? Can't you allow me at least the luxury of worrying like a mother? I fear for them, and Guinevere, too. But I am not a coward any more than you!"

Leodegrance came to her, laughing at her indignation. "If only we could set you against the Saxons, my love. I'm sure they would abandon their huts and return to their own land in terror."

She relaxed and smiled ruefully. "After all these years, you still enjoy teasing me."

"After all these years, you still respond so quickly to teasing." He kissed her, still laughing. "Now I am going to spoil our daughter."

They were interrupted by a maid with the information that a messenger had come with news from Lord Cador. They both forgot the quarrel and hurried out to meet him.

Guinevere had finished washing and was dressed by the time Flora came for her. The older woman looked tired as she laid out the brushes and combs to arrange Guinevere's hair. Guinevere was making a point these days of showing Flora that she no longer needed a nurse to supervise her washing and dressing. But her mother said that a lady always needed a maid to attend to her hair, so she submitted to having it brushed and scented and braided into two long, golden chains.

"Some might say that this is Saxon hair," Flora would often croon. "But don't you believe them, my love. Their color is like old straw, left too long in the sun; but yours is true gold, burnished like a shield, red in the firelight. I could weave you a crown of it and you could find no better."

Guinevere hardly listened. She was accustomed to her hair being a source of wonder to those around her. She rarely thought about it, except when she had to have it washed or when it came undone and caught on branches while she was riding. She never even wondered why she should look so different from her family. Her parents and brothers were all dark of hair and eyes. To them she seemed a sort of changeling, a radiant gift. She didn't even have the Roman nose they were all so proud of, although there was still time for one to develop. But Guinevere wasn't of an age to care. She knew only that she was safe and loved and that was as it should be.

Even though she had gone with her family to the mountain refuges, she had never felt danger. Her existence was protected and she was kept apart from the rest of the society. Only occasionally did rumors of Saxons or tales of great battles and warriors enter her life, and then only as stories, told and sung by wandering scholars. She didn't know that their quiet, ordered, civilized way of life was already an anachronism. For a hundred years no true Roman citizen had lived in Britain, but her parents and their few remaining friends and relatives behaved as if the emperor would return any day, leading fresh legions to reinstate Roman rule.

These were not important concerns to Guinevere. Caesar and Saxon were equally distant to her. Already she had forgotten her fear in the night. It was high May, a glorious morning, and she was going riding with her father. Her joy at this rare treat was only slightly dimmed by the fact that she would first have to spend an hour in the chapel for prayers and then two more with her tutor. There was always a lot to look at during prayers and she had finally talked old Tenuantius into closing Cicero for the summer and letting her read Ovid. The *Metamorphoses* was almost as full of spring as the day outside. She hummed happily as she crossed the garden to the little family chapel. At the door, she carefully smoothed her robe and arranged her veil so that it covered her hair and fell across her forehead.

The stone building was far older than the others in the complex. It had been there when the Romans came. Guinevere's great-great-grandfather had found it, and the hot spring hidden in a cavern nearby. He had painted over the crude drawings of horses and men on the building's walls and tiled the floors with a mosaic of Apollo. Later, when the family had converted to Christianity, some of the tiles were removed and fish and the Greek letters Chi Rho added, as well as a nimbus about the god's head, making him into the image of Christ. The hot spring was farther inside the hill now, but it still provided the water for the heating pipes and the baths.

The rest of the household had already gathered around the altar. Leodegrance and Guenlian insisted that all the house and stable servants attend morning and evening prayers. There were also some young men and women who were being fostered in the house, and Guinevere's parents were very serious about their religious training.

Flora always stood between the family and the rest of the servants. Guinevere thought it was her way of telling them that she was almost a member of the family. But today she noticed that Flora didn't exactly face the altar but turned more to the west as if she were worshiping at some other shrine. Guenlian gently nudged her and she returned to her prayers.

As she had hoped, the lessons for that day were not hard. Tenuantius was preoccupied with a letter he had just received purporting to be an exact copy of a newly discovered epistle of St. Paul. It was all in Greek, a language the copier didn't speak, and Tenuantius was spending all his waking hours and most of his dreams trying to decipher the badly formed letters. He barely listened as Guinevere progressed from the Age of Gold to the iniquities of the Iron Age. He didn't even stop her for one of his lectures on the derivation of the proper names. So Guinevere enjoyed the story without interruption, until Tenuantius signaled that she might leave.

As soon as she was released, she rushed to her room and began to pull on her riding shoes, leather slippers attached to thick leather thongs, which were wrapped around wads of cloth reaching up to her knees. She tied them carefully so that there was no space at her ankle between the leather and the cloth. Then she hurried to find her father.

The air in the courtyard was still. The sunlight streamed in between the branches of the fruit trees or bounced off the dusty white walls. The rays were brilliant and seemed thick enough to hold. The only movement was that of the motes in the light, slowly twirling, spinning down. The only sound was the slap-flop of Guinevere's shoes on the stone walk. At first she didn't notice the strange silence. Then she stopped. She was almost to the stable gate and still there was no noise. She was vaguely annoyed.

"Where is everyone?" she muttered. "Have they forgotten that I was to ride today?"

She stamped her foot. "Very well, I'll just follow them myself."

The horses were all still in their stalls. The stable seemed deserted, too. Guinevere felt that someone was watching her. She swung around and saw the outline of someone standing in the shadows behind the open gate. She stared and then realized that it was only Caet, the stableboy.

"Caet, you frightened me!" she reproached him. "Where is my father? Where are the guards and the men-at-arms? Don't they know I am to go riding today?"

Caet stepped into the light, but the shadows seemed to come

with him. He was truly one of the Old People, not Celtic or Roman or Saxon, but one who must have sprung from the earth itself. His hair was a dark, sooty brown and his eyes gray. He was small, hardly taller than Guinevere, although he was four or five years older. He rarely spoke and therefore was considered simple by the garrulous families who lived in the area. His ancestors had been slaves for three hundred years. Leodegrance had freed his parents and he had been born free, but only in name and he knew it. Guinevere had played with him when she was small. He had made her toys and steadied her when she first learned to ride, and she was very fond of him in her unthinking way. She knew he wasn't simple, but had never bothered to find out more about him. If she had paid attention, he would have given himself away many times. Even now he was staring at her so intently that it made her nervous.

"Caet, please go and find my father for me," she smiled politely. "Tell him I am waiting here for him. I'm not letting anyone leave without me."

Caet bowed and left.

Soon after, she heard the clatter of many voices. She ran to Leodegrance as he approached and hugged him reproachfully. "Father, you had forgotten me!"

"Not at all, my love," he replied. "But I can't take you with me today. A message has come from our cousin, Cador, and I must spend a few days riding to the villas of the other landholders to consult with them. Now, don't be disappointed. There is nothing we can do about it. Come to your mother and perhaps we can think of something else you can do today."

Guinevere didn't complain, but she wasn't happy. He had promised to take her out! She didn't understand how anything could be that urgent. He could leave tomorrow. Nevertheless, she trotted obediently beside him as he thought lovingly of his docile daughter.

Guenlian smiled at the pouting face. "I think it would be good for you to get out in the sun today, even if you can't ride. I was going to send the maids out to the meadow near the forest to gather herbs and wildflowers to dry for winter possets. You and Flora may go with them."

7

Guinevere looked at her imploringly. It was a poor change from galloping freely through the woods with one's father to primly picking flowers in a meadow with one's nurse! Still, it was better than nothing. They were so careful about letting her go out of the compound alone these days.

So, a short time later Guinevere and Flora with the maids and foster girls went off across the fields. They were dressed in light, loose robes with their arms bare and only a narrow fillet around their waists. The girls were laughing and swinging their baskets, for this was a holiday to them. Although she wanted to run with the others, at least, Guinevere followed with Flora.

"You stay with me, my dove," the old woman ordered. "I'm too old to trot around like that and I need your strong shoulder to help me."

Guinevere laughed at that. "Why, Flora, you can run faster than any of them. I've seen you. The time I fell from the walnut tree, you were across the court so quickly that you almost caught me. And when you found that Caet had pulled hairs from Sybil's tail to make me a ring, why, you chased him completely around the house and caught him, even though he had a good start of you."

Flora's lined face grew sharp. "Are you making fun of your old nurse?" There was a warning in her voice that Guinevere knew well.

"No, Flora," she answered meekly, although there was a teasing look in her eyes. "Would you like to lean on me for a while?"

"For a bit." And Flora rested her arm heavily on the girl's shoulder, causing her to stagger. Guinevere set her teeth and bore it. Sometimes Flora could be very aggravating.

Soon they came to the meadow. Tall, scented grasses and flowers covered a series of small hills. At the western edge of it, with no prelude, the forest began. It was as if someone purposely kept the area clear, as if the forest was not allowed to encroach on that spot. The flowers waved, blue, white, red, and yellow in the warm sun, and the young women happily began to gather them. They flitted through the grasses, singing and laughing, and then finally sat on a little mound near the center of the meadow, to sort the blooms and buds and tie them in bunches, gossiping all the while. The long-forgotten queen buried beneath them would have smiled to see their pleasure and rejoiced that the world had changed so little.

Flora spread her shawl in the shade of a large oak tree and sat down to rest. She looked very tired and Guinevere noticed the silver glinting in her hair with a pang of remorse. Perhaps the long walk had really wearied her.

"Now, my dear," the nurse told her. "You may walk a little into the woods if you like or stay with the serving girls and other ladies. But if you go, be sure to stay to the path and don't walk more than a hundred steps in. The sun doesn't reach very far into that forest and it's easy to lose your direction. I will rest a while, since I was robbed of my sleep last night. Now take your basket and your cape and bring me back something beautiful and rare."

Delighted, Guinevere gave her an apologetic kiss and skipped into the woods. Flora leaned her head wearily against the tree. She was getting old, she thought: too old to be leading a double life.

The forest started so suddenly that within a few steps it surrounded Guinevere. From the brilliant sun-drenched field she found herself in a cool, green opaque light. The path was soft with centuries of pine needles and spring rain. Here grew the tiny, shy flowers that Guinevere loved best, lily of the valley and star flowers. Others were delicate shades of red and lavender with clear yellow veins in their fragile petals. She had no name for these, which made them all the more remarkable and mysterious. She knelt so that her face was next to them and brushed one with her cheek.

"I cannot pick you," she told it softly. "I tried once, to take you home to mother, but you crumpled and died in my hand. Stay here, where you are fresh and beautiful. I will find something else for Flora."

And gently she left the little flower, safe among the ferns. Deep among the leaves, dark blue eyes shone approval.

Guinevere wandered here and there through the trees. She didn't even pretend to stay to the path, for she was sure she could find it again. She went far more than a hundred steps because she

9

had long since forgotten to count them. She was intensely happy. She was alone, a wonderful event in itself, and there was something rare and beautiful to be found. The sunlight scattered itself about her in such giddy patterns that she hardly noticed its slow downward slant. It was late afternoon and she was far into the forest when a sound in the bushes startled her into awareness.

"Flora will be furious!" was her first thought. She piled together the herbs and flowers she had picked, along with a few smooth stones and other curious things she had found. They were dumped randomly into her basket. A wild perfume arose as the stones crushed the plants. She stared about her as if she expected the path to appear at her feet. It was then that she realized how far she had wandered.

"I've lost myself, how stupid!" Guinevere was not overly concerned, for in her whole life she had never had a difficulty that someone hadn't quickly helped her out of. Being lost in a forest with night approaching wasn't any worse than climbing too high in the walnut tree or having a horse run away with one. Someone had climbed up and carried her down and someone had raced after her and calmed the horse. Someone would soon come to find her. She wrapped her cape about her shoulders and composed herself to wait.

After about fifteen minutes it occurred to her that she might just as well walk a bit toward home and help those hunting for her. After an hour of walking she began to wonder if she hadn't missed them somewhere. A little later she noticed that the shadows under the trees were getting longer and darker.

"If they don't come soon," she reasoned, "it will be dark and they will have a lot of trouble finding me."

She began to feel a whisper of concern then, as shreds of tales about forests at night came back to her. As a small child, she had been warned that ghosts and monsters walked the woods after dark, hunting for children to carry away to the underworld to be slaves. Guenlian had informed her daughter that they were Christians and civilized Romans and didn't believe in such nonsense. In matters of that sort, Guinevere always trusted her mother over Flora. However, the dimming light made strange shapes among the trees and undergrowth. From the corner of her eye, Guinevere saw huge, scaly hands reaching out for her. When she turned to face them, they vanished into the shadows. She wasn't panicky yet, but nervous. She found what looked like a narrow path and stumbled onto it. Tree roots rose from it, and stones that were eager to trip her or bruise her feet. The twilight above her head was deepening to night and a few pale stars glittered.

She was beginning to give way to fear, stumbling, her dress ripped from encounters with branches, her hair dusted with bark and cobwebs. She sank down, tears starting. Suddenly a light shone before her. It was somewhere behind the bushes; a silver gleam. It couldn't be a lantern or torch, but perhaps the reflection of one off a shield. Guinevere plunged toward it, paying no attention to the stones and grasping branches. As she came to where she had seen it shining, the light moved on. Gasping with exertion, she tried to call out.

"Here I am! Wait! I'm just behind you! Please, stop! Wait for me!"

It was still moving away, becoming only a dim glow in the dark. She ran faster.

"Soldiers of Leodegrance! It is I, Guinevere!"

Still the light moved away from her.

On and on it went, always just too far away to be clearly seen. She was not aware of time or the forest about her, only the ache in her side and the dryness in her throat and the silver shining before her.

Suddenly, the light vanished. Guinevere gave a deep sobbing cry and dove through the thick stand of berry bushes where she had seen it last. Scratched and bleeding, she tumbled onto the main path, not far from where she had entered the forest that afternoon.

As she lay there, panting and coughing, her body numb with exhaustion and relief, she noticed something shining on a branch above her. Curious, she pulled herself partway up and crawled over to it. It was a long, thin strand of something silver. Guinevere couldn't tell whether it was reflecting the moonlight or if it gave off a light of its own. She reached up and gently pulled it down. It wasn't thread or wire.

"It's too thick for hair and too fine to be anything else," she thought.

Then, in spite of her pain and weariness, Guinevere smiled.

"Something rare and and lovely," she almost laughed. "Now I shall have a gift for Flora."

She started to put it into her basket and then realized that she had dropped it long ago. So she sat in the middle of the path, resting, passing the thin, silky light between her fingers.

A few minutes later she saw the good, honest gold and red of real torches and heard the worried voices of her father and the guards. With a joyful cry, she ran to them.

As soon as she saw her father's face, she knew she had done something terribly wrong. It was gray with worry. His normally firm chin was trembling as he gathered her up. He only trusted himself to whisper her name. He held her close before him on the horse, his free arm wrapped about her so tightly that it hurt.

At home, nothing was said beyond the exclamations of Flora as she saw the scratched and bruised arms and feet. Guinevere was given a warm herbal bath, and ointment was rubbed on the wounds. It was not until she was safe in bed that her parents came in.

"We don't want to hear any explanations, daughter," Guenlian told her sternly. "You wandered away thoughtlessly, and any fear or pain you might have had was well deserved. You caused your father and the guards to spend several extra hours of hard work hunting for you, when they were already tired from their journey today. Flora should not have let you enter the woods alone, but you are old enough now to know what you should and should not do and to observe the limits set for you. Flora will not always be near to tell you what is right or wrong. Obviously we have not taught you well enough where else to seek guidance. For the next two weeks, instead of riding with your father or playing in the fields, you may spend your afternoons in the chapel, praying for wisdom and maturity and studying the works of the Holy Fathers. Perhaps there you can find counsel."

Guinevere nodded mutely. She had never seen her mother

so angry. Leodegrance said nothing, but the look on his face was enough. Her eyes pleaded forgiveness. Guenlian sat on the edge of the bed and held her closely. Leodegrance rested his hand on her head.

"Never frighten us like that again," he whispered.

They covered her tightly and blew out the light.

Later, in their own room, Guenlian reflected. "It doesn't seem right to make religion a punishment. Couldn't we have thought of something else?"

Leodegrance frowned, then kissed his wife gently before he spoke. "I think we have made her feel the enormity of her disobedience. She may be rebellious for a while, but it is necessary that she be put into a position where she must think about herself and her place in the world."

He sighed. "The contemplative life is not a bad one for her to pursue for a few days. Would that we lived in times when we all might retreat for a while into philosophy."

Guenlian had finished her nightly ritual of washing and creaming her face. She wiped the cream off with a linen towel. It was made of pounded almonds, oil, and herbs and the scent of it lingered through the night. She slipped in bed next to her husband and brushed her hand across his face.

"Our life was our choice, my love. We could have run to the mountains or gone to Armorica and lived in relative tranquillity. I am proud of you and of our children. Who knows, someday we, too, may have time for philosophy."

For answer, Leodegrance kissed her again and blew out the light.

Flora was angry with Guinevere, too. She had been reproved by her employers, gently but decidedly, for letting the child stray from her sight. That and her own guilt made her grumble under her breath as she came in to check on Guinevere before she retired to her own room.

Guinevere was still awake. She had been thinking.

"Flora," she asked timidly, "may I have a cup of water?"

Flora frowned and snorted but brought the ewer and cup.

"I don't know why I do anything for you, naughty child," she muttered. "Bringing all this worry and trouble to me and to your dear parents who love you more than you deserve. Why did you go roaming like that, when I told you not to?"

"I'm sorry, Flora," Guinevere sighed. "But I've been scolded and I'm going to be punished, so can't we be friends again?"

She stopped, remembering the gift she had found and leaped out of bed to find it, spilling the water.

"Oh no," she said, "I'm sorry for that then, too. But I just remembered. I found something for you, just as you asked me—something beautiful and rare."

She had pinned it to the folds of her dress with one of her hairpins. The dress was still lying on the bench outside her door. Carefully, she unfastened it and came back holding the mysterious silver strand.

At the sight of it, Flora's whole manner changed. Her back straightened, her head tilted proudly, her carriage was all at once far different from that of an old serving woman. She stared in wonder and then lifted her hands, palms up to receive her gift.

Guinevere held it out to her. "I found it for you," she repeated. "I don't know what it is, do you?"

She asked because of the look on Flora's face. As she laid it across the old woman's hands, Flora gazed at the strand reverently. Her expression was one of awe and, perhaps, fear. Guinevere stared at her, puzzled. She hadn't expected such a reaction.

"Do you like it? Do you want it?" she asked. "Have I done something else that was wrong?"

Tears now flowed down Flora's face, but her voice remained steady.

"Of all the things you could have brought me, this is the one I longed for most. But if you have done the right thing, I cannot tell. Only the god—"

She broke off. With a fierce gesture, she drew Guinevere to her and held her, much as Leodegrance had on the way home. Then, just as quickly, she released her.

"This is a great treasure for me, my dove, greater than you can imagine. But it is also a great burden. You did not do right

14

or wrong but the only thing you could have done. It is part of the Design."

With this strange remark, Flora set Guinevere back in bed, and, taking her lamp, left the room.

Guinevere lay there, trying to make sense out of the events of the day, most of all Flora's part in them. But her thoughts wouldn't follow a logical pattern. As she tried to piece it together, the silver light would burst in, now bright, now dim, until it blurred everything into mist and she fell asleep.

CHAPTER TWO

$\mathcal{S}$ummer drifted in. The days were hazy, hot, and dry. The spring rains had ended too soon and the cold well within the compound was so low that water for bathing and washing had to be laboriously carted up the hill from the stream running out of the forest. The hot springs, hidden deep within the tor, were of such a high mineral content that they ruined clothes washed in them and made hair stiff and malodorous. The baths they were used for were only for health, not cleanliness. Servants were encouraged to reverse the process and take themselves down to the stream to wash, which they did with bawdy good humor. The gardeners lovingly sprinkled Guenlian's flowers to keep some color in the house. The rest of the ground on the tor was brown and barren. There was no grass, only pale, sharp stalks that cut even through sandals if one stepped on them the wrong way. These days seemed designed for inactivity, but the inhabitants of the compound went about as if there were always too much to do.

"Hurry, hurry, we must be ready." The swishing robes and slapping sandals quickened the pace. "Faster, faster, the time is almost gone."

The farmers and field-workers were out from earliest light until the last rays flooded the land with a bloodred glow. Weeding, hoeing, carrying buckets and buckets of water to feed their peas and beans, oats and barley. The people in the house bustled from one chore to another; mending, washing, tending the animals. But always, as they hurried, everyone would be looking somewhere else; over their shoulders, across the fields; casting a glance at the dark woods, so close, and the hazy mountains too far for flight. Then they would quickly return to their work.

Rumors swooped across the fields and into the house, fluttering from one low voice to another: We are winning at last. We are losing again. The Irish have made another raid on the Cornish coast. Duke Cador has repulsed the invader in the north. But the Saxons are still coming, pushing in from the ocean like a great tide. They have taken Eboracum; they are moving ever north and west, closer and closer. There was a battle at Caledon. Victory or defeat? Who knows? There are tales that we lost a thousand men, that Arthur surrounded the Saxons and starved them into surrender. Who knows? And what of Arthur, this strange boy-king? Who is he? What is he doing? Are the stories about him true? Who knows? What have *you* heard? What will happen to us? Are we safe, should we flee? Who knows?

Into this tense world one day ambled a calm young man on an old, tired horse. It had once been the mount of a soldier and still showed signs of its breeding, but its day had been past for many years and the plodding walk at which it carried its master was the best it could now manage.

Guinevere was not affected by the nervousness with which everyone else conducted their lives, but she found that with all the bustle, she was often in the way. So she had taken to sitting up with the guard in his watchtower by the gate. There was a good view of the road from there, and one felt closer to the trees and sky. Therefore, she was the first to see the visitor. She let out a whoop of delight that brought even Guenlian running from the house.

"What is it, child?" she gasped. "Your brothers? Oh, it's only St. Geraldus. Oh well, he's a dear lad. It will be good to have him with us again."

But she sighed as she went to tell Flora to have a room made up for their guest. Her sons had been away nearly a year now. They would have been a much more welcome sight.

"Come in, my boy." Leodegrance had heard the commotion and came to greet him. "Tell us the news. Where have you traveled lately? Is it true that the Saxons were beaten at Caledon?

You should know. Come in, come in! Quick, water for our guest!"

"Husband," Guenlian reproved as she joined them. "We should ask the good saint for his blessing on us and our home before we ply him with questions."

"Yes, of course," Leodegrance marveled at his wife's self-restraint. She was as eager as he for word of the battle.

Guenlian offered a cup of water to the man, who drained it at once. He wiped his mouth sheepishly and then raised his hand in some embarrassment, to bless the household.

"You will want to refresh yourself from your journey before we talk." Guenlian smiled as she took the cup back. "Caet, see to the good saint's horse. Anna, tell Filius to bring a bath and clean robes to St. Geraldus in his room."

"We have had to close the bathhouse during this drought," she explained. "Now, come right with me and I'll show you where you will stay."

She bundled him off so efficiently to wash and dress that Geraldus had no chance to say more than "Thank you" and "Certainly."

Leodegrance grinned. He was very glad he had married a woman who could think faster than he. He noticed the disappointed faces of the servants and fosterlings. They were all eager for the latest news, too. Better to speak with Geraldus privately, in case he had something disheartening to say. Then the whole household could hear a carefully worded version of it after dinner.

Everyone brightened up considerably at Geraldus' arrival. Though most of them were only nominally Christian, which was a prerequisite for their freedom, they all felt sure that no harm could come to a house where angels lived. It was common knowledge that angels accompanied St. Geraldus wherever he went, serenading him with heavenly music that only he could hear. Also, he was a cheerful, friendly sort, who ate and drank with everyone else and bathed as often as any Roman. He was also not above singing a few very secular songs after meals, entertaining the hall with tales of battles, magic, and thwarted love. He was certainly different from the usual monkish beggar who came to the gate.

They had little use for these peripatetic "holy" men who believed that by making their bodies as loathesome as possible, they would be closer to God. Flora refused to attend to them when they came.

"Closer to God," she sniffed. "I wouldn't sacrifice a lame cow to a god who'd own that sort. It would have to be a god without a nose."

Guinevere followed her mother as she went through the house overseeing preparations for the evening meal. Guenlian murmured to herself as she planned and organized.

"Lark pie would be nice, but not filling enough. It will have to be a chicken, too. Better tell Rhianna to tell the cook to have someone kill a chicken. At least there is enough for a nice, green sallet. Thank goodness these gardeners have watered, bless their dear, bent backs. I must remember to reward them. Now, wine . . ."

She noticed Guinevere, humming along with her at her elbow.

"Guinevere, dear, go tell your father we need more wine."

"Yes, mother." Guinevere ran off happily. She liked the bustle that came with company. She found Leodegrance in the stables, inspecting a late-born foal.

"Father," she panted. "Mother says we need wine for dinner. May I go with you to get it?"

"Yes, yes," he answered. "I'll just wash my hands. Did you bring a pitcher?"

She nodded. He gave some last instructions to Caet about caring for the spindly new animal and followed Guinevere down the side of the tor.

About halfway down the incline was a well-concealed cave. Whether it was natural or manmade, no one knew. Some thought it was the tomb of one of the giants who had roamed the earth years ago, as the Bible stated. Others suggested that it might be a passageway from one world to the next, as the Old Religion preached. Most of the peasants, whose ancestors had lived there since time began, simply said it was a dangerous place and refused to go near it. Leodegrance only shrugged at the speculations with the good nature of a man who has had time to worry only about the immediacies of life, and is not bothered with what comes after.

"It's big, dark, and always cool," he decided. "A fine place to store wine and winter roots."

He never sent any of the servants down there, though, even those who professed not to be afraid. Whenever a new supply of wine was needed he would fetch it himself, even if it meant leaving his guests.

But not only supplies were kept in the cave. Guinevere and her brothers had long ago dared each other to explore the mysterious cavern. The boys had gone first, one at a time, without even a candle, to show their courage. Then they had generously taken their little sister in to see it, too. Leodegrance and Guenlian had been furious when they first discovered this, for Guinevere had had strange and horrible dreams for weeks after her visit, which had to be explained.

She soon got over her fear, though, and demanded to be taken in to see it again. There was something compelling about the enormous table, round like the moon, deep in a dark cavern where no company would ever sit. Leodegrance had wisely ruled that the children could only enter when he was with them. Only then might they stare at the table, hidden in the gloom beyond the torchlight. Guinevere, at least, kept the bargain.

While Leodegrance opened a new jar and poured the wine into the flagon, Guinevere edged over to the table. She ran her hands over the wood, watching her fingers move in the flickering light. For the first time, she noticed grooves in the top, lines that might almost be letters. Slowly, she spelled out what she felt. "S-I-E-G-E-P-E-R- . . ."

"Stop!" Her hand was jerked roughly away. "That is not for you to touch!"

Guinevere stared at him in horror, rubbing her wrist. She was too startled to cry.

Leodegrance held her close in apology. His voice was more gentle.

"That table is very old and has strange powers. I do not know them all. It is not even mine; I only hold it in trust for another. What is written on it is not for us to know. Why do you think I keep it down here in the dark? Even touching it could be dangerous. You must never do it again."

He kissed her softly, to show he was not angry, only worried. Guinevere nodded. Her eyes were wide. She didn't really want to touch it again. There was something strong and powerful about it, something she was afraid of. Still, she wished she could see it in the light. Not for the first time, she wondered how her father had come by this thing and whom he kept it for, but she knew he would never tell.

He laid his arm on her shoulder as they climbed back up the tor. She threw hers about his waist and smiled back at him. The beating sun drove out the chill of the darkness.

Preparations for dinner were well under way when they returned. Geraldus had been bathed and rested and was making polite conversation with one of the fosterlings as they waited. She was trying to decide whether she should treat him with the respect due a saint or the coquetry needed to amuse a handsome and eligible young man.

Guenlian was truly pleased to have Geraldus stay with them. She encouraged him to spend several weeks each year under their roof. She liked him. He reminded her of her own sons. He was a charming guest who enlivened the meals with his conversation. He knew all the local gossip and much of the distant news. He could sing the old sagas that pleased the servants. She was sorry for him and his problem. If he occasionally acted a bit odd, speaking to the air or swatting at unseen flies, well, that was to be expected from a man who heard voices. Guenlian wasn't entirely sure that Geraldus was, in truth, a saint, but she knew he was a good and kindly man. And his manners were impeccable, which, after all was something even harder to find in a guest these days than claims to sainthood. She also heartily approved of his family ties.

Geraldus' family was one of the old Romano-British liaisons. They were descended from a rather obscure officer of an undoubtedly noble Roman family who had fallen in love with a Welsh princess and decided to settle. Her father was unable to give her much but a line of one hundred fighting ancestors, so they had settled on a smallish estate well up in the Pennines, where they raised cattle, sheep, and horses—fine horses. The family kept to themselves as a rule, sending messages of support in times of trouble and swift cavalry mounts when the invasions threatened their safety. During some of the darkest days, Guenlian, first alone and later with her children, had found a friendly refuge with them, and she did not forget.

Geraldus had been born into this tranquil, airy world. He belonged there, a gentle child, full of light and music. He showed little interest in Roman history or literature, slightly more in philosophy. He mastered reading only enough to study some fragments of Pythagoras on an old papyrus manuscript, which was fast crumbling in the damp climate. He spent most of his time in the hills, watching the clouds and the sheep and playing his pipe. He always had an air about him as if he heard and saw more than others did. His parents feared he might be simple. But no one doubted his word when, at the age of seventeen, he announced that he had begun hearing voices. When asked what the voices told him, he had replied cautiously, "They seem to be singing."

At that, the faces of his dear friends and relatives had lit up with a holy awe and they had backed away from him, reverently but swiftly.

"Angels!" they whispered. "It is only natural that one who lives so close to God would one day hear the heavenly choir."

Then they racked their brains to remember any slight or offense they might have given this chosen one. To be on the safe side, they brought him gifts, most of which were useless to him. That didn't matter. It didn't pay to be in disfavor with the Almighty, especially in these uncertain times.

After his announcement, Geraldus tried to resume his normal life. He continued to spend most of his time in the mountains, tending his sheep and playing his music. He was already a brilliant piper and did well on the small Celtic harp. He would have done justice to a Greek lyre, if he could have found one intact. At first the voices didn't bother him too much. If angels wanted to serenade him, he wouldn't object. The "choir" generally hummed the same four or five tunes, all variations in one octave. It was boring, but easy to ignore. Geraldus did wonder about the quality of heavenly taste, but, being modest, decided that it was probably a lack in himself that failed to appreciate their sounds. After a while he noticed that when he played his pipes, the voices would make a clumsy attempt to follow him. He liked them for that. It seemed very thoughtful of them to take an interest in his music, too. Also, an appreciative audience was something he had always lacked. Sheep are not strong on lyric and melody.

Slowly he began to recognize the different voices. Some picked up new tunes instantly, while others grumbled on in the same old monotone, no matter what he played. He grew comfortable with them, though his opinion of their ability grew less. Some days they would all sing together charmingly; on others, the cacaphony would be unbearable. There was one pure alto with a slight vibrato who consistently followed his playing beautifully. Geraldus fell half in love with it. Finally, it occurred to him that these were probably not the voices of angels. He concluded that a celestial choir would simply have more good voices. There wasn't one tenor who could stay on tune and the sopranos were positively shrill. Even his alto was a little too sultry for true piety.

His attempts to explain this to his family and friends were brushed off as attacks of modesty. They had decided that there was a saint in their midst, and they would settle for nothing less.

He became more involved with the voices than with the people he could see. He spent more and more time with them, or, at least, paying attention to them. They were always with him. As they showed signs of improvement, he started coaching them out loud; playing to them; practicing scales—until his family wondered if having a saint among them was really such an honor. The question was finally resolved one night at dinner.

Several guests had been invited from the surrounding estates. They were all old friends who were content to overlook Geraldus' new status. The meal was a good one and the wines were old and strong. Everyone was enjoying himself immensely when Geraldus suddenly stood up, pointing his finger at something across the room. He glared into space, seemingly at nothing, and shouted fiercely.

"If all of you don't stop screeching and groaning in my ears you can go back to wherever you came from!"

He then upset his wineglass and fingerbowl with a sweeping gesture and stormed out.

Naturally, the guests thought he meant them. There was some confusion as a few accused their neighbors of being the source of the noise. Fights were breaking out at the lower tables by the time Geraldus' parents had managed to calm down those at the main one. It took quite some time before everyone returned to their meal, and a new cask of wine had to be opened to soothe the hurt feelings.

The next day, Geraldus' parents decided that it might be better for everyone if their dear and holy son went to a place more suited to his nature—a monastery, perhaps or some other retreat far, far from sinful man.

They told him at once, as kindly as they could, but Geraldus was listening to an alto solo and heard only a fraction of what they said. His face was dreamy and peaceful and it gave his mother a moment's sorrow to have to give him up to God. But she was a devout woman and assumed that God would see that he ate properly, dressed warmly, and didn't overtax himself. And it would be nice to be able to entertain again.

So, a few days later, Geraldus set off on foot down the mountain. He was supposed to strike out toward the west to an Irish monastery on the coast, but he soon discovered that he could survive quite well on his own. His fame had spread through the mountains and he was greeted enthusiastically whenever he appeared. He sang well, didn't steal, and left a blessing on each house he stayed at. The reverence of his hosts was occasionally tiresome, but the food and lodgings were usually good and he enjoyed the society of different people. After eighteen years in the company of sunrises and sheep, human companionship can be very interesting. At one stop he was given his horse, a creature of a philosophical nature, whom he named Plotinus. Plotinus apparently didn't mind music as he plodded along, and they got along well.

Geraldus was always glad to rest a while with Leodegrance and Guenlian. The food was excellent, the wine superb and the conversation interesting. Best of all, they respected him without placing too much emphasis on his supposedly saintly attributes. They asked a blessing on arrival and departure and nothing more. He liked them.

When he had washed and put on the new, soft robes that were left for him, Geraldus joined the family at dinner. He fervently hoped that the maids who had brought him the bath had not stayed to watch him from behind the curtains. He had thought he felt a draught and more than once he had discovered a maid, or even a fosterling, outside his chambers, curious to discover if saints were made the same as other men.

Leodegrance wanted serious news, however, and Geraldus' concern over his privacy faded as he found himself flooded with questions.

"Yes, sir," he repeated between bites. "This young King Arthur is supposedly doing marvelous deeds against the Saxons, and it's doubtful that we'll have to worry about them coming this far again, at least while he is in command of the army."

"We have heard such fantastic stories of him," Guenlian complained. "If we believed them all we would be sure that he was a giant with flaming hair, a magic lance in one hand and an invincible sword in the other. He must not feel the need of a shield, or does he carry it in his teeth?"

"He does indeed have a fine sword. Excaliber, he names it," Geraldus answered. "And there are many tales of his finding it. All agree it is beyond the skill of modern man to forge such a blade. As for the other tales, I do not know. They say he once went into battle carrying a cross on his shoulders, but that is hard for me to imagine. A man has enough to weigh him down when he fights, without adding a cross as well."

"Perhaps it's a metaphor?" Guenlian suggested.

"Perhaps it's all nonsense, made up to fool the ignorant louts who like that sort of thing!" Leodegrance snorted. "We've heard about his battles, how he slew this and that ridiculous number alone and saved the day. Assuredly we've had no Saxon incursions near here and it's the first year in many a long summer that we haven't. But I want to know who this boy is, this lad who says he's king of all Britain. Not that it's much of a title now, with Saxons eating away at one coast and Irish raiding at the other. Do you know who he is, where he comes from?"

"I've heard it said that he was nurtured at the northern estate of Ector, a fine man who is oddly self-effacing. But as to his parentage, I know nothing, only that there is some mystery about it and that it is somehow tied in with the prophesies of Master Merlin, made so many years ago. I was not born then and do not know the correct words for all the prophecies. . . ."

"Merlin was half out of his head when he spouted all that!" Guenlian began. Merlin was second cousin to her and she thought his dabbling in wizardry did not reflect well on the family. "The poor lad had been dragged from his home, slandered as a devil's spawn and threatened with horrible death. Anyone would babble under those circumstances."

Leodegrance interrupted her. "I'm sure you know that shortly after that episode, all Merlin's family were killed in a sudden raid on their home. The horror of it unhinged his mind and he totally lost his reason. Indeed, he disappeared for months afterwards. We try to be very gentle with him regarding those times and never refer to them if we can avoid it."

Geraldus was unconvinced. He was familiar enough with the story to know that Merlin had been spared because he had been able to solve King Vortigern's problem through his second sight. Geraldus had also encountered Merlin many times in his travels and had been deeply impressed with him. There was no sign of a weak mind that he could detect. In this house, however, he was a guest, so he kept his thoughts to himself.

"I almost forgot," he announced. "Until we spoke of him, your magnificent dinner and delightful wines had pushed Master Merlin from my thoughts, and also my reason for arriving here now. I am here at the bidding of Merlin to inform you that he will soon be traveling this way, probably at the end of the month. He hoped you would have a place for him for a few weeks. He wanted me to warn you that he might be accompanied."

Guenlian smiled graciously, mentally already assigning rooms and wondering which of the stock should be slaughtered.

"I am always happy to see my dear cousin," she said, adding

wistfully, "So many of our people are gone now, either killed in the raids or fled over the sea. It's good for one to have family about."

Guinevere heard this at her end of the table, where she sat almost in darkness. She was not so thrilled that Merlin was coming. He had rarely spoken to her in the past and then had glared at her so fiercely that she was half afraid of him. He always made her feel as if she had done something terribly wrong. She tended, therefore, to be silent and evasive with him. Now, thinking of him, she withdrew from the conversation around her. As her attention wandered she noticed something odd about the people in the dining hall. There seemed to be too many of them. And there were people she had never seen before.

They flitted among the guests, now sitting, now standing, and she couldn't focus on them clearly. As she tried to stare at one, the person would melt away and another would appear just out of her range. She tried to see them clearly for several minutes with no success. Then, just as she had given up and returned to her meal, she noticed a laughing woman with long black hair sitting directly across the room from her. Guinevere stared fixedly at her but the woman didn't fade. She smiled directly at her. The woman was seated next to one of the local small landowners. Potius had happened to be in the neighborhood that day and had been invited to dinner. Such luck didn't often come his way and he was doing his best to stuff himself with fresh meat and fine wine. He never glanced at the woman, even though she was almost touching his elbow.

As he lifted his cup, she gently tipped it toward her own mouth. His meat was whisked from his plate even as he was reaching for another piece of bread. The woman really had no manners at all, thought Guinevere, but the expression on Potius' face was so startled that she couldn't help laughing out loud.

"My lady?" the page behind her spoke softly. "Is there anything you desire?"

Guinevere glanced up at him. She smiled politely.

"No, I am quite content."

When she turned back, the woman had gone. Old Potius

was holding his cup before him possessively, peering right and left in an effort to find the one playing tricks on him. Guinevere realized with a start that he had not been able to see the woman. Why not? she wondered. The woman had been right beside him. She looked around the table, noticing that her parents and Geraldus were still conversing. Every few seconds, he would get a distant look and brush his hand across his hair, or against his ear, as if trying to shoo a fly. Guinevere stared intently, not at him but at the space just over his shoulder. Slowly the woman materialized. She saw Guinevere's puzzled stare and winked. Guinevere returned to her dinner, blushing, and did not look up again.

The end of the meal was so long in coming that she found herself getting sleepy. Their dear old butler and wine steward, Pincarna, had evidently decided that she was old enough to be served all she liked, or perhaps he had just forgotten to give the order to mix her wine liberally with water. At any rate, while the conversation had sparkled and the strange people had fluttered around, Guinevere had listened and laughed. Now that everyone was murmuring and the music had started, she realized vaguely that the wine was slowly rising and her head was slowly falling. Flora found her sometime later, sound asleep with her head on the table.

"Where is the pretty woman with the black hair?" she murmured, as Flora gathered her up to carry her to bed.

"There was no woman there tonight that you didn't know, child," Flora answered. She was puffing a bit and put Guinevere down. "You must walk the rest of the way. I'm too old and you've grown too much for me to do that any more."

"Yes, Flora," Guinevere answered groggily. "But there was someone else there. She drank Potius' wine. How silly he looked, staring at the empty cup. I wonder if he thought he had drunk it himself and forgotten it?"

"You've had too much wine yourself, young lady," Flora replied tartly. "Now I'm putting you to bed!"

Guinevere sank back to sleep, hardly noticing that Flora was helping her out of her clothes. Her arms were limp as the night-shift went on.

Flora's eyes were bright. She didn't seem to be paying attention to the child. She muttered all the while she smoothed covers and folded robes. But Guinevere was too deeply asleep to hear.

"Another sign," the old woman grieved. "Another sign. She grows apace and I cannot stop or change it. Soon, no doubt of it. Perhaps even by the winter fires. How can I bear it?"

She cried out and touched the golden hair reverently. She tried to calm herself from the shock of this new knowledge and old grief.

"If they didn't demand the best, they would not be gods and our gifts would have no meaning."

With this remark, she carefully tucked the blanket about Guinevere and went to her own room, there to sit up all night, staring out her window at the chapel. But what she saw in the darkness was impossible to tell.

Geraldus stayed on as the summer waxed. He was welcomed by all, Guinevere especially. He didn't mind being trailed after by a half-grown girl. He was young and laughing and told exciting stories. She adored him and they were together most of every day. Often Geraldus would play his pipes. Their willowy minor key would always give Guinevere an eerie feeling, as if she were someone else and crying or laughing with them. It was most often at these times that she saw the people around the young saint. There were both men and women, all young and comely as far as she could tell. Most of them appeared only as through a mist, and their hair and clothes never stayed still, even on the calmest days. She still had the problem that whenever she tried to look at them closely they would fade and then appear again, just at the corner of her vision.

Although she had realized almost immediately that these were Geraldus' singers, she told no one of her discovery. They didn't appear at all the way she had been told angels would. She felt no religious awe around them, only curiosity and some irritation. They puzzled her, but she was not a questioning child, and so she came to take them for granted as part of being with Geraldus.

Guenlian was glad to have Guinevere roaming about with Geraldus, safe, but out of the way. A visit from Merlin was something that must be prepared for. He was not only Guenlian's cousin but a prophet of great renown, advisor to the late, unlamented king Uther Pendragon and also adviser to this new king, Arthur, about whom there were so many tales and so few hard facts. So the household was turned inside out. Linen was aired, all the walls received a new coat of whitewash, and some were painted over in pastels. Guenlian sighed for a new mural, but those days were gone. There hadn't been an artist of any worth on the island in years. She also worried about the missing pieces in the mosaics on the floors of the main hall and the chapel. The tiny pieces of stone and glass had been imported from the Mediterranean. The few ships that braved the seas these days brought nothing that had such clear, shining tones.

"My love, we can't have everything," Leodegrance remonstrated when she complained. "Those ships that arrive here despite the ravages of the Northmen should be treasured for what they do bring. We have good wine yet, and spices, and you and Guinevere dress in the sheerest of linens and silks. Must you also have artists and potters from Rome and Constantinople? Perhaps you would like a company of Greek players to entertain our guests?"

Guenlian laughed. "We will have them again someday. The Saxon shall not prevail. We will see our daughter married in cloth of gold with the finest entertainment Rome can offer—poets, actors, dancers of all kinds!"

Leodegrance smiled but he knew in his heart that all their fine talk was just bravado. Even Rome wasn't Rome any more. The government had moved East and the Caesars of the West were only puppets, set up and knocked down almost with each change in the wind. Whatever art or literature or music was to be had would be homegrown. They already produced all the necessities of life and could survive, but the luxuries were good to have, too, and they were getting ever scarcer.

"I am reminded," he said, "the pipes leading to the guest rooms are not in the best repair. I am sure that one is leaking. I must send for the smith to patch it before it is needed in the fall."

"Another thing," he thought, as he continued his inspection, "that we are unable to do as well as our forefathers. Perhaps our Age of Iron is disintegrating into something even worse. We all are living in an Age of Clay."

Leodegrance had tried all his life to be optimistic, but it wasn't easy as he grew older. Every year the times grew worse, even if the change was not apparent on his little estate. Sometimes he felt like a man trying to push back the tide with only the force of his own body.

"When my sons are grown!" he would repeat. "They will carry on. The barbarians will not conquer. They . . . will . . . not!"

Civilization was very dear to him, and to him that meant Rome. Not as she was today, perhaps not as she had ever been, save in the minds of a few idealists and dreamers, but Rome still, with all the best that she stood for, republican government, culture, philosophy, reason, indoor plumbing . . . someone must make a stand to preserve it.

The summer was steeped in early gold. The heat turned the earth to a dying ember, baking and smothering all thoughts of cool air or winter chill. Even the mighty forest crackled as wanderers passed through. Guinevere longed to go there again but was not allowed. Something seemed to be pulling her back to the place where she had first seen the silver light, but Leodegrance and Guenlian had been frightened enough by her adventure and were firm in their refusal. So she roamed on the edge, sometimes with Geraldus, sometimes with the maids, but never alone. She saw nothing, but once she thought she heard a call, far away, from someone who wanted her desperately. She went running madly into the woods but was pulled back by her attendants.

"I must go!" she screamed.

They carried her home and put her to bed with mint tea and a guard at her door. Her mother rocked her like a baby. Her father told her stories of the saints. Flora recited arcane charms in old Brytannic. Nothing would calm her. Finally, they left her alone in her room. The moon shone whitely through the window, and a shadow, too swift to shape, ran past. Guinevere cried out and reached toward it. Then she slept. The next day she remembered nothing.

To Guenlian, all these days were nothing but a blurry chaos of work and planning. Guinevere would be all right. These spells were only the result of her being too much alone or with Flora. Geraldus was good for her. Saint or not, he was always calm and sensible.

"I haven't time to worry," Guenlian reminded herself. "The child is almost thirteen. Lord knows the odd things we imagine then. Leodegrance will see to her. Flora is getting old though, and I don't like the way she's been looking at Guinevere lately. She mustn't carry these pagan notions of hers too far. The girl is mine, not hers! Well, Merlin will be here soon, Dear friend! He can explain it all. But I mustn't act as if I think he's truly a seer. He must have some place he can go and not be greeted at arm's length. He's still my cousin. What a time of year for guests! I hope they'll be content with mutton. We'll tell them it's very late spring lamb."

She bustled about, determined to keep her mind from the things she feared and longed for most.

It was late in July. Guinevere and Geraldus were bathing their feet in the creek. Only the woman with the black hair was along and, for a change, no one was singing. Guinevere lay on the bank, her toes dangling happily in the muddy water, her cheek pressed against the earth.

"Do you hear something?" she asked Geraldus lazily.

Geraldus began to laugh uncontrollably. "Do you know?" he gasped. "That is the first time in years someone has asked me that and meant anything but those damned voices!"

Someone pinched him and he batted the air to stop it.

"No, really!" Guinevere insisted. "I hear horses coming. Galloping! Hurry! They are very near! Look!"

She screamed hysterically in his ear as the horses came around the bend and raced toward her, right through the stream. In a moment, Guinevere was lifted, jerked up into the arms of her brother Mark. They were home! So that's who Merlin's guests were! Home again! She clung to Mark, weeping for joy. Through her tears, she saw Geraldus' beaming face.

"He knew all along!" she thought. "Someone should have told Mother."

CHAPTER THREE

Guinevere's shriek echoed all the way up the hill and into the compound, where Guenlian was checking to see that the linen was being properly aired. Her sigh was half fear and half annoyance. Now what had the child done? Then the cheering began from the guards at the gate and she heard the clatter of horses in the courtyard. She dropped the towels and ran to the front court. Sunlight bouncing off the polished armor nearly blinded her. They were home! Her beautiful sons, all of them together. All safe. She stretched out her arms to them joyfully.

She found herself checking them over, much as she had at their birth: hands, feet, arms and legs all accounted for. Her last worry disappeared.

"Mother!" Matthew cried as he lifted her in a bear hug. "Why were you not out at the gate to greet us? Have we been away so long that you no longer care about us? Guinevere was happy to see us, although I hardly recognized her. She is growing up too. Have you found her a husband yet?"

"I remember, lieutenant, that you once knew the proper greeting for one of my rank!" Guenlian answered sternly. Then she relented and held him close to her heart. "I'm heart-glad to see you, my son."

Mark and John pulled her away from him, laughing.

"You favor our older brother still. Have you no greeting for us?"

"Of course I do, my proud cockerels, when you have finished strutting in your armor for the delight of the maids and boys. You are mightily proud of your trappings, children!"

"Children!" Mark scoffed. "We are all grown men now, Mother, tried and proved in battle. If we are proud, it is of the honor of our name and family, not of this rusty metal."

"I see no rust on your helmet. But perhaps the reason for that is not pride in your armor, but rather the discipline of our cousin Cador."

"Come with me brothers," Matthew laughed, "when will we learn not to fence words with our mother? I have never won a battle with her in my life."

Guenlian smiled as she watched the boys striding off to the stables, their arms lightly placed on each other's shoulders. It was as it should be and she was pleased beyond telling with her strong soldier sons. They were truly hers, she gloated, more than the children of any of her friends could be to them. She had carried them all proudly, refusing to go into seclusion as custom declared, and had suffered their internal kicks and punches with delight.

"I am growing Roman children!" she had told her husband.

So she had shot her sons forth into the world, each one squalling bravely. She had given Flora the care of them for part of the time but had insisted that they be kept near her always. She had refused even a wet nurse.

"How will they grow strong and wise on peasant milk, made from beer and barley bread? I will feed them myself with milk from good red wine and meat."

They traveled with her everywhere and she nursed them as she rode. She laughed at those who assured her that she would ruin her figure and her health. Her friends respected her position too much to laugh at her publicly, but they privately speculated on what would happen to children raised so loosely. When women met at their homes or at the few remaining baths, the conversation always drifted from complaints on the degeneration of society to Guenlian with her brood of babies, three sons in six years.

"They seem to be everywhere children shouldn't be," one

barren matron would cluck. "My dear, those boys have the run of the estate. The baby, whichever one that is, crawls about on the floor when there are guests to dinner! And Leodegrance only grins and warns you not to step on him!"

"She should never keep them at home with her," another would moan. "The first winter illness will take them all, how well I know." And she would sniff lugubriously.

"That would certainly be a fine stop to the Roman army she seems intent on building. It appears to me that she is determined to replace the whole twentieth legion by herself. If she continues like this, she may get delusions of imperial splendor. I wonder that Leodegrance allows it."

"Well, it's obvious why he doesn't stop her. All those children. You know what men are like!"

And here the conversation would take another turn.

The gossip never bothered Guenlian when she heard of it, as of course she did. It was always the duty of some dear friend to inform her of what people were saying. It may even have occurred to her that one day one of her sons might try for the purple. Stranger things had happened. But after Mark there had been no more children for many years.

And then, when their hopes were almost gone, there was a fourth child, the last.

Guinevere, silent, even facing her first breath. She hadn't cried out at all but had simply opened her mouth and taken a long, gasping sigh. Then she opened her great, green eyes.

She had focused intently on the face of Flora, who was holding her, enraptured with awe. It seemed to the old woman that the wisdom and mystery she had worshipped all her life lay in that deep, clear gaze. The silence was so complete that Guenlian began to panic.

"Bring him to me," she commanded. "Why do you wait? Why doesn't he cry? Is the child dead, deformed? Tell me at once!"

Flora wrapped the unresisting child in swaddling and brought her to lie beside her mother.

"It's a girl," she breathed. Guenlian sensed the strange tone of wonder in her voice.

"That was to be expected, I suppose. I can't always have boys. If she's strong and healthy, I see no reason to grieve. Take off those linens and let me examine her."

But Flora was reluctant to give up the baby. She appeared almost reverent and refused to take her eyes from the baby's face.

"She is not like the others," the nurse whispered. "There is a light about her, a divine aura. I believe she was sent to us by . . ."

She clutched the child too tightly as a fearful thought occurred to her. The girl finally cried out.

"Stop your superstitious nonsense and bring me my child, Flora." Guenlian hardly ever used such a tone of command. "We are Christians and civilized, rational beings, and we do not believe in signs. You know I will have no divining or prophesying over my children. Even Merlin knows better than to try to tell me their future. They will be whatever God and their own abilities decide and I leave that to them."

Flora obeyed. She put the baby on a pillow next to her mother's head and left the room.

Guenlian didn't notice. She was filled with the wonder of her daughter. The crying had stopped, but it had done the baby good. Her face was a healthy pink and the wispy gold hair shone above her red scalp.

"Aura indeed!" Guenlian laughed and examined the baby further.

Her eyes were remarkable, the color so pure for a newborn. They were just the color of the first spring leaves, a soft yellow-green. Guenlian checked her hands, uncurling the fingers to see their length. She ran her hands down the bent legs and arms, turned the baby over, looking for birthmarks or blemishes. There was nothing. She was as perfect as any new human being could be.

"What a fool Flora is," Guenlian whispered. "You are no angel or goddess, but a beautiful Roman child. You will have my mother's name, Guinevere, and we will raise you to be a strong, brave woman, just as she was."

Guenlian remembered all these things as she watched her daughter racing to join her brothers on their way to the stables. Guinevere was far from spiritual or even dignified as she hopped along beside John. He was obviously teasing her about something, for Guinevere blushed and tried to reach his head to knock his helmet off. He swept her up and she climbed to his shoulders, enjoying the view. Her laughter sparkled through the still, hot air.

"Can you spare a greeting for an old cousin, Guenlian, or do your children take up all your time as they do all your heart?"

Guenlian came back to the present with a start.

"Merlin, dear cousin!" she exclaimed. "I am delighted to see you here. Our blessed Geraldus has been awaiting your arrival for days. But I see that he, too, is off with the boys. Never mind. He will soon return. Until then you must make do with my poor greeting. You honor our household now that you are the sage advisor of two kings. Your laurels become you, do they not?"

She paused to look more closely at him. He was outwardly robust, but his eyes were veiled by worry and sorrow and his jaw was more firmly set than when they had been children together, or even at their last meeting. She linked her arm in his as they strolled to the house.

"Whatever your cares are now, let them rest while you are with us. Forget Saxons, Irish, and Picts! Turn away from the feuding lords! We will banish them all!"

She laughed and his face softened as he smiled in return.

"Dearest Guenlian. I don't worry about the Saxon raiders or the mulish country lords. I leave that to the fighting men and the diplomats. There are deeper cares within my heart. But, if they are more serious, they are also more distant. I will take your advice and rest awhile with you. I have a mind to hunt with my old friend Leodegrance and his pack of cubs. And an evening in your hall is always a welcome change from the conversation of men who know nothing but tales of battle and glory and can hardly read their own names."

"I didn't know that such men dared speak to you, Merlin,"

Guenlian laughed. "They all seem to be much too afraid that you will enchant them to have much to do with you."

He returned her smile.

"It's true. I see their hands flickering as I pass to ward off my evil glance. But some of the mightier lords feel that discourse with a wizard enhances their social standing as well as proves their courage. So I listen, night after night, to rambling talk of armor and horses, women and feuds. It will be a joy to listen again to the children's tutor, what's his name? The way he goes on about Virgil and Seneca! You would think they had been old friends of his! I doubt that one in a hundred of these so-called Roman soldiers knows of the fall of Troy or the founding of Rome. Arthur and I have discussed this many times. It grieves us to realize that these men have forgotten their past. They know the names of their ancestors to the thirtieth generation, but they know nothing about them. Those who truly are of Roman blood can't even pronounce their names correctly. But now we are spending all our strength simply defending Britain. There is no time for history lessons."

"Is the war going so badly, then?" Guenlian asked. She glanced abruptly toward the stable, where rowdy laughter could be heard.

"No, as a matter of fact, it's going very well. You may calm yourself, cousin. I am aware that you don't like to hear of my visions, but I can assure you that Britain will remain ours for our lifetimes, at least. Arthur is an able general and a fine man. He is doing what no one thought could be done. He is unifying the clans of the north and the settlers in the south and west. As you know, they normally spend their time fighting each other; now they march side by side, for love of him."

Guenlian seized her chance. "We have wondered about this Arthur. Geraldus has told us only a little, and the stories of him often seem to contain as much myth as the ones we hear of you. I have heard that you know his family?"

She waited for a reply.

Merlin sighed. "Yes, I did. His parents are dead. They were unable to care for him, even before. So, when he was born, I took him from the arms of the nurse and gave him to old Ector to raise as a foster son. Arthur spent his whole life there except for the times I took him traveling. Now you know as much as he knows."

"You haven't even told the boy his own parentage!"

"When the time comes, he will be told, as will you all. But it is not necessary to face yet and I would wait."

A frightening thought flashed into Guenlian's mind. Something in his voice, perhaps. But unlike Merlin, she never listened to her intuition. She suddenly realized that they were still standing in the courtyard.

"Forgive me, dear one. I said you should rest and not be bothered, and I have kept you here standing and answering questions! Come. I will show you your room myself. I'll send for hot water and towels, too. We have had to close the baths during the drought. However, we can give you a hip bath in your room. Not as pleasant, I know, but adequate for washing off the dust of your journey. When you are rested, come join us on the patio. We have a fine view of the sunset, and Pincerna has been overseeing an exquisite dinner in your honor."

They arrived at his room. It was well furnished and beautifully decorated. Merlin's smile widened as he saw the well-stuffed mattress and soft pillows. He gave Guenlian a quick hug of delight.

"I may not make it to dinner," he chuckled.

"See that you do, or Pincerna's heart will break," she answered and closed the door behind her.

They had parted happily, but once alone again, they each sighed. Guenlian shook herself and hurried to see about the water, and Merlin gratefully threw himself upon the bed.

Guinevere's joy, however, was totally untempered. Her brothers were home! She had felt recently that being the only child at home gave her too much attention of the wrong sort. Now her strong, adult, laughing brothers were here at last. There would be hunting and riding and rowdy dinners that lasted far into the night. There would be singing and pranks again as it had been before they went away, all so young, to fight. And, she gloated, she could again be spoiled and petted and not treated as a young woman of rank who must mind her behavior.

Fairly bubbling over in her happiness as she pranced along after them to the stables, she didn't notice the bitter, admiring look Caęt gave them as they entered.

It was dark inside and almost cool. The smell of horses and hay struck them at once. All four breathed it in happily. The smell was uniquely that of their own stable, their own horses. They stopped a moment until their eyes grew to show them the shapes in the dark.

Guinevere was still jumping up and down.

"Have I grown?" she teased John. "You haven't seen me since last fall. I've grown a lot, I know it. Soon I'll be as tall as you."

"Then you'll have no more rides on my back!" he grinned. "You already weigh more than my saddle and armor combined. No use Guin, you're a child no more."

But he didn't really believe it. He laughed as he hugged her tightly and lifted her as he had all her life.

Suddenly he stopped. His expression changed almost to one of alarm. Gently, he put her down in the doorway so that the sunlight struck her and shone through her summer-thin gown.

"Oh, Guinevere!" he sighed. "You have grown."

She blushed. She was vaguely aware that her body was not as straight and flat as it had been even a few months before. But the change had been too gradual for any eye but Flora's to see. Now she saw her brothers looking at her as if she were a stranger. She felt a chill run through her. Her eyes began to fill.

John saw this and smiled tenderly. "Dear one, I don't love you less for turning almost into a woman when my back was turned. It only took me by surprise. I suppose I felt that you must be some sort of fairy child who would never change. Brothers! Mark, Matthew! Come! We must greet our sister again. The child we left last autumn has been transformed during our absence! May I present to you the Lady Guinevere!"

41

They stared at her a moment.

"God's Blood, I never noticed!" Matthew exclaimed. "Do you want to make me feel old? I felt myself a man already when you were born. But in truth, you'll soon be of an age for suitors. Well, you have three stout warriors to defend your honor. I place my sword at your command!"

With a flourish of mock pomposity, he drew his short battle sword and laid it at her feet. The others followed.

Guinevere refused to be intimidated. She adjusted an imaginary cloak and veil and extended her hand to them. They were teasing her again and this she could deal with as she had all her life. There was a challenge in their eyes even though they loved her so very much.

"I accept your valorous offer and give you my tokens to carry with you into battle in my name." She looked about for something to give them. She was wearing very little on this hot day—as had just been made apparent—and no jewelry or scarves. Her hair had tumbled down again and she quickly tugged at it to get three strands.

"I have only these three golden threads to give, but they were gathered at great cost." She rubbed the place on her scalp where she had pulled.

"I hope," she added in a more normal voice, "that you appreciate this gift, remembering all the strands you had for nothing in the day when pulling my braids was one of your favorite sports."

"We will cherish them to the death!" vowed Mark, with a melodramatic whap to his chest. "Oops! I've dropped mine in the straw. Well, give me another, sister dear, and I'll cherish that one to the death."

Happily they finished seeing to the horses and returned to the house.

Caet spent an hour that afternoon searching in the straw, until he found one long golden strand. Carefully he placed it in the leather bag around his neck where he kept his treasures.

Whenever Guinevere thought of that summer in later years, she always saw it ringed in gold and silver. Colors were brighter, music more touching, and the happiness was so intense she could taste it.

"It was the last summer before," she would say.

"Before what?" someone would always ask.

"Before everything." Her eyes would then cloud and the questioner would know to ask no more.

But at that time she didn't know that it was the last anything and wouldn't have understood if someone had told her. So she simply enjoyed it with all her heart. She wanted nothing more in her life than to live like this, with her parents and brothers, spoiled and loved forever. They were content, too, for her to remain so, for to her family, Guinevere was the essence of all their dreams: a happy, innocent creature, beautiful and untouched by the grief and conflict outside her narrow world.

There were many riding expeditions, into and through the woods. Everyone made so much noise on these that it was no wonder they saw nothing but themselves. Guinevere's dreams became vague and the strange longing she had felt ebbed. They went on picnics and had great banquets that lasted until the summer dawn. Geraldus more than earned his keep at these. He knew more legends and songs than one could hear in a month of banquets. His honey voice carried them into whatever tale he told, making them laugh or weep without even realizing it. Sometimes Guenlian wondered if these stories were not too secular for a saint. However, her duty as a hostess was foremost in her mind, and there was no doubt that the guests were mightily entertained.

The only shadow in Guinevere's world that summer was Merlin. She couldn't overcome the feeling that he disliked her, although his manner toward her was always irreproachable. It made her very uncomfortable when he was around. She resented his eyes; when they looked at her, she felt she was under examination. Thankfully, he rarely joined the group of young people, preferring to stay with Guenlian or ride with Leodegrance as he oversaw the estate, or even sit by the hour with Tenuantius, arguing points of grammar so intently that the old teacher began to feel there was some hope for the country yet. Everyone was fond of him but Guinevere, but with so much to do and so many friends, she rarely let him upset her.

To Guinevere's brothers, Merlin had always been a figure of excitement and mystery. His mother and Guenlian's had been cousins and therefore he was Family, part of a tight unit against whom nothing might be said. But even in their remote and sheltered corner of Britain they had heard strange stories of him: his unknown siring; the terrifying string of prophecies he had spun for Vortigern, which had all come true as far as anyone knew. Vortigern had been defeated, although the Saxons he had invited into Britain were still rampaging through the country. There were stories of Merlin's dabbling in black magic to help King Uther with his lecheries, but no one knew much about that. Some even said that Merlin was responsible for the Giant's Dance, the circle of stones in the middle of the great plain to the east. About this Guinevere's brothers questioned him, and he replied that it wasn't true. He knew not how the stones had come there, nor their purpose.

That didn't stop Matthew, Mark, and John from believing other stories. They wondered what had happened to him after the battle of Arderydd, when his whole family had been killed, including his uncle, King Gwenddolau. By listening at doors late at night, they had heard the story of how he was seen wandering among the bodies, raving into the winds, as mad as a loon. He disappeared after that and wasn't seen again for over a year. Even Guenlian had been unable to find out from him where he had been or how his reason had been restored.

Now he was possibly the most important man in all Britain. Only he had the full confidence of Arthur. Indeed, it appeared that he was the one guiding Arthur's brilliant rise to power and magnificent successes in battle.

Guenlian and Leodegrance forbade discussion of Merlin by their children. They insisted that he have one place to visit where he would be treated like a human being and a cousin and not a demon-sprung necromancer. Their policy toward him was much the same as toward Geraldus, and both were grateful. Both had learned that the price for this courtesy was slight. Geraldus was to entertain and Merlin was not to prophesy.

Merlin especially was glad not to be badgered with demands to tell the future. As anyone who had heard his prophecies knew, they were as vague and rambling as the Apocalypse, full of flames and symbolic animals. If Merlin knew what they meant, he refused to make them clearer. Truly, he insisted, he wasn't always sure what they meant. Sometimes they seemed like the spoutings of a stranger, torn from his mouth. He never would have spoken at all if he had had some control over himself. For he had other visions, too, clear ones, when the pattern of the future was spread before him like a view from a mountain top, only obscured here and there by wandering clouds. They involved people, individuals, some of whom he loved dearly. Arthur was one. And Guinevere was mixed up in it somewhere; but he could not see the end, only that she would cause everyone much pain, especially herself. He could never look at the girl without a chill sweeping over him. He had noticed the change in her at first glance and was troubled. If only he could get her away, to Armorica. Anywhere she might be sent to keep her from entering the world of men.

He couldn't help admiring her, though. He saw the way she carried herself with a graceful flow that added to the impression she gave of being not quite of this earth. She was still unconcious of her ripening body, which made her all the more beautiful as she tried neither to hide nor to flaunt it. Even her eyes had been fashioned to arouse wonder. In the sunlight they were as green as grass and by fire they were almost the color of a cloudy sea.

"And she is as heedless as a yearling colt," he muttered as he watched her playing running games with the boys. They had set up a course with sudden turns and bars to jump. Guinevere's agility matched the greater speed of her brothers and the game was a close one. Her arms and legs were bare and her laugh shimmered across the warm meadow.

"Why can't she just stay as she is!" Merlin sighed. "As beautiful, elusive, and emptyheaded as a deer in the woods. Probably as heartless."

He wronged her there, but even a prophet cannot see everything, and Guinevere's heart had not yet been needed for anything more than keeping her blood upon its course.

That evening a courier arrived from Arthur with a message for Merlin, who heard it grimly and sent back a reply at once. The poor rider only had time for some meat and ale before he was sent off again on a new mount. He thought enviously of his horse comfortably stabled for the night, while he raced once again into the dark forest.

Merlin was moody all through dinner. He spoke little, and Guinevere was sure that he glared at her just to keep her from eating. His silence affected all the others, and the meal was a somber one. Afterwards, Mark, Matthew, and John fled to the stables, where they could be sure of at least a game of chance and perhaps some spicy local gossip. Guinevere gladly went with Flora to help in laying out the herbs, fresh-picked, to be dried in the sun the next day. Flora had also been gloomy that summer, but at least she only sighed and moaned and did not stare at one as if one had committed an unpardonable sin.

When all had left but Merlin, Guenlian, Leodegrance and Geraldus, Merlin finally came back to life. Geraldus didn't notice the other three. He was listening to a new attempt by his chorus. It was basically a roundelay, but occasionally the alto would venture out on a melody of her own, which would cause Geraldus' heart to beat ecstatically. Consequently, he missed the conversation until he was called into it.

"I have had a message from Arthur," Merlin began sententiously. "The Saxons have been pushed back south of London and the Picts north of Hadrian's Wall, thanks to the efforts of our good cousin, Cador. They will not trouble us again before next spring, he feels. The Saxons in the south have given hostages, which Arthur turned over to Cador on his trip homeward."

"That is excellent news, Merlin!" Leodegrance exclaimed. "Why, then, do you wear such a dismal face? I could barely eat with your morose countenance always before me."

"Yes, we should rejoice, cousin," agreed Guenlian. "Perhaps this is the turn of fortune we have been waiting and working for all our lives!"

"That I cannot see," Merlin sighed. "Arthur has only asked —against my wishes—if you would be willing to allow him to bring a few of his officers and other men of good family to camp on your land and rest and hunt for a while. He thinks they will arrive in perhaps three weeks."

"We would be honored to entertain such a great *dux bellorum,*" Leodegrance replied. "At last!" he thought. "A chance to see this unknown quantity and judge him for myself."

He said aloud, "The harvest should be nearly over by then, at least of the grains. The grapes will be a bit late. We should be able to support them quite well for a few weeks at least. Tell him we should be pleased to have him share our home."

Guenlian nodded. "Of course. Why do you doubt our hospitality? Is there something about him that we should know, something that keeps you from wanting us to meet him? Tell us now."

Merlin shifted uncomfortably in his chair. The pillow was soft and thick, but he might have been seated on pointed rock for all the comfort it gave him.

"It is not Arthur I worry about, nor his men; though some of them have been brought up more to war and the chase than to fine linen and philosophy. No, Arthur is young still, but he has a good heart and a fine mind. They both need training, as he has spent them primarily on military strategy and earning the devotion of his soldiers. He will not shame me with his manners. But there is a problem which I find very difficult to speak of. I do not wish to put an unfounded fear into your minds."

He hesitated and Leodegrance jumped in.

"You cannot possibly unnerve us more with your problem than you do now with your evasions and hedgings."

Merlin bowed his apology. "Yes, it is unpleasant, but I feel I must speak. The disaster I fear is—Guinevere."

"What! Don't be ridiculous! She is but a child! What could she do to harm anyone?!"

47

Both her parents had risen to their feet in indignation. Merlin quelled them with a look.

"Don't allow your adoration of the child to cloud your judgment in the matter. She is nearly thirteen and shows no signs of the ungainliness or self-consciousness of others of her age. Many of Arthur's 'men' and even Arthur, himself, are barely out of their teens, if that."

"Are you suggesting that they would behave improperly to her?" Leodegrance roared. At the end of the table Geraldus looked up for a moment. Leodegrance lowered his voice. "Her brothers and I would chop down any man who came within arm's reach of my daughter!"

"Never fear anything so obvious. They are not the sort to take advantage of the child of a lord as great as you, although all their hosts' daughters might not fare so well. You might warn the serving maids and fosterlings to be somewhat more circumspect in their dress. Everyone at this place lives in a fantasy world! I truly believe it! But that is not the point. Guinevere is beautiful. You would certainly not deny that. She is also charming of manner and has a special air about her. Perhaps it comes from her family. You have given her everything she could want and protected her as even an emperor's child was not. There is probably not another child in Christendom so lucky. And to all of this you add the most valuable dowry in Britain. Do you not see the dissension she could cause?"

Guenlian's head had begun to ache. She felt tears behind her eyelids but refused to let them through. "Not my baby!" she screamed in her heart. But her face remained calm and her voice was as cool as spring rain.

"Possibly, this is true. We have not considered our daughter yet as a marriage prize. But you are right that she is nearing the age when such things must be considered. However, Guinevere is totally innocent of these matters."

"That makes her all the more alluring . . . and dangerous!" Merlin answered flatly.

"What about her dowry?" Leodegrance interrupted. "I have less real wealth than many of the lords of Britain. No land to speak of, and that will go to my eldest son. Why should anyone think that there is anything else of value I might give along with Guinevere, the brightest jewel of my house?"

His voice was suspicious. He guessed what Merlin was leading to and he wanted it out in the open.

Merlin's voice was kinder, more normal now. He had said the hardest part and he could relax.

"First, there is the honor of your name. You are one of the oldest and best-born families in Britain. You needn't wave modestly; you know it's true and you pride yourselves on it. You should be proud, for you are worthy descendants of the Republic. I would rather have a Roman senator among my forebears than all the emperors combined. Secondly, you have something in your keeping which is of great value. It is not yours, though, no more than it was Uther's, who gave it to you."

Leodegrance clenched his jaw.

"Say no more, Merlin. I shall never release the table to any except one I deem worthy of it."

"How can you do that? You have no idea of its power or its use! Uther knew even less. He was afraid of it and would have burnt it, if I had not insisted that it be given to you. I didn't know why, then. I just knew that you were the one ordained to hold this thing. But now I am beginning to understand. I don't want the table revealed any more than you do. But are you aware that all your children have known of this thing, practically since they could walk? It has formed the substance of most of their dares and fantasies since I can remember."

"Of course, I knew they had seen it. But they are the only ones, and they will be the stewards of it after I am gone. I allow no one else in the cave and the entrance is well secured."

"You don't know that they have told others of this thing? To them it's just a family oddity and of no importance, but others have heard. What better way to acquire such a treasure than to form an alliance with your house?"

He had made his point. To Leodegrance, his daughter was the most precious treasure in his keeping, and the table was a sacred trust. He was not prepared to relinquish either.

49

"You say that you wish to prevent such an occurrence, at least forestall it. What do you want us to do?" Leodegrance's voice was hard in his effort to keep it steady. He disliked Merlin intensely at that moment.

"There are two alternatives. First, you could wrap Guinevere in long robes with her head covered like a Roman matron whenever she is out, and try to keep her inside and away from the guests whenever possible."

"Ridiculous!" Guenlian shouted. "She would never understand such a thing and couldn't be made to remember."

"I agree," Merlin nodded. "It would be illogical and entirely ineffectual. Her wrapping would only make her more provocative. The other choice is to send her away for the duration of the visit."

"That would be no better! Guinevere has not spent a night away from us in her life. What would she think if we banished her from the house, especially with important guests expected?"

"Tell her whatever you think best. Let her know you don't think the company appropriate companions for her, if you like. Assure her that it will be only for a few weeks. Anything. She needn't go far. You could send her to Timon and Gaia. Tell her it's for the good of her soul." Merlin was reaching the end of his patience. "Make it a religious experience!"

They considered this suggestion as best they could. It was hard to decide so suddenly, when ten minutes before they had had no thought of ever letting their child out of their sight. It was clear that Merlin was right. She had to go before Arthur and his soldiers arrived.

It might be possible. Timon and Gaia were brother and sister who, twenty years before, had vowed poverty, chastity, and unity with all God's creatures. They had removed themselves far into the forest and now lived alone, in a remarkably beautiful house that they had constructed themselves, with no knowledge of how to plan or build one. Through some lucky chance or divine intervention, the house resembled the woods around it. A stream tumbled by the door. They kept bees and chickens, collected the fruits and nuts of the forest, and occasionally bartered honey for flour. In short, they lived peacefully, as if the golden age of the world had never faded. Guinevere had never met them, but Leodegrance and Guenlian knew them well. Guenlian had once found refuge there at a time when no other hiding place was safe. They were sure they could trust their daughter to this pious pair without fear. Yes, Merlin was right. Guinevere would be sent on a retreat.

The room was still. Merlin knew they had decided. The only sound was Geraldus, impatiently trying to keep the chorus in time.

"One, two, three, FOUR!" he mumbled. "One, two, three, FOUR!! It's not right yet. Try again, from the beginning."

"How are they, tonight?" Merlin asked. He was another who accepted the singers without interpretation.

"I have a whole new batch of tenors. I have no idea where they came from," Geraldus answered distractedly. "They don't even know how to keep together. Then the basses and the altos want to start on polyphony. We've hardly gotten beyond a simple round and they want to harmonize!"

His voice trailed off into annoyed muttering as the music apparently started again.

"Geraldus!" Guenlian raised her voice to attract his attention, feeling slightly silly in the quiet room.

"Geraldus, dear. We would like to ask a favor of you."

The saint pulled his attention back to them. "What? Certainly. Anything you like. Only please don't ask me to preach. I never know what to say and all this racket makes it hard to keep from repeating myself."

"Nothing of the kind," Leodegrance assured him. "We would like you to undertake a commission for us. We want you to deliver something very precious to Gaia and Timon at their retreat."

Geraldus relaxed. He hated preaching, but traveling was fine. Just the right time of year for it, too, and Gaia and Timon always had a warm greeting and the most wonderful bread and honey.

"Fine. I can go whenever you like. What is it you want me to take to them?"

There was a pause.

"We want you carefully to convey the Lady Guinevere to them for a visit." Merlin spoke for all three of them.

"What? Does she know about this? I had thought she wanted . . ." he stopped. "Of course. Not my business. But I thought that she was expecting to stay here and see Arthur."

This produced a sensation among the others that even Geraldus didn't miss.

"Everyone knows he's coming. It's been in the wind for days. Haven't you noticed the excessive amount of chattering among the women; not to mention the excitement among your foster sons? They've been beating each other's brains out on the practice field all week to be in shape in case Arthur should want them to go with him. All the cacaphony around here is almost as bad as my singers."

"Ouch!!" He slapped his arm. He had felt something very much like a pinch.

Merlin glanced woefully at Guenlian.

"So everyone knows that Arthur is coming. All the more reason for her to go. If I can't keep a piece of news secret, it would be impossible for me to try to hide an entire girl. We can spend a week or two preparing her to travel. But please don't wait longer! I would feel even more at ease if she were sent across the Channel. Don't alarm yourselves. I know that can't be. We will have to hope that a mountain hermitage is remote enough to prevent any encounters. Geraldus, will you accompany the Lady Guinevere to the home of Timon and Gaia in two weeks' time?"

"Of course. I will be happy to oblige you. Now I must excuse myself."

Geraldus left with a troubled face. Merlin wasn't sure if it was because of Guinevere or if the singers had started up again.

He sighed. "The next thing will be to explain to Guinevere, herself. If she has set her heart on seeing Arthur, it will be more difficult. To the best of my memory, Guinevere has never, in her entire thirteen years, been denied anything she has really wanted. This is not the best time to start, but deny her you must."

"You have frightened us quite sufficiently," Leodegrance assured him with anger. "Guinevere will go, whether she wants to or not. We do not need any more of your advice or doom-saying."

Abruptly, he too left the table.

Guenlian and Merlin gazed at each other in the candlelight. He held out a hand to her.

"Forgive me, Cousin. I seem to sow dissension wherever I go." He stared moodily into the flickering flame.

Guenlian thought, "How old he is getting! He can't be much past forty, but his face already has deep lines. And all his life he has lived like this, running another man's errands. He seems to have no refuge of his own. I don't believe his father was a demon, as they say. But there are times when he does seem to be carrying some dreadful curse."

She took his outstretched hand. They sat together in silence, watching the candle die.

ChAPTER FOUR

Guinevere! Guinevere! Unbar the door, darling. Let me come in." Guenlian's voice was low and pleading.

"No! You don't love me! None of you loves me! You just want to be rid of me!"

That's what Guinevere answered, but, between the tears and the blanket over her head, her mother could only guess at the words. Guenlian sighed and decided to wait awhile. She went back to her own room, from which she was trying to direct ten different projects, each to be finished before Arthur and his men arrived.

Guinevere burrowed farther into her covers. Despite the heat, she felt the need of thick wool around her. As Merlin had predicted, she was not submissively accepting the command to leave her home just when so many exciting visitors were coming. She couldn't believe that anyone would want her away from them. She felt confused, frightened, and betrayed. If she had known how the hurt in her eyes stabbed at her parent's hearts, she might have been comforted. But they had stood firm, and she never guessed the fears that preyed upon them. They were all against her! Flora, her brothers, even Geraldus. Her best friend! He had only patted her shoulder and said, "Why would you want to meet all those barbarian soldiers when you could be on the road with me? They probably care nothing for music. And in this heat, having to entertain! You will be so much happier in the cool forest with Timon and Gaia. Then, in a month or so, when the weather is better, I'll return for you."

"A month or so!" This to a child who had not spent even a night away from her parents in her life? Guinevere kicked wildly upon her bed, beating with clenched fists at the injustice of it all.

But nothing availed; not tears nor temper nor pitiable sorrow. Everyone was kind, loving, sympathetic. All the same, two weeks later a stony-faced Guinevere sat on her horse next to old Plotinus and waited for Geraldus to finish loading her things on the pack horse. Everyone in the household was there to see her off, but she kept her face veiled and refused even to say goodbye.

She scarcely bent when Guenlian reached up to hold her for one last moment.

"Please, my darling," she whispered. "Believe that this is for the best. We only want to keep you safe."

"Where could I be safer than here?" Guinevere sobbed from behind her veil. But she didn't return Guenlian's kiss.

Geraldus was finally ready. Gingerly he mounted his ancient horse and they set off.

Soon they were out of sight of the compound and into the forest. The air was still but cooler. Soft swishes and crackles filtered from the trees and bushes by the path. The birds had already hidden from the sun and only an occasional chitter was heard above. The hard-baked trail was broad and well traveled. The marks of a thousand horses had worn it smooth and free of obstacles, which was well, for Guinevere still sat tautly upon her horse, holding the reins slack, seeing nothing about her. Geraldus was humming with a dreamy expression. Occasionally he would slip into a tune, although he mainly seemed to be singing counterpoint. Finally Guinevere glanced at him and saw the woman with the black hair and laughing face seated daintily behind him, sideways, not even holding on. She noticed Guinevere and made a wry face. Then she started tickling Geraldus' ear with the fringe of her belt.

Guinevere refused to be tricked into undignified laughter. She stared coolly at the woman and then turned her head away. Her heart still raged at the unfairness of her life.

"What am I?" she fumed to herself. "A slave to be ordered about? A doll to be cast aside? I am almost a woman and they treat me as if I were a baby. I will never let anyone else do this to me again. I will control where I go and what I do!"

Her mind wandered to grand visions of herself as mistress of her own house, ordering her servants about. But the home was strangely like her own and the people the ones who had always cared for her. It made her uneasy to think about it existing without her parents and she tried to think of something else.

The air was pungent with late summer flowers and dry pine needles. The sun warmed her and Geraldus' humming belonged to the day, soft and peaceful. Her hands began to gather up the reins and, after a moment's thought, she hitched up her robe and threw her leg over the horse. Riding astride might not be dignified, but it was much more comfortable. Her long, brown legs dangled contentedly against the horse's flank.

Geraldus turned around and smiled. "I'm glad to have you with me," he said. "It's lonely sometimes traveling, even with my voices."

The last knot in Guinevere's stomach relaxed and she smiled back. "With the crowd you bring with you, I feel that we're traveling in a caravan. I don't see how you can be lonely with all this company."

She indicated them with her arm, especially the woman riding with Geraldus.

He flashed her a puzzled grin. "Can you hear them, too?" he asked in amazement.

Guinevere laughed. "How could I? I'm not a saint. But I can see them all around you sometimes. They fade in and out. The clearest one is the woman behind you."

Geraldus' jaw dropped to his chest. Then an eager light came into his eyes. He groped at the air behind him, but the dark-haired woman slid off before he could reach her.

"Do you mean to say that you can see them?" he gasped.

"Do you mean to say that you can't?" Guinevere was just as puzzled. "You always seem to know where they are. I just assumed."

"How could I not know where they were, with all that caterwauling! They have always been just sound to me. But that woman. Is she still here? I can't hear her. Is she near me?"

"Yes, over there by that willow. She's laughing. She's always laughing."

"What . . . what does she look like?" Geraldus' voice trembled.

Guinevere squinted. "She's hard to see all the time, she moves so. But she has raven black hair fastened only by two jeweled pins at the sides. It falls to her knees and keeps swirling around her. Her face is pretty, but she doesn't look the way I thought an angel would."

"Forget that, child," Geraldus pleaded. "Tell me about her face."

"A straight nose, large eyes, rather pointed chin." The woman impishly covered her face with her hands. "And beautiful long fingers," Guinevere concluded enviously. She had always been rather embarrassed by her short, unaristocratic fingers.

"She has a green sort of gauzy gown on. I can't quite see how it's put together. There seem to be a lot of loose pieces sewn to the waist so that her legs can move freely. There's not very much of it on top." The woman laughed. Guinevere frowned. "I don't think Mother would approve."

"Never mind your mother." Geraldus spoke sharply. His eyes were straining to see into the shadowy limbs of the tree, but he saw no one there . . . His fingernails dug into his palms and his thoughts were astonishingly secular.

"She's gone now," Guinevere told him flatly. "They all are. Sometimes they do that."

"Oh no!" moaned Geraldus. "Do you think it's my fault? Oh, Guinevere, why didn't you tell me you could see them?"

"I didn't know you couldn't," she explained anxiously. "Please Geraldus, don't you be angry with me too. Everyone is acting so differently toward me lately. I won't be able to stand it if you change too. I'll tell you all I know. Really! She's just a woman; not very special except that she laughs so much. There are lots of others who are funnier. There's the man with the long face who's always pulling on his ear, and the short one whose robe is too long, and many other women. I just can't see them as well. But if you want, I'll look very carefully. I'll tell you exactly what they look like. . . ."

She stopped. He wasn't listening, but still was gazing raptly into the trees. His arms reached out and then flopped to his sides.

"I don't hear them anymore," he said. "Let's go. We still have a long journey before us. We'll have to camp in the woods tonight."

For the first time, he noticed the fear on Guinevere's face. "Don't worry," he sighed. "I'm back now."

His knees jabbed old Plotinus, and they plodded on again.

The remainder of the trip was made in silence. They soon left the main road and entered the forest on a thin trail so covered with moss and pine needles and decayed leaves that the hooves of the horses made no sound. Geraldus stared bleakly straight before him, his ears straining for just one note. His heart was beating so loudly that he wondered if the noise of it was not keeping them away. His body ached in a way he had often felt before, but not so strongly. He refused to put a name to the feeling. Guinevere could see that he was suffering, but couldn't understand. Was he upset with her because she could see these beings? Was he angry because she thought they weren't angels? She paused. But if they weren't angels, what were they? She forgot her resentment as she tried to work out this new mystery.

Finally Geraldus signaled a halt in a secluded natural clearing, just off the path. There was a stream nearby where they could wash. He took the blankets and bedding off the pack horse, cut some long branches from a nearby sapling, and made a lean-to bedroom for Guinevere.

"There," he said when he had finished. "It's not what you're used to, I know, but you should be comfortable enough. I'll be right out here by the fire if you need anything, and it's not likely to rain on a night like this."

Guinevere was delighted with her bedroom. It was a three-sided tent on a frame, draped with luxurious silk and woolen hangings. A thick straw mat had been placed on the ground and covered with the bedclothes. There was a curtain that could be let down in front for added privacy or warmth. Guenlian had sent the most costly and elegant of her own hangings in an attempt to pacify her daughter. They were much better than Guinevere was allowed at home.

"I feel like a queen in here, Geraldus. Come in and see! Oh, look! Mother even sent her own vanity box for my brushes and perfumes! See, it has a painting of my grandmother on it."

It was an ivory box, inlaid with semiprecious jewels. On the sides were Christian symbols, fish swimming across one and a Chi Rho on the other. On the top was a portrait of her grandmother, painted on wood in the manner of the last century. It was a good likeness, Guenlian had said, and Guinevere had always loved the proud, dark woman with the huge, sad eyes. It was Guenlian's greatest treasure next to her children, and Guinevere knew it, although she didn't understand how any object could come to mean so much to one. She softly caressed it and put it back in the oilskin wrappings.

Geraldus was building a fire, more for light and companion-ship than anything else, for the night would still be warm. They had bread, meat, and fruit for their dinner, and he brought fresh water from the brook to mix with their wine. He tried to show some interest in Guinevere's delight and was indeed glad that she had lost her sulkiness. But he could only think of his alto. The voices had never been quiet this long before.

"What if she doesn't return!" he moaned. "They must come back. I won't try to touch you again, if you don't wish it. I promise! Anything! Only come back! Don't leave me alone!"

He shrank back into himself, frightened at the intensity of his emotions. "I'm used to them, that's all," he told himself. "We were just beginning polyphony. Oh, but what shall I do without her?"

He tried to imagine himself back home again, on the moun-tains, herding the sheep and wandering alone. It did not cheer him. The fire crackled and flickered its best, but Geraldus saw nothing.

In her tent, Guinevere was happily pretending to be Cleopatra, sending Mark Antony out to do battle for her. Plutarch's *Lives of the Noble Romans* had been one of her earliest books, even before the gospels. And, although Tenuantius had added morals at every opportunity, Guinevere had only caught the glamour and grandeur of the stories.

"Begone, minion," she snapped at an imaginary slave. She thought of what might happen if she ever spoke to Flora or even Caet in that manner. Better not to consider it. But the thought reminded her of a new problem.

She poked her head out.

"Geraldus!" she called. "Mother forgot something. Who will comb my hair?"

Geraldus lifted his head from his hands. "What?"

"I said, there is no one to comb my hair. What shall I do?"

The saint brushed his fingers through his shoulder-length hair. Although other men of the day wore their hair short, it was considered more holy to let it grow, and he had. But as for combing it. . . .

"Can't you do it yourself?"

"I don't think so. Flora always combed and rebraided it every night and morning. It's very long. I don't think I could reach."

This problem was too much for Geraldus.

"Why don't you just not do it tonight? We will be at the hermitage tomorrow and then Gaia can comb it for you."

That settled the matter in his mind and he went back to his worries. But Guinevere was still perplexed. She had been told every night of her life that horrible things would happen to her if her hair were not combed, scented, and braided again at least once a day. She fumbled with the knots in the plaits and loosened them until her hair was flowing freely about her waist. Then she discovered that she couldn't comb one section without another getting tangled. Also, it was difficult to keep it from getting too near the lit grease lamp. She cried out in vexation, but Geraldus was straining to hear his chorus and didn't notice.

She had given up and was trying to braid it again as best she could, which was very badly, when she felt a tug at the back. The bone comb was slipping through her hair by itself! She gave a startled yelp and the laughing woman appeared. She put her finger to her lips. Guinevere nodded and sat docilely while her hair was expertly arranged. She felt the braids being wound about her head and fastened with something. She put up her hands to feel and found the little jeweled pins. The woman tossed her dark hair off her face and smiled tenderly at her.

"Oh, thank you," Guinevere whispered. "May I keep them?"

She nodded and kissed the girl gently on the cheek. Then, laying her finger on her lips again, she slipped out of the tent.

Exhausted, Guinevere blew out the lamp and went to sleep. She never thought of telling Geraldus that she had seen the woman again.

The next morning was cloudy, which matched Geraldus' mood perfectly. He scolded the weather, the woods, and even his long-suffering horse. Guinevere had found that even silken sheets can't make a pallet on the ground as comfortable as a bed. She hadn't slept well and had had the strange feeling all night that something was watching her. She had even slipped out of the tent at dawn to look but had seen nothing except Geraldus curled up next to the ashes of the campfire.

Still, the adventure of the journey was growing in her, and during the silent morning as they rode she woke up more and more. The forest had overgrown the path they were taking, and it was clear that no one had traveled that way in a long time. In some places there were tangles of wild flowers and berries. In others the deer had trampled the grass and undergrowth down almost flat. In those spots one could see far into the woods, between the trees. Occasionally, Guinevere thought she could see a flash of silver, as of something running swiftly by. There was something familiar about it; it wasn't water and it wasn't metal. Then she remembered the light she had followed the night she had been lost.

She almost turned her horse to chase it now, but the form vanished. She trotted up to just behind Geraldus; there wasn't room to ride abreast.

"Geraldus," she called softly. "Look into the woods. I keep seeing something, but it's not clear."

But Geraldus didn't lift his head.

"It's no use. I can't see them. They won't let me. Now they won't even sing for me. I wish I'd never tried. Now I'm alone. All alone!"

Guinevere wanted to say something to comfort him, but she really didn't know what. She was sorry Geraldus felt that way, of course. But he wasn't really alone. He had lots of friends who liked him whether he heard angels or not. And, after all, she was there now. Why wouldn't he listen to her?

"I'm sure your voices will come back," she began. "But this is something different in among the trees, something silvery. Won't you look?"

He glanced to either side. "I don't see anything. I told you I wouldn't. Do you think it would help if I prayed for them to come back?"

"I suppose so. If they are angels they will hear you and, if you are deserving, they will grant your request." She spoke as if from a textbook.

"Guinevere!" Geraldus shouted, rising to sit up straight. "Damn the angels! Don't you understand . . . ?"

He trailed off. Her puzzled, frightened expression shamed him and told him that she knew nothing of what he felt or longed for. There wasn't even sympathy in her eyes, only confusion.

"Merlin was right," he thought as, after a moment, they went on. "She is years younger in emotion than her age would allow. Perhaps she has a heart, but so far no one has laid any claim to it. Poor little girl! I hope life is kind to her and she doesn't find that she can love only when all she loves is gone, like me."

For a time he forgot his own grief in worrying about his charge. Suddenly he felt something brush against his ear, something soft and silky. He almost turned around to reach for it but wisely remembered in time. He closed his eyes tightly as the tears squeezed through his lashes. Someone was humming. Soon she was joined by the tenor, flat again, and two sopranos, somewhat improved. With a gasp, Geraldus joined in.

Guinevere saw the translucent green of the woman's gown, and heard Geraldus trying counterpoint again. She smiled. It was nice that they were back and Geraldus was happy again. How silly he had been to worry so much. Perhaps now he would help her to find out what that light was.

CHAPTER FIVE

T he ground began to slant upward as they climbed the hill to the hermitage.

"We have only an hour or so more to travel," Geraldus called. "But we might as well stop and finish the meat for our noon meal. Timon and Gaia won't have animal flesh anywhere near their home."

Guinevere slid from her horse. "Yes, I know. Mother told me. I suppose I won't mind it for a few weeks, but I can't imagine how they could give up meat entirely. I don't see how I could live without an occasional pork pie or chicken leg. I wonder if that is what is meant by Christian denial?"

She shook her head sagely and bit into her meat avidly. Geraldus laughed.

"No, I can't imagine you ever living in a hermitage, wearing rough wool and eating beans and barley bread."

Guinevere laughed, too. "No, I'm afraid I much prefer to let someone else pray for my soul while I attend to the needs of my body."

They carefully removed the greasy traces of their lunch and started again on their way.

As if to make up for their earlier absence, the troupe of singers had been growing all day. They crowded into the narrow path all around the horses. Some even climbed onto the pack horse, who didn't seem to notice the extra weight. Guinevere had tried at first to look for the silver light, but she gave up. Even though she couldn't see the singers clearly, they made an effective screen against seeing anything in the woods. Geraldus was far ahead of her by late afternoon, but his loud complaints could be clearly heard.

"NO! No! That's not it. DUM da da da da DUM, and then the sopranos join in. Try it again!"

Despite his bluster, even Guinevere could hear the jubilation in his voice.

The shadows of the trees crisscrossed the path before they arrived at the clearing where Timon and Gaia lived. They appeared to be nowhere near a place of human habitation. The forest was thick and dark about them. Suddenly, they rounded a bend in the path and the whole group spilled out into a large open space, where the ground had been scratched bare by thirty generations of chickens. The sound of water splashing over rocks mingled with the constant drone of bees.

In the twilight it was hard to see the house. It took Guinevere a moment to recognize it as one. It was made of stone slabs that had been dragged into position and lined up to form a lopsided square. Then wood and clay had been used to fill the spaces left, except for the doorway. Later, Guinevere would see the window in the back, not made of the thick, greenish glass they used at home, but of some sort of cloth that had been rubbed with wax until it was translucent. In the wooden door was a small oval of real glass, with a blue Chi Rho painted on it. The roof was clay and wattle with a hole in the center for the smoke to escape.

It was beautiful, in a wild sort of way, but Guinevere fought back a surge of depression at the thought of living in it. It was not the sort of place for a pampered Roman lady to stay. She wondered how one of such a good family as Gaia's could tolerate such a place. As she was thinking this, the door opened and a woman came out.

All thought of protest left her mind as Guinevere stared at Gaia. Somehow, she had imagined Timon and his sister as a kindly elderly couple. After all, they had lived in the forest for twenty years and had been grown when they came there. Gaia did not fit Guinevere's image at all.

First, she was tall, taller than most of the men Guinevere knew. She had had to duck her head to get through the doorway.

Added to this was her bearing. Guinevere knew at once that Gaia could belong here as she would anywhere. She was a complete arrogant aristocrat. Her home was a palace simply because she lived there. She wore a white linen robe with some sort of woven belt and plain bronze shoulder pins. Her head was covered, but the black braids wound tightly around her forehead showed only a few streaks of gray. Her face was lined, but more by wind and sun and self-control than age.

"Timon!" she called. "They are here."

She waited in silence as Geraldus and Guinevere dismounted. Guinevere edged shyly behind Geraldus, who didn't seem the least bit intimidated.

He strode up to Gaia, hugged her tightly and, to Guinevere's amazement, gave her a smacking kiss.

"The kiss of peace," he said, laughing, and Gaia's hard face relaxed.

"Peace be to you," she responded. "I suppose you have brought your usual company with you."

He nodded.

"There is a crock of honey mead by the house and new-baked bread for you," she called to the air.

Immediately, the throng around Geraldus disappeared.

"And this is Leodegrance and Guenlian's baby." She held Guinevere at arm's length, staring fiercely into her eyes. "She doesn't favor anyone in the family whom I ever met. So, you are making us a visit? Are you willing to help with our work and obey our rules? It will not be what you are used to and I, for one, will not pamper you."

Guinevere had no doubt of it. Trembling a little, she answered, "I will do as you do, as far as I am able."

Gaia released her. "Good. We will see that you are not given tasks above your ability."

She turned away and began to discuss old friends with Geraldus. Guinevere felt she had been dismissed. She stood apart, feeling ignored and hurt. The conversation was animated. It appeared that Gaia knew Merlin well and had a high opinion of him. This didn't make Guinevere feel any better. Also, they had once been host to Arthur, when he was a boy.

"Yes," Gaia was saying. "Merlin brought him for a short stay. He was a pleasant boy: didn't talk much but was curious about everything. He spent more time with Timon than with me. I can't believe he's grown up to be a warrior; a man whose job it is to kill and destroy."

"He's a good man," Geraldus answered stoutly, "though still very young. His duty now is to drive out the invaders, to make this island safe for ones such as we, who will not fight. I don't believe he glories in battle."

"I hope not," Gaia answered grimly. "I would hate to regret ever having given him shelter."

All this time, Guinevere had been standing by the house, outwardly docile and inwardly raging. She had worked herself up to a fit of righteous fury when she saw a man step out of the woods. Her jaw dropped. If Gaia had been surprising, Timon was unbelievable.

He was an enormous man, as tall as his sister and wider. He looked like a great, brown bear, with thick hairy arms and legs and a flowing beard that covered his face and twined itself into his shoulder-length hair. Guinevere half expected him to spring at her, growling and gnashing his teeth.

He gave a huge grin when he saw her face and stopped a good distance away.

"Is this the little girl come to visit us?" he asked and his voice was so soft and gentle, coming from his rough face, that Guinevere almost wept with relief.

Gaia stopped her conversation and returned to Guinevere. "Of course it is, brother. Why don't you get her baggage and show her the place we have for her in our home."

"Guenlian has sent far more luxurious things than she should have, I fear," she added to Geraldus. "We will not chide her now about them, but slowly try to wean her from a love of worldly things."

"You will have a hard time weaning that one from a love of comfort," Geraldus replied jokingly. "She has been surrounded by it so completely that it would never occur to her that there was any other way to live. Don't mistake me," he added hastily. "She is not indolent or haughty. I am truly fond of her. She has just known one way of life and believes that all people would live that way, unless, like you, they deliberately choose another."

Gaia only shook her head at such ignorant innocence.

Geraldus spent the night and departed the next morning, enriched by gifts of honey and mead and with his chorus dancing happily about him. Guinevere sighed as she watched him go. She felt that her last hope of rescue was gone.

It was not really as bad as her misery made it seem. Life with Gaia and Timon was much better than with most hermits. They were not really as fanatic as was the fashion. They lived in a clean, dry home and washed their clothes in the stream. They ate such food as nature provided and were not above improving their vegetables by cooking them and even adding herbs. Timon even used the honey and angelica to make mead, a sweet and potent sort of liquor. Still, their days were guided by prayer, work, and meditation in even amounts, and it was a hard change for Guinevere.

They awoke at dawn and prayed in the clearing as the sun rose, thanking God for the gift of the day. Then they each worked for an hour or two before eating a breakfast of eggs, honey, and bread. Then they went to a private place to pray again and to ponder the mysteries of the universe. At least this is what Gaia did when she meditated. Guinevere couldn't imagine Timon wondering about such things.

At first she had rebelled, though silently, at the life. The jobs given her were not difficult, but she felt they were menial. The sight of Gaia washing her own clothes was enough to stifle her protests, but not enough to cause her to resign herself to the work.

The constant solitude irritated her, too. At first the command, "Find a quiet spot, free from distractions and there meditate," had seemed ridiculous. Obediently she had gone a little way into the forest, found a pleasant spot under a pine tree and composed herself to think of religious matters. But she didn't know how to start. The prayers one recited each day at mass and at vespers somehow weren't right out here. Oddly enough, she could only think of Ovid and his story of creation, the Golden Age of men and gods.

The years went by in peace and Earth, untroubled,
Unharried by hoe or plowshare, brought forth all
That men had need for, and those men were happy,
Cherries or black caps and the edible acorns,
Spring was forever and a west wind blowing
Softly across the flowers no man had planted,
. . . . and there were rivers
Of milk and rivers of honey, and golden nectar
Dripped from the dark-green oak tree.

That story had always been dearer to her than those in the bible. She had been studying the *Metamorphoses* all summer and loved it. She could almost see the happy men and gods laughing together in the untainted forest. The oak across from her shimmered as if about to pour forth the golden nectar. Streaks of sunlight dappled the air. Guinevere murmured the words, the rich Latin softened by her British tongue. The stillness was perfect and beautiful. Her eyes closed.

She awakened sometime later with the feeling that someone was watching her. She had felt this often recently and it made her vaguely uneasy. She had been dreaming again, something heartbreakingly joyous, and it had hurt her to wake. There was only a wisp of her dream left, something about mingled silver and gold and a feeling of great speed and freedom. She tried to grasp it a moment longer, but it was gone.

Timon and Gaia had a strict rule that meditation must never be interrupted, and that was probably why no one had come looking for her. But she feared they would be angry and think she was shirking her duty if she stayed away so long. She hurriedly gathered her robes about her and tried to smooth her hair. As she left, she thought she heard a sound, as of some large animal, in the woods behind her. She turned to look. There was a thicket of bushes and vines to the left of the path. The leaves shivered. She saw a splash of silver and then it was gone.

She made her way back slowly, wondering. She had no fear of this thing, only deep curiosity and a strange longing.

"What can it be, this silver light? Why does it follow me but never let me catch it?"

She returned to the same place for the next few days. But she saw nothing more.

After a week or two, Guinevere became accustomed to the pattern of life at the hermitage and, oddly enough, she found that she enjoyed it. She wasn't given much work to do and she could hardly continue to resent having to wash dishes or help prepare the meals when her hosts, as wellborn as she, did so too.

She grew to love Timon, who had at first seemed so huge and menacing. He was a gentle, easygoing person with no pretensions, either of holiness or nobility. He rumbled about in his garden or among his bees in perfect contentment.

Guinevere preferred working with him, even though it was more strenuous, to staying in the dark hut, enduring Gaia's silence and accusing stares. Gaia always spoke civilly to Guinevere and was never unkind, but her whole manner was as forbidding as if she had raged at the child and beaten her. There was an air of barely controlled passion about Gaia, which Guinevere, who liked her emotions placid, could never get used to.

So she made a habit of offering to help Timon in the garden every morning. He made her a hoe from a stick and a sharp stone, tied together with a complicated array of knots, and he helped her whittle a shorter stick into a dibble for planting winter grain.

"Why don't you make it longer?" she asked. "I have to keep bending over and it hurts my back."

"A lot of reasons," he told her with a grin. "It's good for man to bow over the earth. You can see it better; you can smell its richness and, as you look down, you can give thought to the words of the scriptures, 'Dust ye be and unto dust shall ye return.' "

"That is gruesome," Guinevere said. "I am not at all sure that I came from dust and I don't mean to think about turning back into part of someone's garden."

He laughed again. "I find the thought rather pleasant, myself. One day I shall be part of the corn, making bread for unborn children to grow strong on. However, I trust you won't need to consider the matter for many years to come. Nevertheless, it will do you no harm to kneel close to the earth. Your eyes are more often on the sky."

Guinevere took the reprimand from him meekly, even

though she once would have been furious if anyone other than her parents had spoken to her so.

"It's not just the sky that I look at," she tried to explain. "The sky itself is boring, so empty and constantly blue; but the clouds, racing across the sunlight; the changing patterns they make on the leaves and grass, especially when the wind is wild. Sometimes, when I lie under the great oak trees at the top of the hill over there, when the sun is bright and the wind dancing all about, I believe I can hear music!"

She stopped a moment to see if Timon was laughing at her fancy, but his face showed only gentle understanding. So she went on.

"The ground contains many marvels, I know. I have considered the mystery of the blade of grass and the blind earthworm," she sighed. Their priest was very fond of drawing morals from the least of God's creatures. "But there is something about the things that move freely upon and above the earth that pleases me more. When I see a flock of geese streaming above me or catch a deer in the woods a moment before it leaps from sight—I don't know —I ache for them. I want to sprout wings or hooves and follow and follow."

She paused, a little embarrassed. She had never told anyone of that before, had hardly put it into words herself. Until she came to the hermitage, her days had been too occupied to allow more than the vaguest feeling of longing for . . . what? She smiled shyly at Timon. He smiled back in perfect understanding.

"How old are you, Guinevere?"

"Thirteen, last month."

"Ah," his voice was tender. "You are growing up. Not just in your body, everyone must do that, but in your heart. There are new questions that your childhood answers won't fit. You are beginning to feel the force of the world beyond yourself. Ah, well. I've always thought that in this well-ordered universe there must be answers for everything somewhere, if we know how to find them. Just don't grieve if the answers don't seem to be the right ones. You might not be asking the right question."

Guinevere nodded amiably and went on hoeing. She understood little of his philosophizing but enjoyed hearing him speak.

Long years later, she would remember his words when the questions became dire and the answers were all wrong.

One morning, a few days later, they were surprised to hear the sound of a horse approaching up the narrow path. Guinevere rushed out with an expectant smile. Surely it was someone to see her, perhaps to bring her home! But as the rider came nearer she realized that this man had never been to Guenlian's home. He must have been a monk. He was wrapped in a brown robe that may have once been gray wool but had probably only felt the touch of water when its owner had been caught out in a storm. In the bright sunlight, the filth ground into it shimmered a slimy green. Guinevere wondered if she would be obliged to receive a kiss of peace from him. She shuddered. The hands holding the reins were nearly as grimy as the robe. She heard Gaia come out behind her and sensed from the sudden gasp that she was not pleased with the visitor either. Gaia was as repulsed by filth as she was.

Suddenly, Gaia strode past Guinevere, brushing against her roughly. She held up her hand as if to repel the man as he drew nearer.

"Begone!" she shrieked. "You are no longer welcome in our home, Nennius. We warned you never to return!"

The horse halted. The man threw back his hood, revealing a fine Roman nose and eyes startlingly blue. Nothing more could be seen of his face for the brown mat of beard which covered it. His hair stuck to his forehead and glistened like his robe. He smiled; his teeth were stained and crooked.

"Now Gaia," he whispered. "You have no call for such a lack of hospitality to a fellow Christian."

Guinevere started. His voice was cultivated and proud, each word formed as if chiseled in stone.

Gaia grew stiff in her rage. "Christian! The word is desecrated by your tongue! Temptor! Purveyor of filth! Hypocrite! Go at once! Return to your decadent world. You shall never cross our threshold again!"

His smile faded. "You are as closeminded and foolish as ever,

Gaia. I will go if you really wish it. But I do not come alone, my dear. I have brought many worthy friends with me."

He patted the leather bag slung behind him.

"Look, my Gaia," his voice caressed her. "Gospels, saints' lives, even a copy of *Pastoral Care* and the new one by Boethius. Wouldn't you like a discussion with Dame Philosophia?"

His leering eyes never left hers as his fingers fumbled with the strings of the bag. Gaia stood stiff with hatred and yet seemed almost mesmerized. Violently she pulled her face away from his gaze. She threw a last epithet at him over her shoulder and raced back to the hut. She stumbled over the lintel and yanked the door shut behind her.

Timon had arrived to see her exit. He strode up to the monk, his face more stern than Guinevere had ever seen it. He grasped the reins tightly and turned the unresisting horse back down the trail.

"See what you have done to my poor sister," he chided. "Why do you return to torment her?"

"Do you see what your sister has done to me?" Nennius answered. "What other man would wait as I have for so many years?"

"Only a fool, Nennius," Timon answered. "Only a fool. You know Gaia better than anyone left on earth and yet you come here every year bringing the two things which tempt her most. You are cruel beyond words."

"Cruel? Foolish? I am not the one. Let her ask God what she has made of me through all these years. Would He not have planned better things for us both? It is she who is the fool to waste our lives; and you for supporting her in her insanity! Bah! I am sick with it." He ended suddenly.

"I will be back next summer; and the next and every year until I am too feeble to climb the path. She will give way yet. Good-bye, Timon. Watch over her. God and eternity will show us who the fools are."

Guinevere had stood astonished throughout the interchange, and she might have been a tree in the forest for all the attention anyone had paid her. She only started to come to life again after Nennius and his horse had disappeared once more into the trees. Timon turned around and only then seemed to realize that she was there and had witnessed the entire scene. He came and put his arm around her gently. From inside the hut could be heard the sound of wild, bitter sobbing, choked in vain.

"Let's walk for a time, Guinevere," Timon whispered. "She doesn't want us now."

The day was ripening and the woods about them were busy with the scurry of birds and animals. Summer would soon be over and the squirrels were busy filling hollow trees. They didn't care about strange human grief. Everything was preparing for the winter. A hard one, Tim guessed; the birds were already migrating, weeks ahead of their time.

They wandered quietly for a while, both pondering what had happened. Finally they came to her space in the woods, the little stone seat beneath the tree. He motioned her to sit and then paced back and forth across the clearing several times before he decided to speak.

"You need some explanation for this and I will tell you only if you realize that it is a sacred secret, never to be spoken of again, even to me. Above all, you must never let Gaia know I told you. Do you understand?"

She nodded.

He stood for a while, trying to find words to explain. How could she understand? Finally, he began.

"Gaia has truly loved only two things in her life, books and that man, Nennius. She cares for me, of course, but not the way she loves him. Yes, still. She denies it but I know. She could live happily without me anytime. Perhaps that's why she doesn't send me away, too. You can't imagine how she was when she was younger. I was always the stupid one; strong but not much for learning. In another time I might have been bought subcommand of a legion. I'm glad it was too late for that. But Gaia! She was brilliant and so beautiful!"

"She still is," Guinevere interrupted.

"Yes, she is still both. And that is her great grief. It's all the fault of that philosopher Pelagius! When his theories came to her she dove in, arguing them with every scholar who visited. I don't understand them! Even if I did, I don't see that it much matters

74

whether Christ was man or god or a bit of both. Then more preachers came, each one gloomier than the last, all telling us how to live a Christian life and divest ourselves of the worldly goods we loved so sinfully. Gaia listened and debated and read the scriptures and all the commentaries she could find. In the end she got the idea that she was doomed to everlasting torment if she didn't give up the ways of the flesh. But hot baths and cool wine never mattered to her, it was all Ovid and Lucretius and Plutarch and Virgil and, of course, Nennius. You mustn't think he was always like that, all filthy and smelling. He does that . . . well, I don't really understand that, either. Anyway, he was once a nice, clean-shaven Roman and a brilliant philosopher, too. They were betrothed by their own decision and our families were pleased. They seemed to be very happy in their own argumentative way. But then she decided that if she loved a thing, it must be sinful. She kept fretting because she couldn't get close to God while so surrounded by the World. She gave up all her books, even the Scriptures. She says that if she reads even one holy word all the wicked voluptuous ones will all come back to her. She daren't even be near a book. Every waking moment she prays that the longing will be taken from her. And, although she has never said a word, I think she fears that if she ever lets Nennius pass over our doorstep, her longing for him will be too strong to deny."

Guinevere sat listening, wondering. She couldn't understand why anyone would want to give up someone they loved, or that anyone could love something so much as to fear it was idolatrous. Gaia's sobbing still echoed in Guinevere's heart and she felt a strange thrill of pity for her. Suddenly, Gaia was human.

Timon saw her, sitting there so innocently, her forehead wrinkled with the effort of understanding. He worried about her.

"Guinevere," he said earnestly. "If you ever decide to devote your life to God alone, be sure you do it because you love Him more than anything else, not to deny your love for something of this earth. The earth isn't so awful. After all, God made it, too."

He shook himself, having said his piece. Again, Guinevere was reminded of a great, shaggy bear. He smiled at her. "I should finish the story. When Gaia turned eighteen, Nennius wanted to be married at once. He said that they had already waited longer than was necessary, but then she decided that since living with Nennius was what she wanted most, she had to get away from him at once. So she came up here. We all fought her. Father even tried to bring her back by force, but nothing worked. In the end they sent me up here to watch out for her. She thinks still that I only remain because of my promise, and that is another of the burdens she carries," he chuckled. "She can't believe that I am happier here with the animals and the bees than I ever was with all those educated Romans. Well, that's all. We've been up here nearly twenty years. Nennius declared that if she wouldn't marry him, he would become a monk, too. But he wouldn't give up books for anyone. So he travels about the world, hunting for manuscripts that can be loaned for copy, and brings them back to Britain. Gaia won't even look at one. But every time he returns, he comes here first, hoping to break her down."

Guinevere listened with growing wonder. It was a very romantic story, but silly, somehow. What good was Gaia to God up here, miserable? She felt vaguely that there must be an answer somewhere, that something in Gaia's beliefs had gotten turned around and a word would set it right. But it was beyond her. She shook her head and smiled at Timon, who was kneeling, breaking up a clod he had kicked loose, crumbling it until the soft dirt ran between his fingers.

"You won't mention this to Gaia, now," he cautioned again. "She thinks she's fooled everyone into thinking she's abandoned her early desires years ago. It would shame her terribly to think that others knew her weakness."

"She is the strongest person I have ever met," Guinevere answered. "I know I wouldn't have the courage to say a word to her."

"You mustn't be afraid of her, either, you know. She has a good heart; it just never occurs to her to use it."

They went back to their work, hoeing the beans they had planted when Guinevere arrived. Already the first tiny leaves were unfolding, close-huddled to the soil. Guinevere had never noticed this precarious beginning before, this first fragile advance from the dark ground into the sun and wind. It amazed her that they throve so, that anything so tiny could have a chance. When

Timon reminded her that even the great trees around them had started as seedlings, she flatly refused to believe it.

He laughed at her. "Do you think that they sprang full grown from the earth one morning, complete with bark and branches?"

"Well . . ."

"I suppose you think that I arrived in the world six feet tall and wearing a beard?"

She considered. "Do you know, I think you must have!"

She walked around him, staring up at his great mane of hair, tumbling over his broad chest and shoulders. He could never have been a fat, limp, pink baby. Her imagination, never great, could not conceive of this at all.

He roared in delight at this limit of her thought. "So be it then. I can't argue with you any more than I can with Gaia. Let us simply tend our garden and leave speculation to the scholars."

They continued their work in companionable silence. In the hut Gaia cried until she fell asleep.

CHAPTER SIX

The days slid by, summer waning as the garden flourished. Guinevere had long since meshed with the rhythm of Timon's work cycle. She trotted after him, tending bees, cultivating the soil, exploring the forest in search of its treasures. He often gave her some small job to do quite alone. Before she would have felt put-upon, but now she accepted the responsibility as an honor. She hunted for early berries and gathered the angelica to steep with honey and water for mead. Her times of solitude grew more precious to her than she ever could have imagined. In her special meditation spot she felt most at peace. There she would sit motionless for hours, waiting. Sometimes she sang to herself or chanted poems. At first these were by the Latin poets or the church fathers, but they seemed jarring and too civilized for such a place. So, without noticing it, she began to chant the old British songs, the ones the people who worked in the fields knew. She had heard them repeated every year, each in its own time. The farmers and fieldmen, the potters and weavers, the dairymaid and the stablehand all knew the proper songs. One to call the wind upon a hot afternoon, one to make the name of one's true love appear in the water; another to protect the new calves from sickness; more to bring the deer to the arrow. Flora had hummed them all to her when she was a child, and more. Perhaps the old woman thought she was too young to remember, but they were her first music and they were forever printed in her memory.

One day, on a deep sunny morning, she found herself sitting in the warm grass pungent with the smell of rotting fruits, and she began to sing the prayer for bringing flowers from the earth. Flora would start humming and reciting it to herself every winter solstice and kept on until midsummer's day. Sometimes, when she had thought herself unwatched, Flora's hands had moved over and upon the brown, barren ground in certain patterns. Guinevere thought it was a kind of dancing for the fingers and had learned to imitate it in her room. But she had never tried it out-of-doors, near summer's end, with life already blooming flamboyantly about her.

The grass quivered as she touched it, and she smiled. A comfortable warmth ran through her hands, like that which came from spiced wine by a winter's fire. She sang low and caressingly, in the same loving tone in which Flora had sung it to her. She could sense the movement of growth far under the green mat. Nearby, something watched her with joy in its sorrowful velvet eyes.

"The time is coming," it thought. "She will be ready to find me and, for a while, our lives will run together. I will no longer be alone. For a time."

A giant crystal tear sizzled in the grass.

Guinevere finished her song with a laugh. She patted the grass she had just blessed as if it were a pet kitten. Then she realized that it was nearly time for breakfast and she had promised Timon that she would help make a new hive, as the bees were getting ready to swarm. She skipped from the glen without a backward glance. Behind her, an orchid broke from the earth and reached toward the sun.

Occasionally, when Gaia was thoughtlessly cruel or Timon very busy, Guinevere wondered when Geraldus would come back for her. She worried that they had forgotten her at home, learned to live without her. She didn't panic. It was just something that settled at the back of her mind and caused her lower lip to stick out. She usually forgot it a moment later, so great was her contentment with her life. But still, she would sometimes stare through the tiny front window at the stars and wonder if anyone missed her.

She needn't have worried. In the midst of trying to feed and entertain what seemed a whole company of soldiers and petty lords, Guenlian missed her terribly. The minute the men had come galloping across the shallow stream, horses sweating and armor gleaming, she had known that they had been right to send her away. They weren't quite barbarians (after all, one had to remember they were fighting for Rome). A few were even moderately well mannered. But they were soldiers, trained from childhood to kill in battle. And when life consists of taking up a lance and shield and charging into a dirty, bloody melee every few weeks, there is not much time for gentility. These men certainly showed it. They wore their muddy riding boots to dinner and drank their wine in long gulps. Their voices were too loud and their language a bastard Latin. Merlin was right in saying that few could read their own names. And even though strict orders had been sent down, more than one serving maid hid deep purple bruises beneath her thin robes.

Guenlian shuddered but bore all their boorishness with dignity and apparent unconcern. Such was the power of her name and station, not to mention her own regal appearance, that no one ever quite got out of hand.

Matthew and John were more than slightly embarrassed by their comrades' manners. It was strange how different these men appeared in their home. There were many hunting trips, and during the breaks in these, the brothers tried to make it clear to the men that even with the drought, baths could be provided for those who wished to follow the old customs. There was a lot of ribaldry connected with this suggestion, but most of the soldiers took the hint. They mocked but they admitted, too, that they were powerfully awed by this glimpse of Roman life. It gave them new insight into what they might have if the invaders were ever completely ousted from Britain.

It had been planned that way by Merlin, of course. He and Arthur had discussed it before they came. A few weeks of civilized life would give them all something to imagine for themselves.

Leodegrance had sighed when they explained it, but resigned himself to the inconvenience in the name of Rome.

So the hordes of soldiers came to the villa. During the day they hunted in the forest. It was mostly for sport and to keep themselves occupied, but there was no denying that the game they brought back was vital to keep them all fed. Not all the sheep and cattle on the place could have satisfied those carnivores. At night they feasted in the great dining room, or tables were set up in the atrium under the stars. To make more room, Guenlian said. To save spending the next day mopping, she thought.

Mark was the only one of the brothers who preferred to stay behind when the others rode off. At first he explained that it was to help oversee the land and free his father for pleasure, but later he confided to Arthur that he had simply had enough of seeing things die.

"I'm home now," he sighed. "And I want to think of nothing but food and a clean bed and how nicely little Rhianna has grown since I was last here. It seems a pity. She's almost sixteen now. Soon her parents will decide she's ready for marriage and send for her. Then she'll have to go back up into the mountains and live in a leaky stone house with her fine strong herdsman husband. And all her beauty and grace will be wasted unless a wandering monk should stop by or a merchant come to bid for their horses and wool. I have no doubt that she will be supremely happy."

Arthur smiled at his friend. They sat alone on the ground, leaning against the old stable wall. The stone was still warm from the sun, although it was well past midnight. The roistering hunters had all long since staggered to their beds, or lay curled where they had passed out under the tables. But Arthur was restless and not as drunk as his men. He had gone wandering and found Mark in the stable. He was feeling talkative and Arthur was content to let him ramble on, hearing little of what he said. They were facing the court and the lamps were still lit in a few of the windows. Arthur gazed at the scene hungrily. The house alone was more than he had ever imagined. It was a piece of art unto itself; mosaics on all the floors and murals on the walls; statues carved into the lintels and columns—and windows! Real glass windows of a cool, rippling green that made the room inside seem mystical and soothing. And Mark called it home. He had never known any other.

Arthur remembered his fostering place. It was in the north, too near the sea. It was cold and damp all year 'round. It was only an old fort, adapted for family living. The rooms were tiny, originally intended for storage or as watchtowers. The walls were thick stone, with narrow slits in them, not to admit light but to fire through at attackers. When the wind was strong, they would be covered with oiled skins and then there would be no light at all. The walls were smeared with smoke and grease, and the entire household slept together for warmth. Cleanliness wasn't a word in his vocabulary until he met Merlin.

He stared angrily at his hands. Big, rough, clumsy. He wondered if the Lady Guenlian had cringed inside when she had touched them in greeting. He felt terribly uncomfortable and out of place in this ordered, cultured world, but his whole heart longed to be a part of it, to live like a gentleman, a Roman citizen, although he was rather vague on just what those terms entailed. To live in a place like that and feel as though one belonged there; he laughed bitterly at himself. He knew what he was, for all Merlin's teaching. He was a soldier, a man who could make other men follow him into battle. When the battle ended he was no one again: a man with no family, no station, no place in the cosmos, certainly no place in a society where everyone was related and every man knew his cousins to the seventh degree. He pressed his lips together tightly and tried to pay attention to what Mark was saying.

Actually, Arthur was being too hard on himself. He had made a very strong and favorable impression on Leodegrance and Guenlian. Even before he spoke they were pleased with his air of quiet control. But their prejudice showed in their failure to approve of him completely until they had heard his voice. Under Merlin's careful training, his Latin was pure and clear. He knew the correct phrases and when to use them, although he still had a hard time recognizing words when they were written down. For all his rough, barbaric appearance, they decided that he was acceptable as a general for their sons. In their minds it was but a small transition from that to leading the country. Everything he said and did on his visit only confirmed this opinion.

And, although she didn't admit it, there was a lonely, lost look about him that touched Guenlian's heart and made her want to mother him as she did her own children.

"Who is he?" she asked Merlin one night as they sat alone on her private veranda. "You know who he is, you've said so."

Merlin nodded. "He is a boy with a great gift for making other men believe in him and a certain talent for military strategy. He hasn't done much else, yet. He's not far over twenty, you know."

"He looks younger," she commented. "I suppose it's because he's so fair. That mop of red hair and all those freckles make him look like a boy. He can't be shaving yet. His body still outraces itself, all arms and legs and nose. Mark still has that coltlike appearance, and he's only seventeen. But I did not ask you his age or talents. I want to know where he comes from, who his family is. You have hinted mysteriously to many people that you know his parentage but won't reveal it. Is there something shameful about it? Is Arthur likely to go mad in a full moon? I'll not believe you if you say his father was a peasant or a slave. Crude as he is, there's good blood there, I'm certain."

Merlin frowned and answered bitterly. "You're wrong, Guenlian. His father was a slave; the worst kind, a slave to himself, to his own base desires. He was full of uncontrolled temper and lust. They were his master and they overcame him in the end."

He stopped suddenly. He had said too much. He cursed himself. Guenlian was not a simpleminded country wife. What might be obscure to most people would be clear as crystal to her, raised as she was in the eye of the storm, surrounded by politics and intrigue. Too late he remembered what good cause she had for knowing of a man who allowed his body to control his reason. He studied her carefully in the candlelight. Her face was closed. She remembered. In the cool night she could still smell the rancid wine on his breath and the hot, clumsy hands pawing at her robes. She shuddered.

"By whom?" she asked sharply.

Merlin saw there was no use prevaricating. Actually, he was

relieved to be able to tell someone. He had feared he might die before it was time to reveal the secret, and that could not be permitted.

"His own legal wife," he said.

"I can't believe that. There was a six-month child, born soon after the marriage, but it died, of course. They never live when they come so early. She had no others. They said it was a judgment. She believed it, poor woman."

"It was a full-term infant. I received him still wet from his mother, the birth bloodstains on his fingernails, and rode out with him at once. I found a wet nurse and kept him with me three months. When I was sure he would live, I sent him to Ector for fostering."

"It was true then. There were rumors even at the time that Uther had gone to Tintagel the night that Gorlois died and forced himself upon Igraine. I never understood why she consented to marry him. I thought it was out of fear, but she was carrying his child even then." Her voice intensified in anger. "He raped her with her husband's murder on his soul, and you connived it for him!"

He shrank from her. "It had to be, Guenlian. It was an evil piece of business and it sickened me, though I was as young then as Arthur is now and didn't realize what she must have suffered. But that is the way it was ordained and I could only guide the events. Even as I must do now."

"Why did you never let anyone know the child lived?" She didn't doubt his story. Though she understood nothing of the burden of prophecy, she never disbelieved anything he said.

"You know what it was like after Uther died. The man had as many enemies among his own followers as among the Saxons. The babe was born too early. There would always be doubt about his parentage. But even if his legitimacy were proven, there were twenty factions that would have been happy to see him dead. I thought it better to let him earn his kingdom. I've watched over him as much as I could, taught him, taken him with me when I was able. I've tested him, too. He has his mother's character and sense of honor, though he has his father's looks. He will make a good man and a just ruler. Still, we don't know if there will be anything left for him to rule. And there are many yet who would refuse to follow him knowing whose son he is. You cringed, yourself. But remember Guenlian, dear cousin. The boy doesn't know himself. He thinks he is Noman. And as that he can be both proud of what he has accomplished and humble in the splender of nobility such as yours. You are the only one alive now who knows. Even Igraine was told the child died. Can you forget it and treat him as you have before?"

She shook her head. "I can't forget where he comes from, but I can try to forgive it in him. I have found no sign of Uther in the boy, apart from the hair. That would give him away if it were known any son existed. Igraine was a gentle woman. The best of her family. She was kind to me and risked much to help me escape from court with Leodegrance, that I might be spared the horror she lived with every day. For her sake and for her heart in him, I will be kind."

"Thank you cousin," Merlin smiled. "I may have made a mystery for you where none was needed. You know I could never take the straight path. Also I feared, as you might, that he would inherit Uther's lustful nature. If that happened, I would have let Arthur remain a man at arms on the northern borders and given up our hopes for a dynasty and a united country. So, I did what I thought was best."

He looked to her for approval, but her face was closed again. He felt uneasy as she smiled politely across the small table.

"Would you care for more wine?" she asked.

Automatically, he stretched his glass out for her to pour the wine. As he did so, he realized that there were people in the room behind them. Had they heard?

The movement suggested that they were just passing by. Merlin sipped his wine in silence, waiting for the voices to fade. But almost immediately, Mark entered the room, followed by Geraldus and, lastly, Arthur. Poor Arthur, Merlin sighed. He held his arms stiffly at his sides, like a soldier at inspection, but he appeared to be simply afraid of bumping into something priceless and destroying it. He stood behind the others, near the door, so obviously out of place and ill at ease that Guenlian's heart melted. She smiled at him.

85

Mark spoke first. "We three have been thinking of going hunting for a few days by ourselves. We don't want all that howling pack around us all the time. Can you think of a diplomatic way for us to get away without offending every minor princeling and warlord in Britain?"

"You value your own company rather highly, my son. Why should anyone question you and your friends going on a private hunt?"

Arthur shuffled his feet. He didn't want anyone to think he had too high an opinion of himself.

"Mother," Mark smiled. He knew when he was being teased. "You know exactly how much in demand we all are. Why, I can't even go to comb my horse without someone coming after me to ask my advice on a point of protocol. Now, dearest mother, will you help?"

She shrugged away his caress gently. "Of course. There is no reason why your brothers and father cannot manage to entertain our guests for a few days. Perhaps they could be taken on a ride to the seashore. I doubt if many of our highland-bred lords have ever walked upon a sandy beach."

"The very thing!" Mark turned to his friends. "Can't you see the Lord Colum splashing in the waves and hunting for shells?"

"From what I know of him," Merlin interjected, "I would guess he'll spend his time examining fortifications and complaining that those appointed to keep watch for the Saxon invaders were not doing their job."

"Now, cousin Merlin," Mark chided. "You always see the dismal side of things. Colum may frolic like a naiad in the surf. I know your gloomy ways. From the way my mother was staring into her glass when we entered, I'd wager that you've been sitting here all evening foreseeing early and horrible deaths for us all. We need no more of that! Arthur, Geraldus, and I are going hunting! We have decided on it. What's more, we will not bother with boars and stags and such prosaic quarry. We are hunting mythical beasts only. What say we find a dragon or two, a griffon, or perhaps a unicorn? We may even find a satyr lost in the woods. No more nonsense about meat for the table. Pack our bags with pigeon pie! We shall go on a quest!"

He struck a heroic pose and drew his sword. The candlelight struck it and turned the steel to shimmering silver. Guenlian smiled fondly. For all his foolishness, there was something grand about him. She wished he *could* find a satyr. Of all her children, Mark was the only one who knew how to dream.

Geraldus laughed and Arthur at least relaxed.

"It's settled then," Mark said. "Like the champions of old, we start at dawn, marching alone to our destiny."

"I do think, dear," Guenlian interrupted, "that you might take a few others along. Perhaps Caet, to care for the horses. He's been moping lately and a quest is just what he needs."

"Could we take my foster brother, Cei, with us, too?" Arthur blurted and turned red again.

"Well, all right," Mark bowed to the voice of prudence. "Perhaps I'll ask a couple of others. But don't you add anyone, Geraldus. Taking you along is the same as inviting a cohort. You'd better warn your friends, Arthur, about his odd habits of waving his arms about and screaming at the air. Not that I mind. It's very entertaining. But some people might think it annoying, or assume that he is coming down with St. Vitus' Dance."

So, still laughing and talking, the three left again to make their plans for the morning. Merlin sighed wistfully as he saw how Arthur relaxed as soon as he was out of Guenlian's line of vision. He leaned back on his cushions when they were well away. Guenlian still studied her glass.

He drew a long breath. "Will you keep my secret, cousin? Even from your husband?"

"Yes, as long as you ask. I think I'd rather. Perhaps no one ever need know. Poor boy! There is something endearing about him. I hope his life will not be too hard."

"Let's not think of that now," Merlin answered. "As your son so wisely said, we need no more prophecy. Good night, my dear."

"Good night," Guenlian smiled. When he had left, she let herself slip back on her couch. Memories she had blotted out for years were flooding back. Those awful, barbaric years after Ambrosius died, when his brother, Uther, was warlord of Britain. He was a tall, sinewy man, with a wild flaming beard. Guenlian cringed at the thought of him yet. His voice was loud, even when he tried to whisper, and his whispers were vulgar and oily. His lecherous tastes were well known, even after he married Igraine. She and Leodegrance had come to court once, just before Matthew was born. She had returned home for his birth but come back a few months later to be with her husband. It was then she had caught his eye, her hips slender again but her breasts full and round with milk for her son. One night he had sent her the best tidbits from his own plate and ordered her wine poured from his cup. The very thought of eating what he had touched revolted her. Thank God Leodegrance was wiser than poor Gorlois! He had gotten his family away at once and yet connived with Igraine somehow to keep Uther's wrath from falling on them. Poor Igraine, no one ever believed she had been forced to marry Uther. All her children taken from her, all her dignity, all her pride. How glad she must have been to die!

"Guinevere, my dearest child," Guenlian whispered, "I'm so grateful that you're away from here now. I wish so that you could always stay there, high in the hills, away from all the filth. But, oh, how I miss you!"

She drained her glass and lay there, watching the candle flame until it sputtered out. Much later, Pincerna found her there, asleep. He called Leodegrance, who gently carried her to bed.

Arthur, Geraldus, and Mark set off at dawn the next day, happy and eager. They took only Caet and Cei and three other friends who they thought would appreciate a quest. They rode out bravely, singing at the top of their lungs. Early risers came out to wave them good-bye. They saluted one and all as they went through the gate and across the river, and their voices could be heard long after they passed from sight.

Two days later, Guinevere woke up with a feeling of intense joy. She had been dreaming again, she knew. But that feeling had never before stayed with her after she awoke. This time she didn't feel as if she had left something precious behind in her sleep but that it had come with her into the waking world. Today, even

Gaia's stern face could not depress her. She had stopped wondering about Gaia. It was Timon she loved, Timon who teased her and worked with her and yet spoiled her much the way her family did with affection and complete acceptance. When time came for meditation she fairly danced her way among the trees off to her special place.

"That child has no idea of the seriousness of life," Timon laughed as they watched her go.

"She will have," Gaia answered bitterly. She stalked back into the hut. Her meditations were spent in its darkest corner. Nature had no lure for Gaia.

Guinevere had dressed herself that morning in a long white robe fastened at the shoulders with plain gold brooches. She had another chain of gold about her waist, but her feet were bare. Gaia had carefully combed her hair into tiny braids, woven about her head, but when Guinevere got to the clearing, she decided to take them all down, just to see how it would feel to run with it all streaming and floating behind her. She slipped the jade pins back on either side of her forehead, just to keep it out of her eyes. Then she ran and danced and whirled until she went round and round in a blinding gold circle. Even after she stopped, the hair continued to swing back and forth like a living thing, keeping time to her dance.

It was through this golden mist that she first saw it fully. It stood on the other side of the clearing, in the shade. Slowly, she brushed the strands away from her face and stared. Her heart beat loudly and her body was still, as if frozen. A passerby might have thought he had come upon two statues from legend, so still were they. The country maiden and the fabulous beast.

Even in the dark beneath the trees, there was a silver glow about him. His coat was pure white and his cloven hooves polished to a deep shimmering purple. His mane and tail were silver, not dull gray, but as shining as the molten metal poured from the flames into the mold. Guinevere knew at once where the single strand she had found had come from. But the most awe-inspiring thing about him was the slender spiral horn rising from the center of his forehead. It was as long as her arm and reflected the light in hundreds of colors, like mother of pearl, as he shook his head. Dark lavenders and blues predominated, but there were flashes of every other color, from orange to green.

Guinevere was too intimidated by his beauty and his wildness to step closer to him. She sank slowly to the ground, her eyes never leaving his face. She was praying harder and more sincerely than she ever had in her life that this marvel, this creature of dreams, would not run away.

The unicorn bent his head, as if bowing to her. He lifted it and stared at her directly. Guinevere caught her breath. A thousand nights of longing came back to her and she held out her arms. Slowly, the creature came to her and gently, humbly, laid his exquisite head in her lap.

"There can't be any greater happiness than this," Guinevere thought. Now she knew what her dreams had foretold. She lifted her hand and caressed his shining mane. Her hair fell across it and gold and silver mingled, floating in the light breeze. Her heart ached with the mystery and beauty of it all. The unicorn didn't move under her touch. It was so still, she wondered if it could be asleep. Timidly, she looked down and carefully brushed the hair from over his eyes.

The deep blue eyes caught her and held her in a visionary world. They wrapped her in emotions she had never known and couldn't name. Sorrow and joy twined about each other, and a fierce calling swept her into his mind.

No one saw her in that moment. The great passage she took into his loneliness and experience were only reflected in the mirror of the changes it made in her. All that her beauty had been up to then was nothing to this moment. It shone like an exploding star, as her mind and soul were linked to those of the unicorn, the most elusive and perilous of all the mythical beasts.

Guinevere felt his joy in finding her; one that overcame all the desperate grief that clouded his spirit. She smiled at him.

"I have been looking for you a long time," she whispered.

"Not as long as I have hunted you," he answered in her mind. "From the moment of your birth, I have been seeking you, only knowing in my heart that somewhere you must exist."

"Will you stay with me forever, then?"

The blue eyes darkened to violet. "There is no forever; I will stay until I must leave you."

"I won't let you go, ever!" But even as she spoke, Guinevere sensed that he was not speaking his desires but only what must be, and that he would never go from her by choice. He had truly been created for her, as she must have been for him. She was bound by the wisdom in his mind and he by the innocence in her heart.

He lay his head down again, his spiral horn rested in the crook of her arm. They might have stayed that way for years. Guinevere knew only the breath of the wind about her and the comfort and contentment of finding one's perfect dream fulfilled.

The unicorn stirred, as if troubled by nightmares. Guinevere came half back to reality as she patted him gently.

"Don't worry . . . what was that?" she started.

There was noise in the woods, a clanking of metal and the swish of branches being pushed aside.

"There's someone coming! Who could be so far from the roads?"

"Only a hunting party," the unicorn replied.

"Perhaps. But they are making far too much noise unless they have already sighted the quarry. They sound very excited."

"They have found the tracks of an animal that they thought never to find. Of course they are excited."

"What animal?" she asked, and then, unbidden, memories of legends came to her. The unicorn and the maiden. "Not you!"

The unicorn lay still, his head drooped upon her lap, resigned.

"You knew they were coming, didn't you?" she demanded. "Did you think I sent for them to trap you?"

His eyelids trembled and a burning tear fell on her robe.

"If you believed they would come to kill you, why did you find me?"

"It is my destiny. I have sought you all my life. For one hour of peace, for one day to be joined to your life, for these I accept my fate."

"But I do not accept mine," she spoke so quietly he didn't

hear her. He only caught the determination in her mind. "I cannot see you die. I've only just found you. You are perfect. No one must destroy you. Go. Now, before they see you. I will never let you be caught. Only remember me, remember me and come back to me if you can. I will die without you!"

She stood up, pushing him to his feet. He shook his head as if coming out of a heavy sleep.

"Please," she begged, "Run, give me the hope of a moment again with you. Run!"

The glorious animal rose to his hind feet and pranced, pawing the air. He still made no sound, but he directed at Guinevere a joy so intense that she felt bathed in the grandeur of it.

"I will find you," he promised and then he was gone, leaving only the print of his cloven hooves in the grass to remind her that he had been there at all. She stood where he left her in the center of the clearing, uncertain what to do. The voices were coming closer and words could be distinguished.

"They go this way!" one shouted. "See here? Clear and sharp. Hurry, I want to see what kind of thing could have made these!"

There was louder clatter as more people tried to push their way through the high undergrowth. Just as they broke into the clearing, Guinevere turned, so that the sun shone from behind her. She couldn't see the men as they appeared on the edge of the clearing. They entered one at a time, each saying something to the one behind him. Then they saw her and stopped.

Guinevere heard the first one gasp. She wasn't afraid of them, now that that her precious unicorn was safely away. But they seemed afraid of her. She smiled to reassure them.

She had no idea how she appeared to them, still bathed in the radiance of her encounter, with her hair undone and the sun creating an aureole about her. She only wondered at their strange behaviour.

The first man stumbled forward, his eyes never leaving her face. The other two followed. Just as she was about to greet them, they dropped to their knees, bowing their heads. This startled her, especially since she suddenly recognized one of them. While they were looking down, she ran for the safety of the trees and hurried back to the hermitage. She disappeared as swiftly and silently as the unicorn before her.

A moment later, Geraldus and Mark arrived in the clearing. Arthur staggered to his feet, his eyes glazed with awe.

"We have seen a vision," he breathed. "The holy Virgin herself."

Cei looked at him oddly. "No, there were flowers all about her. She was a goddess, surely, the guardian of this place."

Caet stared at them both.

"It was Epona," he said firmly. "I heard the whinny of the celestial horse, just before we saw her."

Geraldus looked at Mark, who shrugged. "There were too many branches in my way. I saw nothing."

Then Geraldus spied something in the grass, near the place the vision had been. He walked past the still-befuddled men and picked it up. It was a small jade pin, set in gold filigree. He nodded, his guess confirmed.

"Guinevere."

CHAPTER SEVEN

 rthur remained convinced that he had seen the Virgin Mary in the forest and nothing anyone said could change him. Mark and Geraldus tried.

"But you didn't see," Arthur protested. "How can you doubt my word? She smiled at me as if blessing all my endeavors."

They wanted to tell him that it couldn't be. But they were hampered by their unwillingness to admit that it was only Guinevere. There was something strange about the whole episode, they thought. Why hadn't Caet recognized her? He had known her ever since she was born. They shrugged and kept silent. Certainly, this only renewed Arthur's confidence in the divine approval of his cause.

"I shall have her image painted on my shield," he insisted. "She shall be my protectress and my inspiration. If only you had seen her, too. You would then understand. She was so beautiful and so remote, and yet I could feel her kindness and wisdom surging through me, just from a glance."

Mark and Geraldus gave up. There was no point in trying to argue with a fanatic. Besides, his "vision" seemed only to have strengthened him to do what he had already intended, rid the country of the Saxons. That was all to the good. So the next week Arthur and his men rode off, full of the righteousness of their cause and also the joy of gracious living and aged wine. The inhabitants of the compound watched them go with relief. Now they could return to normal.

"And now," sighed Guenlian, "My Guinevere can come home."

She sent Geraldus and Mark to fetch her. They went eagerly, hoping to hear from her what had really occurred in the forest.

Guinevere came racing to meet them as soon as they appeared in the clearing. She had heard them singing at the top of their voices long before they arrived, in counterpoint with no melody. But she was oddly reluctant to return with them.

"I am very happy here, and there is still so much work for me to do," she told them. "Perhaps you could come back for me when the harvest is over and the honey gathered. It will be just a few weeks more, after the frost. Please!"

Mark was startled, not so much by her words, which he hardly noticed, but by her appearance. She was radiantly beautiful, as always, but her expression had changed. There was a shadow on it now of worldly knowledge and sadness that one shouldn't acquire living in a mountain retreat. There was something strange and slightly frightening about her, and he made up his mind that she should come home without delay.

"Guinevere," he said sternly. "Our parents have missed you very much. Mother is lonely for your company. Matthew, John and I must go back to our units soon to train for the spring invasions. Will you not come home to wish us godspeed?"

Guinevere's eyes filled. How could she tell them? "If I go now, I'll never see it again. Who will let me go into the forest alone to seek him? How will he even know where to find me?" she thought.

Unbidden, a voice came to her: "We are one heart now. I will follow you until the end. Wherever you go, even into the deepest cave or the most distant shore, there also will I be."

Guinevere blinked. Had the others heard it? No, they were all still watching her, waiting for her response.

"I will come with you," she sighed at last. "I do not wish to cause my parents sorrow and I would be sorry to miss seeing you off. But I did want to see how Timon collects the honey."

So Guinevere went home, after bidding farewell to Timon and Gaia. She discovered that she really was eager to see her parents and friends again, once the fear of losing her unicorn was gone. Warm baths and meat pies also had not lost their charm. She settled in as though she had never left. But something about her had changed, and the ones who loved her noticed it, although they didn't know whether to worry about or approve of the difference.

"She is gentler than she used to be," Leodegrance remarked. "She seems to see other people more, to be more sensitive to them."

"But I feel she is drifting away from us," Guenlian fretted. "There is some secret she has that she will not share. I see it in her face. Our sons were never like that."

"Our sons never let us know they had secrets, but there must have been many." Leodegrance smiled. "It should not surprise you, my love, that our daughter is growing up. Perhaps her dreams do not include us anymore."

"I'm not ready for that. She is still a child. Merlin has unsettled us all with his baseless worries. My dearest only girl-child. I won't lose you yet!"

"She won't leave us for many years, Guenlian. Don't weep, now. We have our daughter. She has just grown introspective from being in that quiet place. It can only do her good to wonder about things a bit instead of accepting life without question. But, if you think she has gotten too dreamy, we'll wake her up again. There will be more fosterlings here this winter and some close to her in age. The company of her own kind will bring her to life again."

Guenlian had to be content with this, even though she felt that something was going on that was more than adolescent vagueness.

Guinevere didn't feel herself to be any different. She thought others had changed while she was gone. This frightened her a little. Home was the one place which must be immutable; the steady center of a spinning world. Even the tiniest alteration disquieted her.

Flora worried her most. She had aged during the summer. Her movements were faltering and she often had to stop and sit a few moments before she could continue her work. Guinevere mentioned this to her mother with concern.

"Yes." Guenlian was glad to know that Guinevere cared enough to be aware of the change. "She is really a very old woman, you know, although she appears so vital that we forget it. Her children were all grown long before she came to take care of mine. I believe that Caet is really her great-grandson, but she doesn't speak of her family. I have tried to cut down on some of her duties, but she is proud and very sensitive. You can help her, if you will, by giving her as little to do as you can. If I remember Gaia, she must have taught you a great deal about taking care of yourself. She was never one to pamper her guests."

Guinevere laughed. "Is that why you sent me to her? Yes, I can make my own bed now and need not be reminded to wash my face."

"That is not a bad start," Guenlian said. "I have neglected your education in that area badly. My dear mother always said that you should never tell a servant to do something you can't do yourself. How else will you know if they are doing the job properly? How else will you be able to train new people? She lived in another time, of course, when women had only the running of their homes to concern them. At least," she paused, "that is how I remember it. How odd! At any rate, one thing I have learned is that even if the winter is fierce, the Saxons are raiding the coast, all the pipes are broken and the entire family sick, linen must still be aired and meals prepared. Are you willing to spend the winter this year learning all the dull routine of maintaining a household? Someday you may wish to run one yourself."

It seemed a gloomy prospect but Guinevere agreed. Winter was all rain and slush anyway, and one couldn't read all the time. Also, it was still a good while away.

As Leodegrance had hoped, that autumn was busy and noisy with the games and intrigues of a house full of young people. Guinevere soon joined in. The unicorn moved to the edge of her mind, not taking up all her thoughts and dreams. He was still there, comforting, caring, but she discovered that she didn't need to be obsessed with him. He was part of her now and there was no need to be constantly in touch. So she was able to awaken more to the people around her.

Matthew, John, and Mark stayed to spend the early fall at home. They had promised Arthur to winter with him and help with the plans for the spring defences. Guinevere treasured every day they remained at home. They rode and ran and told stories in the twilight. She was overjoyed to realize that they accepted her more as an equal now than ever before. They talked with her instead of around her as they had when she was a child. And Guinevere grew to love them as people, not just worship them as her great, distant warrior brothers. Mark had always been her favorite, but now she started to see why. He was quieter than Matthew or John, who seemed always to be laughing at some joke. But he smiled more than they did and there was more understanding in his eyes. He fought for his dream of a safe, unified Britain, not for any particular joy in battle. Matthew especially got caught up in the fighting itself and often forgot that there was any purpose to it beyond finding out if he could wield a sword or spear better than his opponent. He was the best soldier of the three for just that reason. His mind was occupied only by strategy; he was not distracted by ideals. And where Matthew went, John always followed devotedly.

One evening she mentioned her concern for Flora to them and her plan to take over some of her work. They agreed that the old woman needed help.

"It's a fine idea," John said. "But you can't relieve her at the night work, and that is what is wearing her out now."

"What night work?" Guinevere was puzzled. "You know Mother would never make Flora work all night."

"Didn't you know?" Her brothers all smiled. "You never noticed how often she's gone at night? You never wondered at all her charms and potions or the things she gave us when we were sick? You never saw the red and gold robes she keeps in her clothes box?"

"Red and gold robes?" Guinevere remembered the time she had wakened in the night. "But why?"

"Guinevere, Flora is the local high priestess. She must officiate at all the rituals for her people."

"Don't be ridiculous! No one believes those old things any more. And Flora is a Christian, just as we are. What could she be a high priestess of?"

Matthew answered. "Perhaps she was baptized, though I doubt it, but she believes in the old religion and so do most of the peasants around here. They worship a dozen or so gods, but the main one is Epona, the horse goddess. Wait until the winter solstice and see if Flora is in her bed that night. She'll be out seeing to the sacrifices and tending the sacred flame."

"How do you know about this?" Guinevere demanded. More important, why didn't she know?

They all three looked guiltily at each other. Finally John whispered.

"We found out years ago. But we never told Father and Mother and you mustn't either. Flora caught us and nearly added us to the flames, but she never told them about it. We followed her."

Guinevere's eyes were wide. Were they teasing her again? "What did you see?"

Matthew's voice was low and eerie. "An altar in a sacred ring of trees deep in the forest. All the people from the farms and even some from the house were circled around it, chanting in the old tongue, and Flora, Flora stood alone in the center dressed in her robes of red and gold and holding a bronze knife. They killed a calf and sprinkled its blood on the altar and on all the people. Then they burnt it in the fire, as the chanting grew louder and louder. They burnt it whole, without even saving a piece to eat."

"We went many times," John added. "It was much more interesting than daily prayers. Sometimes everyone danced and sang. Sometimes they all moaned and wept. It was about the most exciting thing that ever happened to us, since every time there was word of invasion we were packed off to the mountains to hide. But finally one time Flora caught us. We weren't quick enough climbing back in our window.

"I've never seen anyone so angry," Matthew shuddered.

"We promised we would never follow her again. I would have promised anything."

"Why didn't you tell Father?"

"And be punished again for being out after dark? Besides, I think he knows about Flora. Have you ever noticed that everyone goes to bed early on Midsummer's Eve? And think of the gifts that the people bring to her each harvest time. He never seems surprised, although it would make more sense if they were given to him or the priest."

"They love her, too," Mark tried to explain. "She has been a part of the family since before we were born. As long as she comes to chapel with us and doesn't flaunt the old religion in their faces, why should anyone bother her?"

Guinevere didn't answer. She needed time to think about this. What upset her the most was that she had never thought of such a thing, even with all the clues she had been given. It slowly entered her mind that she hadn't been very observant. When she saw Flora next, Guinevere stared at her as if she were meeting a new person. Flora had always been a servant, nurse, lady's maid to her. She examined the proud, lined face and noticed her straight carriage. She did give the impression of an unyielding personality. Guinevere tried to imagine those strong hands holding a knife instead of a comb. It frightened her. She didn't think of it again.

Autumn blazed itself dry. The harvest was almost finished and soon it would be time for the men to return to their unit. Geraldus announced that he had imposed upon their family much too long and would leave with them.

"I must see my family again before the snow begins in the mountains. It's odd how annoyed they are if I neglect to visit them each year. They are certainly happy enough to see me go. If you can tolerate me another time, you may look for me in the spring."

As it turned out, Geraldus left a few days before the others. He rode out on old Plotinus, splashing across the near-empty creek, his singers gathered around him, all apparently singing gustily. Guenlian sighed as she watched him go. Even though she doubted his sainthood, she was fond of the boy, and it was true that she felt safer when he was with them. Perhaps it was just that he took her mind off her worries. Well, she meant to keep busy this winter, and there was Guinevere to teach. How young and fragile she looked, the wind pressing her thin robe against her, her slim arm waving. She felt a wave of resentment against Merlin. He must be wrong! This was still her child. No one had the right to try to take her so soon.

For all her good intentions, her heart ached unbearably when the time came to say good-bye to her sons. Only Leodegrance's strong presence at her side gave her the courage to send them off as a Roman mother should, smiling and triumphant. She hugged each with a fierce passion when they kissed her, but all she said was, "Don't tarnish your armor or dull your swords"— a proper phrase to send a soldier off. They laughed at her and waved their bright shields above their heads as they left.

When they had gone, she retired to her room and cried all night in her husband's arms. She only allowed herself to do this because she knew he felt as she did. The next morning she coolly gave orders for her sons' rooms to be cleared out to make space for the new fosterlings who were expected. Leodegrance felt no need of such determined reserve. He wandered sadly through the house and out to the stables and stared at the empty stalls.

"They've gone again, Caet," he stated. "I'm proud of them, each one, but I wish every time that they ride out that I were going in their place."

"So do I, sir," Caet whispered bitterly, "so do I."

When he was alone, Caet picked up a stick and jabbed and slashed viciously at the straw stacks and wooden posts. Great dreams burned within him. Arthur's visit had not impressed only the noblemen. Caet had thought that all warriors were like Leodegrance and his sons. Inbred feelings of inferiority told him that he could never be like them. But the others! Loud, slovenly, lecherous, paunchy. Caet scorned them all. He was a thousand times better than that sort. And if that were true, then he, the son of generations of slaves, could also be a fighter. He practiced constantly from then on, toughening his muscles and perfecting what he fondly hoped was swordsmanship. He weighted his stick with rocks to approximate the heavy short sword and cut a young tree to get wood long enough for a lance. When he exercised the horses, he took his weapons along to practice swift, stabbing blows that would slay his opponent without harming the horse. He knew that the Saxons brought no horses with them on their ships and that the mounted soldier was doubly horrible to them. They excelled in tactics that brought the rider down to be met on their own level. So he sent the horse racing toward low-hanging branches and outcroppings so that he was forced to duck or swerve in the saddle at the last moment but still keep his seat— without stirrups, no small achievement.

Caet had his life all planned. He was free. He never let himself take that for granted, even when he did the filthiest jobs. He knew he could leave whenever he was ready. But not yet. There was still a reason for him to stay.

"Caet, you're dreaming again," Guinevere teased him. "You jumped halfway to the ceiling. You didn't even hear me come in. Will you bring my father's horse to the courtyard? I'll get my own. He's taking me riding again! We're going over to see Lord Potius and his family. I can't wait to do some real riding again. All I got this summer was with Geraldus and you can hardly move then for fear of running over one of his singers. I thought I might not have another chance before the rains come."

She ran past him, not even looking at him. Caet watched her a moment and then silently did as he was told.

Soon the rains did come, and the household withdrew into the warm villa. The outside world disappeared or was seen only through sheets of water falling from the porch roofs. All activity was moved inside, and Guinevere remembered that the time had now come for her to learn all those boring household tasks.

Guenlian tried to make it as pleasant for her as possible. The women and girls all sat together and laughed and talked as they carded or spun or sewed. But although Guinevere dutifully ran the drop spindle until her fingers blistered and her back ached, she was not with the others. She was wandering in a forest listening to the wisdom of a fantastic creature. She was feeling the smooth coolness of his horn and the strange patterns its colors made in the sunlight. She was remembering the peace and perfect contentment she had felt on that summer day.

Guinevere loved best to work in the kitchens where the herbs were dried and made into possets and flavorings. The wild scents helped her fantasize and she could almost feel them under her feet as she ran, when the others only saw her sitting at a table, crumbling the leaves in her hands.

Her dreams that winter were no longer vague. She was sure that the unicorn was with her then, listening to her wonderings. Guenlian had hoped that the two of them could grow closer during those dismal weeks, but she perceived at once that Guinevere was with them all only in body. She never laughed or commented on the stories they told. When she was spoken to, she would start and then smile gently at the speaker, asking her to repeat herself. Guenlian shook her head. It was no use. She tried to remember if she had been this way at thirteen. It was certainly an introspective time. Perhaps when her daughter was older, there would still be time to talk together. There were so many things Guinevere didn't know!

Snow fell by the winter solstice and even though Guinevere had intended to stay awake to see where Flora went, she found that after her usual bedtime hot drink, her bed looked so warm and comfortable that she just couldn't stay out of it any longer. So she snuggled down in the warm blankets and never discovered whether or not her brothers had told her the truth.

And one day, late in March, when the wind howled and the trees were still bedraggled with the remnants of last year's leaves, there was the joy of an unplanned visit from Matthew. Leodegrance had not thought to see any of his sons again before summer, when the spring invasions had been checked.

"What brings you all the way back here?" he asked. "That's not to say we aren't glad to see you. There is nothing wrong, is there?"

"No, no, of course not!" Matthew answered heartily. "I was bored stiff with all the training and decided I needed a week with my family. Nothing more."

His eyes drifted from his father to the group of faces behind, fosterlings, maids. He seemed to be searching for someone. Leodegrance was no fool. Nor did he pry.

"It's good to see you, son. You can fill me in on the preparations they are making for the invasions this year. Where does Arthur think the worst attack will come from?"

Matthew made some answer that Leodegrance didn't hear. He had seen the boy's eyes light up and tried to follow them without being noticed. There were several girls there but only one looked his way. Rhianna? How unlikely! Why the child hardly spoke at all. Matthew's style was hardly a shy thing like this. Still there was a glow on her face that was unmistakable.

"Well," thought Leodegrance. "It wouldn't be a bad match. I'll have to discuss it with Guenlian. Amazing!"

No one had ever seen how that shy face could come alive or known how softly Matthew could speak. The week was over too soon for everyone and he rode away again. Guinevere watched until he disappeared. Of all of them, she was the only one whose thoughts were not on him. Her mind was reaching far into the forest, calling.

ChAPTER EIGhT

As the spring days lengthened and the earth dried, activity quickened at the villa. People blossomed out into the fields and woods, planting, visiting, building, or just traveling for the sheer joy of being out. Guinevere began to watch for Geraldus. Even with her dreams, the winter had been dull for her. The talk of the fosterlings and maids revolved around beauty secrets and gossip. Her thoughts were all of her unicorn, so she had little real communication with the others. They, however, never resented her or thought she was snubbing them when she neglected to join in their talk.

They shared the common belief that Guinevere belonged apart from everyone else simply by right of her existence. They never expected her to be like them, so there was no animosity. Still, Guinevere was lonely and longed to be out again. All winter the unicorn had been only a shadow on her wall and a whisper in her mind. She yearned to be with it again, to caress its mane and to feel the cool weight of its horn on her arm. She began to fear that she had only dreamed it. She must know the truth. The first day that was relatively warm and dry, she begged to be allowed to go out walking or riding—alone.

"You are too old to be out alone," Guenlian replied. "Get some of the girls to go or have Caet accompany you."

She threw the words over her shoulder. She was airing the linen, a job she hated. But the winter dampness was in everything, and all the fine clothes would be ruined if they weren't all taken out, piece by piece, and carefully dried and scented.

105

"The girls are all busy or else they won't go out in the sun, and Caet will be helping to clean the stables for the rest of the day. I won't go far. Please!" She was feeling desperate.

Leodegrance hurried by, pulling on his riding gloves. He was going to check up on the sheepfold. Shearing time was coming soon. He saw his daughter's face and paused.

"Let her go, my dear," he smiled. "She has been held in the house too long, penned in by other people. Run off now, Guinevere; don't stay long or I'll not give you permission again."

Guinevere didn't wait for fear of a change of mind. She hugged him joyfully, kissed her mother, and raced away.

Guenlian frowned. "You shouldn't have let her go. She's almost fourteen now. She can't run around unattended in the woods like a child."

"She is a child, Guenlian. Look at her. You kept her by your side all winter long. She had hardly a moment of her own. Didn't she dutifully stitch altar cloths and oversee the kitchen maids? Let her go by herself for a while. You know as well as I that she'll never be a chatelaine. Household cares are as far removed from her as starlight."

"I know it better than you. Wasn't I the one who had to pick out all her false stitching? And the kitchen maids could have bathed in the kettles for all the attention Guinevere paid them. But I don't care about that. I kept her by me because I wanted to keep her safe."

"No one will harm her here," Leodegrance answered, but his voice was not assured.

"I have just heard," he added as if he had only then remembered it. "The Saxons that settled in the southeast last year have started moving north again. They are looting and burning. Cador has been sent to stop them."

"Really?" Guenlian answered carelessly. "Well, he is a good soldier. I'm sure he will have no trouble."

The linen slid from her hands. She picked it up.

"Aren't you going to see to the sheep?" she asked.

"Yes, of course. I'll be back late in the afternoon, don't worry."

He kissed her gently and left.

106

Guinevere managed to hold herself to a ladylike walk until she was safely out of sight of the villa. Then she felt the calling and everything left her mind but the need to be with him, at once. She tore across the field and into the wood to the place she knew he would be. There, standing motionless in a pool of sunlight, was her unicorn. She stopped a few feet from it and just stared at it. Joy filled her eyes. Then it stepped daintily toward her and bowed its head. She wrapped her arms about the silky neck and again became a part of its timeless world.

The rider did not see them as he passed nearby, urging his exhausted horse onward for the last mile. His eyes were fixed straight ahead and his thoughts were on the job before him. He wore the remnants of a Roman soldier's garb, many generations old. Only the breastplate was in good repair. His cloak was of thick wool, too hct for the weather, and it was caked with mud and torn. He didn't slacken his pace until he was across the creek and at the gate. Then he checked his mount and asked to see Leodegrance.

Gone, the sentry told him, looking disparagingly at the man's grime.

"Then take me to your mistress!" he snapped. "I have come from Cador and I've not ridden three days without sleep to be gawked at by the likes of you."

Guenlian and Pincerna were in the dining hall, preparing the menus and planning seating order for guests, when the rider was shown in. Guenlian glanced at him quickly, noting his labored breathing and the dust and mud covering his clothes. She wondered why the day had suddenly grown so dark. She couldn't seem to focus clearly. All she could see was the glare of sunlight on his breastplate, searing her eyes and blinding her to everything else.

"You bring a message from my cousin?" The words were cold and brittle and came from far away.

The soldier saw a tall, stately woman above him on the dais. She was like a statue before him, calm and aloof and waiting. He shifted his feet. All the way here he had been preparing to speak to Leodegrance, one soldier giving a report to another. That would have been hard enough, but he hadn't been trained for anything like this. He didn't know how to begin.

"The Saxons . . ." he stuttered. His voice broke. Why did he get all the bad jobs? "We fought them five days ago. It was a horrible fight, with all of us strong and rested from the winter. They were a far greater force than last year. Some of their ships must have been missed by the watchers. We didn't expect so many and finally had to give way. Your sons were fighting in the rear guard."

"As they should," Guenlian nodded. "Go on."

He had paused again. Guenlian hadn't moved or changed her expression since he entered. He didn't want to go on. She stood there before him as if he were telling her it had rained in the north and the crops might be damaged. Why didn't she help him?

Guenlian couldn't understand at first what he was saying. The light bewildered her. She felt someone move a chair behind her but she didn't sit. She simply stared at the courier, trying to piece together his reason for being here. Finally, the realization hit her.

"Which one?" she asked sharply. What a stupid question. Did it matter which? Was one son less precious than the others? Would the loss of one of them be a lesser blow? Why was it so dark? Only that horrid reflection glowing from that awful man.

His mouth dropped open. "Look at her," he thought. "The queen, no doubt. 'Tell me your news, peasant, and let me get on with my work.' Then I'll tell her."

"All of them . . . my lady," he added.

Still her face didn't change. "I see," she said. "Tell Cador to make arrangements to have them sent home for burial."

"I . . . I . . . can't," he stammered. "It took us two days to regain the place. The Saxons had . . . had . . . looted and burned the bodies. There was nothing left."

There. That was the message. All of it. There was nothing more to be said, nothing he could give her. All he wanted was to be out of there, away from this cold woman with those terrible eyes. She still hadn't moved, not a finger since he had entered.

A last thread inside Guenlian snapped. Not even a shred of them left. Not even a Christian burial next to their ancestors with the proper prayers and godspeed. Nothing. What was this paper in her hand? A seating list. It fluttered to the floor.

"Pincerna," she said at last. "Give this man some food and a fresh horse and tell Caet to ready mine. I think I will go riding this afternoon."

She walked from the room without another glance.

The soldier relaxed with a huge sigh. "And I come here trembling and shaking for fear of telling her, and all she says is 'I think I'll go riding.' " He snorted. "I'd always heard they raised their sons for their own glory. I believe it now. I've got five brothers at home but my mother would wail over my death as if the sun had gone out. She doesn't even flinch when all three go under!"

Pincerna descended upon the man so quickly he didn't know what happened. The butler's face was lined with tears and his voice faltered, but, as he spoke, he twisted the cords of the man's cape so tightly that he nearly choked him.

"Raven!" he rasped. "Bird of doom! Filth! My lady ordered you food and a horse and for her I shall see that you get them. Then leave this place and never return or your mother will most certainly wail!"

He released the terrified rider and sent him to the kitchen with a servant.

Then he raced out to the stables as fast as he could.

The news had sped before him. Caet was leaning against Matthew's new colt, sobbing loudly. Pincerna gripped his shoulders as gently as he could.

"Caet, you must help me. Ready a horse for our Lady Guenlian at once. Then you must take the swiftest horse we own and ride it as fast as you can to find Leodegrance and bring him back. You will have to tell him why. Can you do this?"

Caet nodded.

Pincerna released him with gratitude. He knew the boy would find the necessary strength. That relieved his mind on one count. Now he must hurry. The sounds of horror and grief echoed through the villa like a wave spreading outward, spilling, rolling down the hill and out across the fields. In the whole house, only Guenlian remained silent and dry-eyed.

She had walked to her room; she saw no one as she passed.

She sat on the edge of her bed and carefully picked up her riding shoes. She wrapped the linen around her legs and then laced the shoes over it, watching the leather thongs cross in chi's up her calf. "Christos" she thought. It made no sense.

There was a great force inside pushing outward, hunting for escape. She must go quickly.

She pulled on her gloves and went out to the courtyard. No one dared stop her. Caet stood there with her horse. His face was smeared but he was holding his tears back. He put out his hands to give her a lift up. She took the reins from him and started to put her foot into his cupped hands. Then, just for a second, she seemed really to see him. Her face softened, and bending, she kissed his cheek. He jumped back, startled, and then turned his face away so she couldn't see. He knew now why Pincerna wasn't going to Leodegrance himself. He watched her go and then ran back to the stables. Pincerna was waiting.

"Has she gone?"

"Yes, through the gate just now."

Pincerna patted his back. "Good lad. Now, you know your job. Don't let your grief slow your pace. You are the best rider in the compound and you must prove it today. Leodegrance must be here when I return!"

"I will bring him." Through the numbing sorrow, he felt a thrill of pride. He was the one being trusted; not one of the foster sons or men at arms, but Caet. Pincerna had known that none of them felt as he did and he had discovered Caet's dream to be like the brothers. He would not fail them!

Pincerna took another horse, not fast but surefooted. He was not a good rider and he prayed that he could stay on long enough to complete his work. He rode out the gate and across the creek and then turned sharply, following a newly broken trail into the forest.

Guenlian didn't notice the watchman at the gate or hear his cry of "God save us all!" She didn't feel the water splashing against the horse's flanks and wetting her legs as she crossed the creek. She concentrated on making the horse take her the way she wanted to go and holding back the thing inside her until she was well away from everyone.

Once she entered the forest, she broke off from the main path and let the horse find its own way among the trees and through the underbrush. The awful pushing was at her throat; she swallowed against it, but it was too strong. Suddenly, like a sword thrust into her brain, came the realization. She began to scream. It was like no sound she had ever made before. It was deep and inhuman, a primal wrenching forth of the anguish within. "My children! My babies!" she shrieked as she slid from the horse. The words were indistinguishable, long, drawn-out sobs of words. She fell to her knees and clutched the ground with her hands, her fingers digging into it and pulling out clods of new grass. She ripped the earth and pounded it until she was grimy and bleeding, but the earth didn't notice. All the while her cries poured forth, with scarcely a breath taken. She couldn't stop. She had to kill this horrible pain, to beat it out of herself. She clawed at her chest, ripping her delicate robe and leaving thin lines of blood against her skin. She kicked and screamed and pounded at the uncaring ground until she lay exhausted, beaten, whimpering and alone.

A thousand years passed. She vaguely felt someone lift her gently and wipe her face, murmuring all the while. She didn't resist. She was still too busy fighting the battle within herself to care what was being done to her body. There was no victory that way. She was lifted further and placed upon a horse. A voice was speaking to her but it didn't make sense.

"Please, my lady, hold on for only a moment. I'm too old to steady you while I climb up myself."

She slid forward and limply held her arms about the horse's neck while Pincerna got up behind her. Then he gathered up the reins and placed her head and shoulder against his chest. Then he held her with one arm while he tried to guide the horse with the other.

"Forgive the liberty, my lady," he pleaded. "I must get you home. I must take care of you."

She nodded. It didn't matter. As long as no one disturbed her from her struggle. They went slowly. Pincerna reflected with a grim irony that if he were a young man, this would be romantic and dashing. Now he suspected that he only appeared foolish.

A branch brushed Guenlian's arm. Something stirred. Who was this man? Pincerna? Something about Pincerna. He had told her something once and she had been very sorry but had forgotten it almost at once. What was it about Pincerna?

"You lost your children too, didn't you?"

He sighed. Perhaps he should keep talking, just to keep her from thinking. But this wasn't exactly the story he would have picked.

"Yes, my lady, all of them. Two to the winter sickness, one to the sea, and one more to the Irish raiders."

"Killed?"

"I hope so. They took her on a slaving run one day when she and two friends were out hunting for shells on the beach. I never should have let her go."

He was silent for a while.

"My wife died with one more in childbed and then I was alone with a farm and no one to leave it to, so I just walked away. I would have walked until I died if I hadn't been a Christian, but the hermit who lived on the beach told me I would see them all again if I went on living, but if I took my own life all hell would part us. I don't know if I believed him but I couldn't take the chance. So I walked until I came here and you took me in."

"A long time ago."

"Yes, and I don't want to die now, even if I did then. I can wait if I must to see them. And if you'll pardon me again, my lady, you can, too."

"I needn't. I see them now," she said and her voice chilled him. He tried to force the horse to go a little faster. "I see all of them. That's what I can't bear. If I could envision them as men, soldiers who did their jobs and died fighting, I would be able to live with it. But I only see their sweet, baby faces, their innocent children's smiles and feel them ripped from my arms and slaughtered, thrown alive into the flames!"

Her voice went from a harsh whisper to a shriek and Pincerna could only hold her frantically with one arm and pray for help.

It came. Leodegrance, followed by Caet, heard her and

came. Leodegrance, his face aged and worn, held out his arms for his wife and she went to them, still wailing softly as if she had forgotten how to stop. He took her home and the maids who loved her best bathed her and bound her battered hands. They wrapped her in warm, soft blankets and tried to get her to eat, but she did not seem to understand. So they left her in her own bed and went away to dry their own tears.

Flora wasn't among them. When she had heard the news she had simply collapsed. She was in her room now, awake, but too feeble to move or even speak. Tenuantius, Guinevere's teacher, was the closest thing to a doctor they had, and so he was sent for. He listened to a maid's recounting of what Flora had said before she fainted and gazed for some minutes into her open eyes. Then he ordered a guard set on the door.

"Her mind appears to have totally gone," he told Leodegrance. "For some reason, she blames herself for their deaths and the shock of this has brought on a sort of paralysis. She is very old and may not recover. At this point, it would probably be a blessing."

Leodegrance waved him away. "Take care of her. You know best what to do. Tell me if there is any change." He hurried to be with his wife.

Guenlian was sleeping now, fitfully, with moans and thrashings. Leodegrance sat beside her. From the moment, only a few hours past, when Caet had raced toward him, he had not had a minute to digest what had happened. He could not comprehend yet that his sons were dead, although a dull ache in his heart warned him that he soon would. He only saw his wife, who had been his strength through years of precarious living, lying helpless and hurt before him. With that in his eyes, everything else was, for the time being, remote. He took her hand, willing her to return to him. The shadows of the bedposts lengthened and he realized that it was still daylight, barely time for dinner. He pleaded with her to look at him, to waken and see him instead of the image of her burning sons. Finally, with one great, shuddering moan, she opened her eyes and stared at him directly, sanely. But her first words startled him for they were not what he had expected.

"Where is Guinevere?" Her voice condemned him.

Lord! Where was she? Off in the woods somewhere. She didn't know. She would come home laughing and find him. Someone must go find her.

"Caet!" Leodegrance shouted. Guenlian didn't even start at the noise. She was back in her nightmare. But Caet was there at once. He had not gone back to his work in the stables but lurked near the door hoping to be of some further service, longing to show his loyalty and love and, perhaps, also his ability.

Leodegrance regarded him with affection. "A fine lad," he thought, "I remember his birth. It was the same winter that Guenlian was carrying Mark." A stab of pain caught him and he quickly spilled forth his errand.

"Guinevere is somewhere still out in the fields or woods, Caet. She went for a walk some time ago. She is probably on her way home now. You must find her before someone else tells her about her brothers. Don't say anything except that I was worried about her. Bring her to me at once. Can you find her?"

"Yes, I will," Caet answered. The soldier again, he held his body proudly as he walked out.

But Guinevere was already there. She had felt something wrong, even through her communion with the unicorn, perhaps because of it. Vaguely disturbed and annoyed at having her first afternoon with him spoiled, she had hurried toward home. The field workers had seen her but turned their backs as they saw her approach. They were not working, just standing or leaning on their tools. Before she crossed the creek, she could hear the sounds of wild lamentation from the villa. As she rushed past all the people, they would stop their sobbing a moment and stare at her, but no one spoke. The noise was terrifying. It came from every corner and pulsed against Guinevere's skin as she ran through the rooms, too confused and frightened to speculate the reason for it all.

She came at last to her parents' door, just as Caet was leaving. She never forgot the sight. Guenlian lying in bed, her hair tangled, her face streaked with tears, staring at nothing, and beside her, Leodegrance, hunched brokenly, his head in his hands.

"Mother!" Guinevere cried. "Father, what has happened to her? Tell me!"

Leodegrance raised his face to answer her, but at her voice, Guenlian rose and stretched out her arms.

"My last baby! Guinevere, come to me. I must hold you! I must know I have one child left!"

Guinevere went to her and held her, feeling strange to be comforting her mother, who had never needed anything from her before. It was long afterward that she finally understood what had happened.

In the next few days the whole makeup of the household changed. The fosterlings were all sent home. Their going made little difference to Guinevere at first, for she had had little to do with them, but after they left the villa was quieter, and many of the servants began to leave too, until eventually only a dozen or so of the oldest or most devoted remained. Guenlian slowly forced herself back to life. Twenty years of responsibility saved her. It was her duty to tend to the household, to see that everyone was cared for. Her movements were not as sure, her speech less decisive. Sometimes she would suddenly pull in her breath as if struck. But she survived.

Leodegrance worried her. In the first hours of anguish, he had been too busy giving orders and arranging matters to stop and let his grief out. Now he refused to. He immersed himself in estate problems, took inventories, planned repairs, sent messages to Cador and Merlin so incessantly that most of the horses were usually gone. He pushed himself every waking minute and then simply fell into an exhausted sleep, almost a coma, from which he awoke unrested but determined to go on. He spoke only of business and turned away from every sympathizer, even his wife. His energy was constant and frantic, like a bonfire determined to burn itself to extinction.

Finally one night, near the end of summer, Guenlian found him in her dressing room. He sat alone in the twilight, slumped over and so still that she feared he was dead. But as she approached he spoke. His voice was dull and blurred with tears.

"Our sons are dead," he said. "They are gone and Rome is gone. We are living in a mausoleum, each clinging to our familiar sarcophagus. We have lived out our lives for nothing more than to be the last of our race."

He raised his voice, more life coming into it.

"I'm sick of those platitudinous callers who tell us not to worry, for our boys are in heaven. Heaven! What are they to do in heaven? Sing psalms? They are soldiers, fighters. There is no need of them in heaven. Are there armies in God's country? Is even He struggling to hold on to the skies? Bah! I didn't raise my sons for the glory of heaven. I raised them for Rome. I'll hear no more of heaven and the mercy of God. I have followed the new religion and what has it given me? I got nothing and I'll give nothing back. God doesn't care for me. With all the talk of love I haven't even been given comfort. What has God given us to help bear this blow?"

Guenlian went to him and knelt at his feet, embracing him fiercely. "Each other, my dearest. We have each other! Now that you have come back to me."

For the first time since that awful day, he looked at her. "I thought for a time that you would die, too," he whispered. "You are a great gift. If I were to lose you, I would truly believe I was in hell, for I would certainly have nothing left."

Gently, she helped him up and led him to bed. There they found such comfort as the living can give each other.

Everyone praised Guinevere during this hard time. She was melancholy, but not maudlin. She wept tastefully whenever her brothers were mentioned. She was considerate with everyone, devoted to Flora, who was still bedridden and did not seem to know any of them. She dutifully stayed near her mother, except for a brief time each day when she was sent alone to the forest, "for exercise."

"Poor dear," the maids clucked. "She doesn't want us to see her cry. Let her go; no one would harm such a child."

She kept repeating to herself, "My brothers are dead. My brothers are dead. The Saxons killed them. Matthew will never tease me again or sweep me up on his horse for a ride. John won't tell me any more legends about the stars. And Mark will never sing to me or kiss me good night."

But she couldn't sense the finality of their lives, only the ending of something in hers. She had never seen a dead person. She only knew of battles from sagas and harpers' tales. It didn't occur to her that Matthew would never ride a horse nor John see the stars nor Mark sing to anyone again. Vaguely, she felt that they were still doing all those things, but without her. She resented them for not returning. So when she wept against the unicorn's flank, it was for herself, for the sudden emptiness in her own life, not the destruction of theirs.

Being with the unicorn soothed her without questions or demands. It was always there waiting for her, no matter what time she was able to get away. It told her stories of things she didn't understand. It knew nothing of the world of men except its part in the pattern of capture and death. But it knew how the trees prepared for the winter and the celebration the woodland made with the coming of spring. It told her of how the earth repaid the sacrifices of battleblood by growing all the more lush and green the following year. It knew the tunes the stars play deep on a winter night and even the first notes of the aubade sung by the mountains to the sun chariot in ancient times. All this lulled Guinevere and rested her aching heart. She had not fully cast her lot with humanity and was unaware that she had the choice of becoming one of those amoral, immortal creatures the unicorn spoke of, or one like those who followed Geraldus. She came closer to becoming one that summer than she ever would again, until the end. But she wasn't aware of the decision and so let others make it for her.

CHAPTER NINE

I t seemed a mockery for summer to be so beautiful that year. The rain and sun combined for what was certain to be one of the best harvests in many seasons. Guenlian and Leodegrance spent only superficial interest on it. It was enough for them if they could get up each morning, dress, and accomplish one more day without succumbing to their own despair. After the first vicious tide of grief had subsided, they spoke no more of it. By mutual consent, their conversation was mundane to the point of sterility.

"May I have my blue beads, dear?"

"Of course. Will there be guests to dinner?"

"I think not. I have heard that Potius and his family are emigrating. Is that so?"

"Yes, the old sot complains that he can no longer get decent wine here so he is going back to Gaul to see if he can raise his own. The fool! Wait until he discovers that grapes do not grow already fermented in the cask!"

"Not many neighbors left to come to dinner."

"It doesn't matter. I'm not in the mood for much company anymore." Abruptly, "I must go check the horses. The roan mare has a sore on her left hind foot that isn't healing well."

"Yes, I must hurry myself. I really should be sure the maids have cleaned the dining hall properly. Things have been lax with them ever since Flora has been ill."

Ever so carefully, they stepped around the open wounds, averting their eyes from the festers. Everyone followed *their* own pattern until the whole household felt as if it were involved in some complicated ritual dance, where one missed beat would bring catastrophe.

And the center about which this dance revolved was Guinevere, never a part of the pattern, but always the focus, an object of caution and concern. She spent a part of every day with her unicorn, now that the weather was warm. Constant association with it had left a sort of aura about her. Spending so much time with a creature of fantasy gave her an otherworldliness and a serene attitude that half frightened those around her.

"It's not natural," a stableman flatly declared one day. "She doesn't seem human, that one."

"What are you saying?" a housemaid answered indignantly. "She's as kind and gracious as can be. Grows more like her poor, dear mother every day."

"Sure, she smiles at you and asks after your health, but do you think she sees you? Look at her eyes sometime instead of at the floor. They give me the shudders."

"What do you want from her, to kiss the hem of your robe? A smile and a friendly word aren't enough for your excellency. If her eyes bother you, it may be your own guilty conscience looking back at you."

"You're all addled by that girl. You think she's as pure as rainwater. Look how everyone lets her run off to the forest any time she pleases without a guard or even a maid. She stays there for hours and comes back smiling like she's seen a vision. But nobody asks her where she goes or who she meets. She's probably got a lover from some peasant family and is laughing at you all for not seeing it . . . Urk!"

Pincerna had entered behind him and now grabbed him by the collar. He was almost frothing with righteous anger.

"Get your disgusting body back to the stables! If I ever hear of you repeating such evil slander about the Lady Guinevere, then freeman or not, I'll lash you until there isn't a piece of whole skin left on your body! If she looks even to scum like you as if she's seen a vision, maybe she has. Do you think the saints appear to your kind? Now get back to work and never let me see you here in the house again! Do you understand?"

The horseman was a head taller than Pincerna and twenty years younger, but he nodded and left as if an entire army were chasing him. That night, he stole one of the best horses and escaped. Leodegrance received the news with indifference.

"He won't get far. Our mark is on the horse. No one will believe we gave it to him. In the meantime, we have others."

Pincerna shook his head. The Leodegrance of old would have gone out after the man and brought him back tied face downward over the horse's tail. He wondered if he should mention the accusations the man had made. No, of course there was no truth in them and Leodegrance and Guenlian had enough just now. Still, it might not be a bad idea to send someone out after her, just to be sure she was safe. Whom could he send? Caet? No, it might start more gossip if he were seen sneaking out after her, and tongues were ever ready to spread such tales. Who then? A woman? It really wasn't dangerous in the immediate area. But not many of the servants were left and none could really be spared for so many hours. Of course, Rhianna! It was so easy to forget her, she hardly ever spoke. He had trouble remembering that she was still about the house, the only fosterling who had insisted upon remaining. It probably wasn't good for her to do so. The house was too glum these days. She really hadn't been looking well, lately. This was no place for a young girl now, not even Guinevere, really.

That thought passed through his head with a shock. No, it wasn't a good place for Guinevere now. But who could imagine her anywhere else? One might as well uproot the tree by the gate. Pincerna dismissed that whole idea.

Accordingly, the next day when Guinevere set out, Rhianna followed her. She took a basket with her as an excuse if noticed, but no one questioned her. Rhianna was the sort of person who is easily overlooked. She was seventeen and had a well-developed body for her age, and long, slender legs. But her face was still that of a child and she had a way of staring wistfully at the world around her that discouraged most of the men of her class. They preferred their women round and flirtatious, at least for enjoying before their marriages were arranged. Mark had commented on her figure, but it had never occurred to him to go farther than that. Her meekness made him nervous.

Rhianna was more than fashionably pale. Her skin was almost greenish white and she panted a bit as she hurried to keep up with Guinevere without being seen. Occasionally Guinevere would break into a run and leave Rhianna far behind. Rhianna went as fast as she could, but she knew she couldn't keep up and was sure she would fail in her task.

She had not wanted the job of spy, but it hadn't occurred to her to refuse. Every time someone approached her these days she trembled for fear they would insist she return home. She couldn't go home, not now. And yet she didn't have any idea of what she would do. Like the rest of the house, she could only think one day ahead, no more. But the day for a decision was nearing for her.

Guinevere had disappeared into a tangle of vines and branches. Rhianna waited a minute and then followed her. The growth was very thick—it was impossible to see far ahead. Struggling to remove the vines caught in her hair she didn't stop quickly enough on the other side and nearly stumbled over the two of them.

The unicorn started and rose to its feet. Guinevere looked up.

"It's all right," she said lazily. "It's only Rhianna. She won't hurt you. Let her touch you, too."

But the beautiful creature only shook its mane and backed away from her, vanishing among the trees.

"Wait!" Guinevere called. "Come back! It's only Rhianna!"

Rhianna grabbed her arm. "Don't bother, Guinevere. It can't come back for me. It won't let me come near it."

Then she sank to the ground, coughing and weeping bitterly.

"Rhianna!" Guinevere put her arms around her. "Don't cry so. You are the only one after me who has seen him. Not many people do even that. I suppose he is only my unicorn. Perhaps you'll meet one some day."

"Don't be ridiculous, Guinevere," Rhianna pushed her

away. "A unicorn can only be tamed by a virgin. Everyone knows that. Now go away and leave me alone."

She tried to rise to her feet and stumble away, but went only a few steps before she reeled dizzily, and grasped at a tree to support herself.

Guinevere ran after her and held her up.

"Rhianna, what's the matter with you?" she cried. "Why are you out here? I've never seen you this way. You must be ill. Here, let me help you."

"No, don't bother," Rhianna said fiercely. "I'm not ill; I'm wicked. I'm going to have a baby and soon everyone will know. My family will disown me and yours will throw me out and I'll probably die and go to hell."

She sat down again and cried and coughed some more. The running had worn her out completely and she looked terrible. Guinevere sat beside her, wanting to help but not having any idea of where to begin.

"But I don't understand, Rhianna. How could this happen?"

"Guinevere, don't you know anything?"

"Not about babies. No one ever told me and I never thought to ask."

Even in her misery Rhianna smiled. "No, I suppose no one would." The thought of someone sitting down with Guinevere and explaining sex to her was ludicrous. Still, she would very likely be married someday. "Well, it's no matter. I have no husband and there is but one road open to me." Her voice shook. "But I am weak and afraid. Oh, I wish I had a unicorn!"

"Babies must have fathers, I know that much. Isn't that so? Where is this person, Rhianna? If he became your husband, then everything would be all right. He isn't . . . uh . . . unsuited to us, is he?"

Rhianna flushed. "Where would I meet anyone 'unsuited'? Guinevere, you are amazing. Your brother Matthew is the father and, in case you have forgotten, he is dead. He can't marry me now. At first, I was so glad we had had those few times together. He came back in the spring just to see me. But now I only feel sick and ashamed, and wish we had waited until he asked my parents so we could be properly married."

Her voice drifted off. It didn't matter if Guinevere listened or not.

"I had such dreams. Our beautiful villa high in the mountains. I knew just where it would be. Away from Saxons, Irish, and Picts and away from all those noisy drunken soldiers. Just the two of us. I told him all about it and he laughed and said it would be a fine place to come back to. We could raise horses and when he was old they could be the dowries for our daughters. And now there is nothing left of him. Nothing but this," she felt her stomach, "and this." She held out her hand. On the middle finger was a signet ring.

Guinevere smiled. "I know that. Grandmother gave it to Matthew because he was the oldest and he would wear it even though it was a woman's ring because he loved her so. He gave it to you? How he must have loved you then! Rhianna, you should go to Mother and explain it to her."

Rhianna stiffened at once. "No, how could I do that? She would only think me wicked. She would say I was trying to push myself into your family and cover my shame!"

"Rhianna!" Guinevere was angry. "You know my mother. How can you say such things of her. She raised you, loved you. She will know what to do. What do you want instead, to kill yourself?"

She started. "No, or I would have already. But I think it's the only honorable thing for me to do."

"I don't know what you are talking about. It is true that nobody ever explains these things to me; perhaps I should ask. But I do know that my brother is no longer alive except for that part of him living inside of you; yet you want to destroy that too. I can see no honor in that and I don't think Mother would either."

She added, more humbly. "I don't know or understand how you feel. I don't know much about people at all, but Mother does and I think we should go to her. Now. Please?"

Rhianna's face lit like a sunrise. It was what she had wanted all along, but had been too timid to do.

"Will you come with me?"

"Yes, but you must explain to her. I don't know how. And,

Rhianna, promise me that you won't tell anyone about . . . about my friend?"

The wistful look returned to Rhianna's eyes. "No. It belongs to you. I know what they would do with it. You are right. Even to have seen such a thing is more than I ever dreamed of. I'm really a very ordinary person. When I found that Matthew loved me, I felt there was really nothing more that life could give me."

"It is not the same, I know, but you may say you have another family now, too."

Guinevere held out her arms to embrace her sister. In that silent moment, perhaps all things mythical and true would have welcomed them.

The golden feeling lasted for Rhianna until they came to Guenlian's door.

"Go in first, Guinevere, I can't. My feet won't move."

"No, we'll go in together. Here, take my arm."

It was late afternoon and Guenlian had, for once, run out of things to do. She slumped in her chair, staring out of the window at the patterns the morning glory vines made across the glass. She resolved to think of Nothing, rather than of the darkness that pursued her. But thinking of Nothing only let in the darkness, and she was beginning to slip into despair. Seeing her like this frightened Guinevere, as it had so often in the past weeks. But Rhianna only felt pity and understanding. Didn't she, herself, feel the same sorrow? She went to Guenlian and knelt at her feet, resting her head on the older woman's knee.

Guinevere came with her, feeling out of place. She sat on a stool nearby. Absently, Guenlian patted Rhianna's face.

"Mother." Guenlian focused her eyes. "Rhianna wants to speak with you. She has something to tell you. I think . . . something . . . from Matthew . . . a gift."

She could not find the words. Guenlian had roused herself and was looking at Rhianna intently. Guinevere knew she would not be missed, so she slipped away, glad to be apart from such confusing and deep emotions.

Rhianna lifted her face. It was streaked with tears. "My lady, please forgive me. I truly loved him and we thought it would not anger you when you learned we wanted to wed."

Guenlian regarded her with a practiced eye: her pallor contrasting with her full breasts and slightly rounded stomach. She couldn't believe it. Leodegrance had made some comment that Matthew seemed much taken with the child but . . . then she noticed the ring. Her whole manner changed as she swept Rhianna up into her arms, laughing and crying at once.

"Oh my daughter, my dear! I cannot thank you enough! You poor lamb, don't you see? He is not dead at all. You have brought him back to life. My husband will be so relieved!"

Rhianna wasn't prepared for hysteria from the dignified Lady Guenlian, but being always close to tears herself these days, she clasped Guenlian's hand and sobbed too. With all the weeping, there had rarely been two happier women.

Guenlian quickly composed herself, slightly ashamed of such a wild outburst. She had had enough of those. But she continued to rejoice, not only for this promise of a continuation of Matthew's life, and therefore her own, but also because she now had something concrete to plan for and worry about. It would keep her busy and looking forward. It would keep her living. Grasping the problem at once, she immediately gave all her attention to it. First she had to calm Rhianna's fear.

"You should have come to me at once, my dear. I know what you thought. But you needn't believe that parents are so blind. We saw the way you and my son looked at each other and I know Matthew never raced from one end of the island to the other just to spend a week with me. We had already given thought to suggesting a marriage between you two. I even mentioned it to your mother in my last letter to her. So, you see, no one will be very surprised to hear that you were married when he left last spring. Of course we didn't say anything then because we planned a formal wedding and a settlement of dowry when he . . . returned."

She swallowed quickly and went on.

"As he didn't, we are of course overjoyed that we ignored tradition and allowed you a few days together first. Poor dear, you didn't have much more than that, did you?"

Rhianna was still trembling and crying. Why couldn't she stop crying lately? "I thought, I was afraid you would think I was lying, that I wanted a place that wasn't mine."

"How could you? Another girl, perhaps. No, I always hoped to have another daughter someday, and you are just such a one as I would have picked. Leodegrance will be pleased too. He and your father have always been good friends. Now we must think only of you and caring for you. My grandchild must be strong and healthy and you have obviously not been eating properly, if at all. I will send word to your mother at once. But Rhianna, she has three other children, and I have only Guinevere and you. Will you stay with us, at least for a time?"

For answer, Rhianna only nestled into Guenlian's arms with a sigh of relief. Somewhere in the back of her mind, Guenlian wondered how long it had been since Guinevere had caressed her so.

The truth was that Guinevere had never completely belonged to her family. There was something so fragile and ethereal about her that while they all had loved her passionately, they had never felt completely relaxed with her. Even as they teased her and laughed with her and punished her, they all felt there was a part in her they could not touch that had nothing to do with this world. This constraint was growing stronger as tragedy divided some and brought others closer together. Guenlian, Leodegrance, and now Rhianna had sought each other for courage and strength to bear their grief. Guinevere instead fled to the forest and the comfort that awaited her there. If she had known what would come of it, at the end, Guinevere might have run screaming into their arms. If she had not been only human, she might have had some warning, some protection. But the absurd thing about human life is that one must fling oneself blindly into the future with no idea of what one will find.

The whole household grew more cheerful when Rhianna was introduced as the wife of Matthew. Even though all of them knew there had been no wedding, no one broke faith. Rhianna's parents were written to, and they sent word they would visit at once. So all the servants rehearsed gleefully complete details of the bridal feast: how hard it was to make a good meal on such short notice, what everyone had worn and what they had said. It didn't matter that no one was likely to ask them about it. All summer they had eaten their bread with sorrow and it was more than time to smile again. As far as they were concerned, Rhianna was "a lady born" and if the gentry chose to be a bit lax in the matter of weddings, that was their right. So they pampered Rhianna and showed her marked respect. Slowly she was losing her frightened rabbit look and her posture of hunched misery. It seemed to her that she finally belonged in the world, and since she was naturally too self-effacing to take advantage of the concern of others, she wasn't spoiled by all the attention, only strengthened. The joy of a new life growing before them made everyone look forward to the long months ahead. Even though autumn was approaching, the whole household had a feeling of spring.

Guinevere stayed away even more now. She was less likely to be missed. She didn't resent Rhianna's place of honor and was secretly curious about the baby, but she didn't feel at home around women who could talk of nothing else. Even housework was a more pleasant subject to her. A lot of what they said sounded very disagreeable, and she couldn't understand why they seemed to have relished the suffering so. Guenlian had never mentioned days of pain with her children; had she gone through this too? Guinevere wondered why anyone would want children at such a price. It didn't please her to think of it; she preferred to retire more and more into her own world.

One dreary, foggy day in November she slipped out, wrapping a thick wool cloak about her. She was sick of hearing about labor pains and wanted the restoring companionship of her unicorn. She found him, but for the first time his thoughts were distant in her mind. She caressed his shimmering mane and drew her arms about his neck, but he didn't radiate the warmth she had expected. She was afraid to speak to him aloud but willed him to return to her with all her energy. At last, she felt his thoughts return in her direction.

"I am sorry I worried you," he told her. "I have been thinking a great deal lately when you are not with me. I am the only unicorn. I have never seen my own image, save in the minds of others, and it is never the same. I have often wondered about the unicorn who came before me. The day I awoke in the forest, he met his death. He gave me all of his knowledge, but none of his memory. Was he ever lonely? Did he ever ask himself why he was on earth? Was his life so short that he had no time to think? I don't believe that in all our history, any unicorn has spent so long a time with one human being. Perhaps it is unsettling me. Perhaps unicorns were not made for introspection. I cannot be sure."

"What is it? What is wrong with you?"

He went on. "I have heard, though I can't remember where, that we have cousins living in the sea. I would like to converse with them. When the rains end this year, I will go to the shore to seek them."

"No!" Guinevere clung to him in panic. "You mustn't leave me! Everything is so strange now; the whole world is changing. It keeps running from me. I won't let you go, too."

He looked at her in surprise. "Of course I won't leave you. I can't. We are one soul, for now. I will go when you do."

"What?"

"When you go to live in the castle by the ocean in the spring, I will go too. I thought you would be pleased."

"I am going nowhere. I am staying here, at my home, forever."

His thoughts were puzzled. "I know I felt it. In the spring. I saw the rocks and could even smell the salt."

"You must be mistaken. No one has said anything about my leaving."

"Perhaps not. But remember, when you go, I will be with you."

Guinevere pulled her cloak more tightly about her. "I am going home. I must think. Anyway, it's too cold for me to be out today."

She slipped in the mud as she hurried home. It wasn't fair! They couldn't send her away again. Her only refuge! Why was everything so inside out lately? "No one has time for me anymore! No one cares what I do, even if I stay out in the rain all day and catch the ague and die! No one would care. Even he would only hunt for another maiden to pet him."

The thick fog clung to her cloak and dripped from the hood

pulled far over her face. The mud was so thick on the path that it muffled the sound of the horse coming up behind her. It was some time before she noticed that she was walking in the midst of a crowd. No one else was wearing a wrap or even seemed to be getting wet. They were all completely silent but moved their lips as though singing. Even then she was so concerned with herself that it took a moment to realize who they were. Then she spun around and saw him.

"Geraldus!" she cried, and threw herself at him as he slid from Plotinus' back. "Oh, Geraldus! Why did you wait so long to come back? We have watched for you every day since the spring. I thought you would never come!"

He swung her around, mud and all, smiling with relief at his welcome. Then his face sobered.

"I didn't know if you would want to see me . . . now. I thought I might be in the way."

"Oh no, if you only knew the people who have come by to comfort us and how little comfort they have been. I have been so lonely for you. Everyone else is so different now. Hurry. Let's go tell father you are here."

Geraldus may have doubted his welcome, but the joy with which they greeted him was sincere enough to convince anyone. Mark had been his special friend, the only one he had of his own age, and he had felt Mark's death as much as if his own brother had died. All summer now, he had known that he should visit them again, but he had been afraid. How could he walk in, alive, when all the others were gone? It would almost be an insult. Finally he had worked up his courage, packed his mended robes in a bag, and started out. He was rewarded by the look on Leodegrance's face when they met and the choked answer to his mumbled words of consolation:

"We are glad to see you, lad. You can help us learn to live with this. We will bear it together."

Guinevere refused to let go of his hand as she led him through the house. She babbled on and on of how glad she was to see him.

"Now we can have music and stories again. No one but you can recite so clearly the story of Aeneas. I'm so happy to see you.

Will you teach me to dance? Will you stay the whole winter?"

Geraldus was more than willing to remain, if they wanted him. There was no better or warmer place to spend a winter. The lure of hot baths was easy to give into on icy cold days. Guinevere was still dragging him on to her mother's work room. From within he could hear the voices of several women.

"Certainly, it will be a boy. I carried all my boys just that way and even I can see how he beats on you. He's a fighter already."

"No, Guenlian, a boy I have no doubt. But she has had a craving for grapes and lamb's meat. That certainly implies that he will be a holy man."

"I think you are both wrong, my lady. The child is sure to be a girl. If you had consulted the stars, as I have, you would know that."

Guinevere whispered, "I'll wait for you in the dining hall. A little of that talk is enough for me."

Geraldus entered shyly, nervous at invading such a decidedly female gathering. He saw the three speakers and the object of their speculations sitting mute among them. But Guenlian dropped her sewing at once and rushed to him as impetuously as Guinevere had, giving him a joyous welcome.

"My dear boy! How glad I am that you have come at last. You know everyone here, don't you? Winawe, Rhianna's mother, and her maid Enid? Of course you remember Rhianna, but she has changed somewhat since your last visit. You have heard that she and Matthew were married last March?"

Rhianna stood unsteadily. She was still having trouble adjusting to her ever changing center of gravity. She smiled hopefully at Geraldus. With moist eyes, he bent and softly kissed her.

"You look beautiful, little one," he whispered. "Matthew must be very proud of you. I'm sure he knows all about this and rejoices that he has left something of himself behind on earth."

"Do you really know that, Geraldus? Did your voices speak of him?" She was so innocent and trusting that he could only mumble something reassuring and excuse himself.

"Of course, I'll have someone bring you fresh towels," Guenlian said. "Guinevere can show you to the bath house. I know you know where it is, but we must follow the proprieties. We'll all see you at dinner. We have been too long without your music."

She kissed him again and sent him off. He found Guinevere and she got the linens. The air around him seemed strangely quiet, and automatically he glanced around.

"If you are looking for your singers," Guinevere told him, "they didn't follow us in. I think they went straight to the baths. After all, they have been here before, too. Do they know that father doesn't allow men and women to bathe together?"

"I really don't know if they do."

"You should tell them, in case someone should happen by."

"But Guinevere, you are the only one who can see them and I am the only one who can hear them!"

"Oh yes, well then. I'll stay away. But only until you are dry and dressed again, so don't stay there all afternoon. I have missed you so!"

Geraldus smiled and mused as he watched her skipping back to the house. "There is one person who hasn't altered in the least, in spite of everything. Imagine, mousy little Rhianna and Matthew!"

From inside he heard the sound of splashing and some male voices trying to harmonize on a rather vulgar drinking song. He cringed. Where had they learned that? Now the sopranos were joining in. They would never get it right, if they practiced a millennium. He opened the door.

"No, no, NO!" he shouted. "Can't I leave you alone for a minute? You're flat on half the notes and sharp on the other half. Now, from the beginning—"

ChAPTER TEN

The room in which Flora lay was white and the ceiling low. From her bed, she could only turn her eyes from one empty surface to another. She heard her faithful attendants enter and leave, knew they were feeding and cleaning her and raged at the shame of it. Except when a face bent over hers, she might already have been in her sarcophagus, reclining peacefully in her tomb. More than anything she wished for the dignity and release of death, but she knew it would not be given her until she redeemed herself.

"It is the cardinal sin," her mind repeated. "You withheld the sacrifice. You must pay, you must pay. The punishment will not fall upon the victim. Mother! Most high! Give me strength and I will fulfill the prophecy; only let me move and I will do so in your service!"

They all came to see her every day. Guenlian patted her hand and spoke as if she had lost her reason instead of her body's strength.

"Here's some lovely soup for you. Isn't it just lovely? And here's a warm comforter. Let me wrap it around you."

Leodegrance would come and yell as if she'd gone deaf, "HOW ARE YOU TODAY?"

Caet sneaked in once with a gift of flowers. He laid them on her pillow like an offering at a tomb. But his eyes were sad as he kissed her cheek, and of all of them she felt he best knew the degradation she suffered.

Guinevere came, too, and for an hour every day sat next to

the bed and prattled as always. The only difference was that now Flora could not interrupt. Guinevere never looked at her. Flora wished she would. Even without words she knew she could have made the child be still.

Constantly her spirit railed at her body, admonishing it to obey, and all the while she repeated her prayer: "Give me strength long enough to do my duty, only that long and no more. I must be allowed to atone!"

But the weeks passed and her muscles remained unresponsive. Her terror grew until she barely heard the platitudes of her visitors. Only her own pleading echoed in her ears.

Outside the white room, life was becoming joyous again. Geraldus cheered everyone. He made them smile without feeling guilty. He sang. Although the winter solstice approached, the villa was warm and merry. It wasn't hard to remember the rebirth of nature with the new life growing before them within Rhianna.

Only in Flora's room was it winter. Pincerna and Tenuantius discussed it.

"She won't let go," the butler worried. "Her body is gone, useless to her, and I believe her mind is going too. She doesn't seem to recognize us anymore. Yet she refuses to face her own end. Why won't she accept it? She has had a longer life than most."

"She's not one of us," Tenuantius said, as if that explained the matter. "Tacitus and Sidulus have some very interesting comments on people of her race. You must come by my room some evening and I will read them to you. I have an anonymous commentary which is also very enlightening."

Pincerna shrugged and muttered something about usually being on duty in the evening.

Everyone knew there was no hope and pitied the fierce determination that kept the old woman clinging to life. But she cared nothing for them. She continued her efforts until, late one night, her arm moved. No one saw, no one knew, except Flora. But she knew it was a sign that she would be allowed to atone for her weakness. Every day thereafter she felt the muscles tighten and strengthen and every night she practiced until she knew she was ready. Now she need only await the winter solstice. At the proper time, in the proper place, the demands of the goddess would be granted.

In the fields, the people were making huge piles of firewood and bones. They would be lit at sundown and would burn all through the longest night. Leodegrance knew the bonfires that would ring his home were not for the birth of Christ but for Donn, the god of the dead, and Beltenus, the sun god, who would not return to his strength until his own feast day, Beltane, in the spring. But Leodegrance didn't mind. He had always felt that as long as there was light to burn away the fear of winter darkness and death, the name of the god didn't matter. At least not to him. He had been born on this island, and his father and his father, reaching back almost three hundred years, to the first Roman settlers. He was more than half of British blood, himself, and his ancestors had worshipped a whole pantheon. He understood the old religion even if he didn't believe in it. Therefore he took the precaution of having a bull slaughtered before the solstice and dividing the meat among the tenants. Better that than finding three or four missing, taken for the rites. And each night Flora grew stronger.

On the eve of the longest night, the inhabitants of the villa held a solemn service to commemorate the birth of Christ. Then they had a simple supper of bread and broth and retired early. Sometime later it seemed to a confused Guinevere that she woke to find Flora standing over her in her silken robes, holding a cup of spiced wine. Each year on that night, Flora had done the same thing and later, Guinevere had assumed vaguely that her memory of this must have been a dream. She finished the wine as she had always done, and after that her sleep was dreamless.

She didn't awake even when the strong, bony arms lifted her from her covers and carried her out into the freezing night, nor when she was undressed and placed on the icy altar. Flora worked alone that night, with no other worshippers or acolytes. This was for the goddess alone. She lit the candles and unwrapped her cloak to reveal the red and gold robes, stained with dark, brown blood from a hundred animal deaths. Carefully she sharpened the bronze knife. Serenely she intoned the sanctifying prayers. She was calm. Soon the old sin would be absolved . . . Guinevere would return to the goddess from whom she came and the cycle would be completed. The island would once more be protected. Flora's body should have been feeble from her long months in bed, but her movements in the candlelight were deft. She had no doubt that Epona herself was guiding her hand. Flora was filled with contentment. With gentle love she unbound Guinevere's hair and arranged it around her body. It was time.

Guinevere was freezing; she tried to pull her blankets closer about her but somehow she couldn't make her arms move to reach for them. The cold was piercing and it made her angry. She could hear the wind bellowing outside and felt a draft blowing across her. A strand of hair fell in her face and she wanted terribly to push it away. But her body refused to respond.

"I must still be asleep," she thought. "I must wake up. If only I could open my eyes!"

She tried, but it was no use. In her effort she managed to make a tiny squeak, which sounded to her a frantic scream. "Someone will surely come and wake me now! Why can't I do it myself?" She squeaked again.

Flora didn't hear her. She was deep in her own ritual, hypnotizing herself. This was her supreme night. She was no longer a serving woman or a nursemaid, and she never would be again. The force of Epona was in her now. She belonged to the immortals and knew she would not return. She ran her finger down the blade of the knife. A thin line of blood followed the mark.

With the greatest effort, Guinevere at last managed to push her eyes open a slit. She saw the candles through the curtain of her eyelashes. Nothing else was clear. It suddenly occurred to her that she was naked and uncovered, but all she felt was the cold. Then she heard the footsteps approaching and saw the glint of the knife above her. But still it made no sense. She only longed for someone to put back the blanket.

Then a thought roared through her mind like a storm. "Open your eyes, Guinevere! For your life, look at her! Don't let her move! I'm coming to you!"

With one desperate effort, Guinevere opened her eyes as wide as they would go, and found herself staring into Flora's face. It was white and smooth with madness. She gasped.

Flora started. Her hand trembled. "Epona!" she howled, "help me! Take your own!"

Then Guinevere heard the hooves pounding, hammering, breaking down the wooden door. Its crash was covered by the high pitched, horrible scream of a horse in terror. Flora shrank back as the unicorn bowed its head over the altar and pointed the deadly sharp horn at her heart.

"Renegade!" she accused. "You know she is destined for your Mistress! Epona will not be thwarted. Even her servants cannot prevent the sacrifice!"

She raised the knife again. The unicorn stepped forward. Guinevere now found that she couldn't shut her eyes, and she watched in terror as the knife descended. The bronze blade seemed to move so slowly, inch by inch, closer to her unprotected body. She saw the unicorn rear as if he were swimming through a powerful surf. His forehooves pawed the air above the altar, ready to fall upon Flora, standing on the other side. Flora shook her head, awestruck but determined. And then, too quickly to see, the direction of the knife changed as the old woman plunged it into her own body.

There was blood everywhere. It spurted across Guinevere, burning hot on the icy stone and her cold body. It flooded along her chest and cascaded down her hair, pooling on the floor. And still she could do nothing, not even weep. The unicorn was gone. Had he also been a dream? The candles one by one were snuffed out by the wind blowing in through the open door. The only sounds were the slow drip of blood to the floor and a steady hiss as life streamed from Flora. Guinevere was alone.

The crash of the door and the horrid screech of the unicorn had roused the household. At first Leodegrance thought it came from the fields, where the bonfires were at their height. But then he realized that it was too close. He rushed out into the night. First, he looked to the stables. Was someone stealing the horses? But they were dark and quiet. Guenlian pulled a blanket around herself and followed him to the patio.

"What was it?" she asked. "I thought it came from the chapel. Surely the revelers wouldn't dare to desecrate it."

"I'm going to see." Leodegrance grabbed his cloak and

picked up a stout walking staff. The voices of others wakened by the noise were filtering through the halls now, sleepy, curious, worried, annoyed. Pincerna appeared looking like an old senator in his long robes. He strode through the buildings, trying to quiet people and to find the cause of the disturbance. He met Rhianna in the courtyard.

"You shouldn't be out on a night like this, so near your time," he chided her. "Go back to bed."

"I was awake anyway. I don't sleep very well. I thought I should go see how Flora is. All this commotion must be bothering her, as she can't get up to see what it is."

"Very well, that is thoughtful of you. But just look in on her and have one of the maids tend to her if anything is needed. Then hurry back to your room. You must think of yourself now."

Rhianna disappeared into the house and Pincerna was on his way again, when he heard her calling frantically.

"She's gone!" Rhianna yelled. "Someone has kidnapped her!"

Leodegrance was heading for the chapel but turned back at the call. He found Flora's cell filled with people, all talking at once with Rhianna, looking aggravated, standing in the middle trying to explain something to the person next to her, who was busy exclaiming about the whole thing to no one at all.

"What is the matter with you?" Leodegrance roared. "All of you, back to your beds. We'll tell you what happened in the morning. Someone see to my daughter-in-law, she looks ready to collapse. Geraldus?"

"Here, sir."

"Get your boots on and come with me. Certainly whoever made all that racket has long since left, but we should check and see what the damage was."

They left then, but everyone else continued to mill around, unwilling to miss out if something interesting happened. By common consent, they removed themselves to the dining hall and tried to convince the cooks to check the larder while they waited.

Caet, however, was not among them. The moment he heard the scream of the unicorn he knew where it was coming from and guessed what was happening. He didn't stop to reason how Flora had moved herself. He knew she could do anything if her desire was strong enough. He only ran, barefoot and half clad, straight to the chapel, praying that he might not be too late.

The distant bonfires gave the only light as he stepped carefully through the broken doorway. At first he could see nothing, and then he made out a glitter and slowly, in growing terror, he walked toward the altar.

Guinevere, eyes wide open, covered in blood.

"Oh no," he pleaded. And then louder, sobbing, begging, "No!"

He knelt on the stones, afraid to touch her. "Grandmother, why did you do this?" he yelled, "Why didn't you take me!"

He heard their voices and the sound of their boots and other footsteps nearing the chapel. He struggled to his feet and groped his way to the door, leaning on the lintel post. His cries had brought not only Leodegrance and Geraldus, but the rest of the house, including Guenlian, who had found time to dress properly and even, oddly, put on her earrings. Caet saw her and panicked.

"Don't let her in!" He called, "Geraldus, keep them out! Wait!"

They pushed past him. Someone had remembered to bring a torch. The fire made wild shadows and at first Geraldus couldn't recognize the thing on the altar before him. A mass of filmy gold with patches of red and white showing here and there was all he could make out. Then he shuddered. He realized that one of the white patches hanging down the side of the altar was a human arm and suddenly the mass of abstract shapes came into focus.

"Oh, my God," he murmured. He pulled off his cloak and went to wrap it about her, more to keep her parents from seeing than to preserve her modesty, for he was sure she was long past caring. As he did so, he noticed a faint movement of her lips. She was breathing!

"Someone, help me. She's still alive. Quick!"

Guenlian rushed past everyone as they stood rigid with shock and confusion. She pushed the cloak off and brushed back the cascades of hair from Guinevere's body, hunting for the wound, to staunch it. But she found nothing. She lifted her daughter and ran her hands over her limp back. There was not even a scratch. Finally, she showed Leodegrance.

"This is not her blood. I can find no mark upon her. Where did it come from? How did she get here? Is there a curse upon our house?"

Leodegrance examined her carefully, noting her still open, glazed eyes.

"She has been drugged by someone. She may not have any idea of where she is or what has happened. Quickly, someone, wrap her up and take her to the baths. Put her in a clean night dress and return her to her own room. She may awake never knowing of this night."

"No, I will take her," Guenlian insisted. "My last baby, my strange girlchild. No one shall touch you but me. Where is Flora?"

"What do you mean?" Leodegrance wondered if she had gone mad also. "Flora is bedridden."

Pincerna then remembered the commotion in Flora's room.

"She is missing. Rhianna found her bed empty. Do you think someone has captured her, too?"

Guenlian was busy covering Guinevere and pulling the strands of sticky hair from her face. She didn't look up to speak, but her voice was low, clear and awful.

"Flora has done this thing. She always wanted Guinevere for her pagan sacrilege. I want her found and punished for this."

She then lifted Guinevere alone, although the child was almost as tall as she. No one dared offer her help as she made her slow way to the baths.

Leodegrance stared about him, at the rippling fires in the fields and the carnage glowing in the torchlight. He had reached his limit of understanding. There was no more order in the world. Children died while their father yet lived and children were born when their father had died. A sacrifice of blood with no wound. And it was Midwinter night. The bonfires assaulted the sky as though they would be the sun and light the darkness of the heavens. It was a night for men to go mad. He noticed the thick oaken door, torn from its hinges and splintered on the tiles.

"Am I perhaps mad myself?" he wondered.

The altar was bare now, the room dark. People began edging away, remembering that they had left the cook stirring a spiced ale to take the chill off their souls. Geraldus stayed behind. He watched Leodegrance with concern, unsure of what to do next. And Caet stayed. He had glimpsed in the torchlight the corner of a red and gold cloth behind the altar in the dark alcove where no one had looked. He knew what it was.

Gently, he knelt by his great-grandmother's body. He bent to kiss her one last time when he saw two eyes glittering at him. He inhaled with a rasp of terror too great for noise. Ever after he believed that Flora was no longer in her body then. He refused even to consider what spoke to him through her mouth.

"The sacrifice was desecrated," the voice hissed. "She will not pay, but Britain will. And you. The child was mine. She was destined for me and no other fate. Now all who have her will reap only grief from her. She will come to wish she had gone with me this night."

The glittering eyes darkened and the body went limp. Flora was gone and the Goddess with her. There was no one left in Britain who knew the rituals or had the power. A sudden light hit Caet's eyes. Geraldus had thrust the torch where he was kneeling. His breath came back so quickly that he choked on it and started coughing. Leodegrance looked down at the body. No emotion showed in his voice.

"Guenlian was right, but we will have no need of vengeance now. Take her to her people and have her put on the fire. She would prefer it to a Christian burial and it is better that it be done now, before we begin to ponder this night."

Caet nodded. He went to fetch some of the field workers and others who followed the cult. They would know what to do for her. When he had done that he returned to the stables. There amid the smell of horses and hay, he shivered and cried until dawn.

Guenlian put Guinevere in her bed and smoothed the covers around her. She was sleeping naturally now, but who could tell what she might remember or how this could affect her. Leodegrance waited for her out in the hallway.

"Will she recover?" he asked.

"Sooner than we will, I believe. But I have thought it out. The time has come for us to give her up for fostering. This is not a place for her. There are too many memories and too many horrors. Our cousin Cador has a large castle on the Saxon shore. It is filled with people of her own age and rank. And it is not so far away that we cannot see her sometimes. Oh, my dear, we must get her away from here. Who knows what may happen next?"

"You are tired and frayed by what has happened. Let us think it over and decide tomorrow."

"Yes, tomorrow, but there is no other choice."

They left a guard at the door and returned to their own room. Slowly, the others of the house drifted back to their rooms and, if they didn't sleep, at least all was quiet.

Geraldus had stayed behind to see that Flora was taken care of and to examine the chapel. He had ordered the bronze knife burned with its priestess. Over and over, he paced the short distance from the door to the altar. Under all the marks of many feet there were those of an animal, one with a cloven hoof. He had seen those marks before, but still had no name for what made them. Something made him carefully scrape them away with the heel of his boot. Only then did he return to his room. The air around him was strangely empty of voices. "They must all be splashing in the baths again."

Geraldus felt lonely and sick, forsaken by everyone.

"Lord, why did you do this to me? I am an island, surrounded by voices, cut off from almost everyone on earth. The only people who ever made me feel one of them have been tortured and struck down. There is nothing left. I have nothing to hold on to. I can't live like this!"

He fell on his bed, too tired even to remove his boots, and sank at once into sleep.

He awoke in the hour before dawn. Only one voice was singing, an alto, soothing and low. He smiled without thinking. He felt the pressure of a hand on his cheek and a whispered, "Don't open your eyes. You still can't see me. I was supposed to wait for this, to lure you to our country, but I must have lived with you for too long for I find I can't bear to see you suffering like this. There is little comfort I can offer, but what I have is yours."

Geraldus' heart throbbed in his throat. He opened his eyes but there was no one there. She laughed.

"I told you you could not see me, but I am here."

There was a rustle of blankets and a warmth beside him.

"Do you always sleep in your boots?"

"Are you . . . will you . . . run away again?"

"Not this time. I believe you have made me almost human!"

"What are you? What do you look like?"

"I am just as Guinevere described me, black hair, a straight nose, and pointed chin," she guided his finger down her face. "Long fingers," her hand clasped his. "There is only one thing different."

"What is that?"

"I'm not wearing my green dress."

His hand moved across her shoulder and down.

"No, you're not."

Conversation was becoming more difficult for him; a fierce drumming in his ears drowned everything else out. Fortunately, his alto seemed to feel that she had said enough.

Sometime later it occurred to him that if hearing voices had made him a saint, this would surely reduce his stature to that of lunatic. But he prayed more fervently than he ever had before.

"Lord, if I am mad, please, please, never let me again be sane."

CHAPTER ELEVEN

The sublime Lady Guinevere sneezed again. Her eyes were red, her nose was swollen, and her throat was so sore that she could only croak. It was her third cold this winter and she was completely miserable. Unkind people at the castle implied that it was all her own fault. If she insisted upon bathing and washing her hair every week, she couldn't expect to remain healthy all winter.

Guinevere was at the castle of Cador, a gloomy stone fortress built on the coastline known as the Saxon Watch. Its main purpose was to warn those inland of any new invasion forces. It was not intended for the comfort of its inhabitants. Guinevere had been there three years and was finally resigned to it. She had protested bitterly at leaving her beautiful home and entering a totally different world. But who can fight against fate and the visions of a unicorn? So Guinevere had submitted to the request that she go to her father's cousin for fostering.

Guenlian knew how difficult it would be for her pampered child to adapt to this life, so she had insisted from the first on some special considerations. She told Sidra, Cador's wife, that Guinevere needed a private room, instead of sleeping in the great hall with everyone else in the household. She also needed a personal maid. Therefore Risa, one of the maids at the villa, had gone with Guinevere to the castle; she prepared her bath, combed her hair, and brought her food when she was ill. In all other ways, Guinevere had been forced to adjust. She coughed repeatedly and cursed each one of the moss-covered walls about her with a newly acquired fluency.

"Guinevere?" a voice called from outside the door. "May I come in?"

"Gawain?" Guinevere tried to sit up and push the pillows and blankets into better order. "Yes, please do, I'm so lonely."

He pushed aside the curtain; there were no doors in the tower rooms. "How are you feeling today?"

"About the same. But I'm becoming used to it, so it doesn't bother me as much. Tell me the news."

Gawain smiled at her. He knew she had refused to go to the hall or to see anyone while the cold made her so ugly, but she never minded him. It should have hurt his ego, but he rather liked it. He and Guinevere were so much the same.

"They say that Arthur is coming to visit before spring. He is looking for men for some special new group he is planning. This time, I'm determined to make him notice me."

"How could he avoid it?" she laughed. Even in the late afternoon sun, Gawain's hair glowed with a crimson light all its own. He was the only person she had ever met whose hair could rival her own. It curled forth from his head in a series of living coils and gleamed in the daylight like a nimbus about him. Apart from that, Gawain was a head taller than most people and so vibrantly handsome that respectable matrons had been known to walk into closed doors while staring at him.

Gawain was not amused by her teasing. "This is serious, Guinevere," he insisted. "I've trained for the last five years in hope that Arthur would notice me and ask me to join him. Every time he has come here, though, I've been away. He never comes to Cornwall, where my family lives. I just can't understand my luck!"

Guinevere nodded. "I have never met him, either, for all I have heard of him. Each time he has been here, I have been at home, or visiting somewhere. Every time he visits my parents, I seem to be here. It does seem bad fortune that neither of us can come face to face with the one man the entire island depends upon."

"I won't let it happen again. Nothing will get me away from this castle until I've shown what I can do and have had my opportunity to join him."

They were interrupted by Risa, Guinevere's maid. She spoke to Guinevere, but her eyes were always on Gawain.

"Are you feeling well enough to come to dinner, my lady? I will help you dress if you wish to go down."

"No, thank you. I'm not hungry. If you will bring me some soup and spiced wine when you finish your meal, that will be enough."

"Yes, my lady," she curtsied and stumbled out, still staring at Gawain.

He sighed. "If only they would be willing to do more than just look."

"We were talking about Arthur."

"Yes, well. I was only saying that I won't be passed over this time. I could be a great help to Arthur if he would only overlook my affliction."

"I know that. But it is hard for those who don't know you well to understand. I've never known of anyone with such a curious problem before. We have all seen how, at noon, in the bright sunlight, you can defeat any warrior, on horseback or afoot. You can uproot trees and destroy stone walls. But Gawain, what if an enemy attacked by night? By twilight you are so weak that you need to lean on someone just to reach your bed, and once you're asleep, we can't even wake you! A whole battle could be fought around your tent and you would never know it!"

"Even so, there must be some way I could serve. I can't stand the way people look at me as if I were some kind of coward. Here I am, as strong as an ox in the daytime, and I spend all my days here at the castle or hiding at home. There are times when I wish I had never been born!"

His despair was so genuine that Guinevere forebore teasing him any more.

"Gawain, isn't there some way you could be cured? You have never mentioned how this happened to you. Is it a curse or something that runs in your family?"

He stared at her a moment and then started to laugh.

"Guinevere, I've been here all this time and you still don't know about my family?"

"No, no one told me and it seemed impolite to ask. Do they all have this problem?"

"Not this problem, but . . . well, I don't mind your knowing. Certainly there is no secret about it. My mother is not the type to be subtle or discreet in her actions."

"Your mother?"

"My mother, Guinevere, is Morgan, called Le Fay. She is wife to King Lot of Cornwall and daughter to Igraine, late wife of King Uther. Her sister is Morgause, a sorceress, some say. You may have heard of them all."

He flushed a little as he confessed it, as if both ashamed and proud of his notorious family.

Guinevere was uncomfortable, too. "Oh, I'm sorry. I shouldn't have asked. Really, I should have known. I have heard of your mother. She must be a very interesting person to know."

Gawain laughed again, this time without humor. "So say half the men in Britain."

"I didn't mean that, Gawain. Never mind," she brushed away his apologies. "Didn't you ever ask your mother about your problem? Have you always been this way?"

"Yes, for as long as I can remember, I think since I was born. I did ask her once, when I was angry at what I was missing. My brothers would go exploring at night and I could never go with them. She thought it was very funny and said it must be my father's fault. She told me that she hadn't considered the possibility at the time but it was very nice that one of her children was certain never to interrupt her at night, just when she was busiest."

"What could that mean?" Guinevere ignored the last part of his statement and concentrated on the first. "I have never heard of anyone in Lot's family having to sleep the moment the sun went down."

"My dear, just how bad is your cold? No one ever said Lot was my father. He's a fine man and I like him, but I doubt that he sired me or any of my brothers, either. I don't know who the man was. Knowing Mother, I sometimes fear that it was no man

146

at all but some sort of incubus she conjured up from hell with one of her potions."

"That doesn't seem likely. I've always heard that such demons love the dark and dread the light of day." She crossed herself piously. "May we be protected from them. That is the opposite of your problem so, if anything, he must have been one who loved the day."

"That's true. I hadn't considered it that way. You are a comfort Guin. I hope you feel better soon." He gave her a brotherly pat on the head and yawned.

"Still another month until spring. I must go and get some dinner before I'm too tired to eat. I'll see you tomorrow. Good night."

"Good afternoon, Gawain."

He nearly collided at the curtain with Risa bringing a tray for her mistress. He excused himself as she edged around him silently, staring all the while with adoration.

Once he was out of sight, she collected herself and brought the tray over.

"The soup is cold now, my lady, from the long climb, but I'll heat it again on the brazier and warm the wine also. There are some dried apples soaked in milk if you would like something now."

"Yes, that would be fine," Guinevere held out her hand for the bowl. "Risa, why do you stare at Gawain so? You watch and watch him but you never speak."

Risa started and spilled some of the soup.

"Oh dear! Look at the mess! I didn't realize I was being so obvious."

"I have noticed you and so has he. He would like it if you spoke to him."

"Then he must say something first. I'm not so bold as all that."

She carefully poured what was left of the soup into a small iron pot and let it heat over the coals. Her cheeks were red and she held her face close to the heat to explain it. She spoke again casually, without turning her head.

"Did he tell you he wanted me to say something?"

"Not exactly. But I think he would like it."

Risa waited silently while Guinevere finished her meal. Then she pulled a small roll of parchment from a fold in her robe. "I'm sorry," she said. "I almost forgot, there was a letter from your mother."

Guinevere unrolled the parchment carefully. It was only a short note full of daily happenings. But it brought a greater warmth than the mulled wine.

"Is there any news, my lady?"

"Nothing special," Guinevere smiled. "My niece is demanding that her grandfather teach her to ride. She is an active little person and apparently keeps the whole household busy. She is so pretty and so much like Matthew. I can hardly wait to see her again. The roof in the solarium is leaking this winter and Father is worried that he can find no more tile makers to repair it properly."

"Do they say if there is word of Caet?"

"No, I suppose that if he were heard from they would say something. It does seem odd, the way he ran off without asking anyone. Father was particularly disappointed."

She read on awhile, lost in memories. Risa took the soup bowl and left. The room grayed in the growing twilight. Finally she put the letter down and looked about her. Despite the efforts of Guenlian and her hostess, the contrast between this room and the one she had grown up in was enormous. The floor and walls were cold stone. Attempts had been made to cover as much of them as possible, especially since the proximity to the ocean made the walls always damp and mossy. They had been draped with thick hangings of linen and wool, but the smell of mildew permeated everything. The floors were strewn with straw, which soon grew brown and broken from dropped food and muddy boots. In the great Hall it was far worse, as the animals were allowed to wander about, relieving themselves where ever they liked. The elegant long robes the women wore were crusted at the hems with every kind of filth. The stench was overpowering to Guinevere, but most people, enveloped in their own aroma, soon ceased to notice. Early on in her stay, Guinevere had discovered that water could only be procured by sending servants out to the well to draw it and then carry it in steaming buckets from the great fire in the hall to her room. It was tainted by the sea and no one drank it unless forced to. It was much more tolerable as ale. Guinevere longed to bathe every day, as she had at home, but her conscience would not allow all that trouble so often. Once a week annoyed the household quite enough.

Still, oddly, she had adjusted to life there. In many ways it was more exciting than her backwater home. Cador's castle was part of a long string of watchtowers that had been manned for centuries to spot ships of traders and possible invaders. Messengers were always coming in with information on how the wars were going or to tell what ships had been sighted. The conversation and entertainment in the evenings were also different from the low tones and ancient lays heard in the villa. Life here was noisy and more intense; sometimes even a little wild. People were used to a chancy existence and lived as though they might not see another spring. It frightened Guinevere and exhilarated her. The only thing she could not accustom herself to was the lack of privacy. Outside of her own room she was rarely alone. Even there she had to share sleeping space with Risa. There were over a hundred people living, working, or passing through the castle on any given day. They came from all over the island and a few even from Armorica, Gaul, and farther east. They bumped and jostled, yelled and competed for space and attention until Guinevere's only thought was to run from them all; anywhere, only to get away.

That was how she found her place, a small strip of beach at the end of a narrow path. It was covered by the sea, except at low tide. This night she knew it would be open and, even with her cold, she was determined to go down there, alone. She covered her head with a blanket and leaned her face through the narrow slit in the stones that served as a window. The wind cut her eyes so that tears blurred her vision. But she didn't need sight. She was calling, calling again.

Finally, as from a great distance, she felt the answer come. "I will be with you tonight; wait for me."

Her muscles relaxed and she covered the hole in the wall again with the oiled skin nailed above it.

An hour later, when she knew the rest of the household would be grouped by rank around the hearth, she slipped down the stairs and made for a side door she knew she could unbolt. She held her breath as she passed across the dark corner of the hall, but no one turned. They were all intent on a new arrival's story, something involving a virgin miraculously saved from torture by a monk who turned out to be her lover in disguise. Guinevere had heard many of these stories before and didn't even pause to listen as she hurried outside.

The door opened easily and Guinevere was free. Surefooted, she ran down the dark path. The beach was empty.

She tried to hear the unicorn in her mind, but apart from the constant knowledge of its presence, she felt nothing. Where was he? She reached out to him. It had been weeks since she had actually seen him, although they had communicated almost every day. She felt exhausted and discouraged and wondered if the feelings were her own or his. At first he had been delighted to be with her at the ocean, but as the months had passed he had changed, even as she had begun to grow up. Whether one was connected to the other neither was sure. Yet he was restless now in a way he had never been in the forest, and as Guinevere seemed to grow more and more comfortable in her world, his own contentment grew less and less.

A great wave threw itself upon the stones and wet Guinevere's shoes. When it subsided, he was there, shining like the midnight sea. His spiral horn gleamed in the faint shreds of daylight. Guinevere ran to him. She wrapped her arms around his cold neck and pulled a strand of seaweed from his mane.

"Where have you been for so long?" she reproached him. "Have you found the others?"

He shook his head sadly. Droplets fell from his coat to the sand. "They must be there. I feel there are beings like myself and yet different living out there, just beyond my strength to reach them. I swim out, calling to them, but there is no answer."

He sank down beside her betraying his fatigue. Now Guinevere knew it was his emotions that had depressed her earlier. "I wish I understood," he sighed. "I wish I knew even if I ought to understand. Guinevere, my other self, I fear I have lived too long for one of my kind. We are meant to be born, to sing and to be killed. That is how it has always been. There are times when I want to beg you to call the hunters and let the cycle continue."

She clutched him tightly. "I could not do it. It would kill me if they took you from me."

"You needn't worry," he soothed her. "I am unable to take such control of my fate. If only I could stop wondering, questioning. My own nature is a mystery to me and yet I must discover it. I must know what a unicorn is meant to be. But I am so tired."

His eyes closed and his head fell into her lap. Guinevere bent her face over his and wept for his sadness. She wished she could help him, find his answers. But since she had never questioned anything herself she did not know what it was to be torn and consumed by the need to know *why*. Her miseries were more concrete. So she could only comfort and love and caress his tormented mind with her own peace.

What he gave her in return, she couldn't say, but she returned by first starlight to her room content to be where and who she was. Strengthened and sure, she was no longer bruised by the noise in the hall. Each time she was with the unicorn some of his radiance remained upon her. Gawain happened to glance up as she passed by his sleeping place and thought for a moment that she carried a candle before her face. But he was nearly asleep then and the next morning assumed it had been a dream.

The rumors had been flowing in and out of the castle for months. Everyone knew that Arthur had finally built up a unified force that was slowly pushing the invaders, particularly the Saxons, back to the sea. London had been saved from becoming a Germanic town and only the southeast areas and a few settlements of the invaders in the northeast remained. The autumn past he had scored a great victory over the most important of the Saxon warlords and forced them to leave hostages before they retreated, as a token of their sworn oath never to attack again. Now word had come that some of these hostages were to be brought to Cador and housed at the castle until proper treaties were made and conditions for their release ascertained. Opinions were mixed about the new arrivals and loudly voiced.

"Why should we take in these Saxon pigs and treat them as royal guests when we know how they have treated our own people in the places they have conquered?" spat a young soldier named Cheldric. "They should be kept in chains by the door and made to howl for their meat like the animals they are."

Another answered him. "Arthur has some idea that we should treat them well so as to prove to the Saxons that we are civilized people. As if they would know a civilized country! They even refuse to live in the towns we have had to abandon to them. Instead they build ugly wood huts and crowd into them pigs, cattle, and wives."

"If Arthur insists that we treat them well, I will, at least, not harm them," Cheldric muttered. "But I will sleep with my knife in my hand if they are allowed to roam about unguarded and unfettered. You'd best, too, Mauron, if you don't want your throat slit by night."

The person who heard most of these comments was Sidra, Cador's wife. She was a strong, proud woman who was saved from being a tyrant in her home by a sense of humor and a firm belief in her own ability to manage people without their knowing it. Certainly she had succeeded so well with her husband that he never realized he had not made a decision in his own home for twenty years. It was she who fed a hundred people a day and found places for them all to sleep. She had managed to get Guinevere a private room without anyone whining to her that she was showing favoritism. She kept guests, fosterlings, and servants busy maintaining the castle and doing the chores without anyone feeling put-upon or ill-used, and lastly, she had the rare talent of being able to listen to the crudest of stories without embarrassing the narrator or lowering her own status. This was crucial in a place that was full of soldiers, where no one could speak above a whisper without being heard by a dozen other people. It was generally understood that she knew everything that went on and kept order partly through the implied threat of using that knowledge.

Sidra was not beautiful. She had dark brown eyes and light brown hair, now almost totally gray. Her face was pleasant but not exciting, and scarred from a childhood case of smallpox. Her marriage had been an arranged one, and it had taken her husband several years to realize that it was the best thing that had ever been done for him. When it finally dawned on him, he went to her immediately and told her so. He was not a man of action for nothing. Since then her life had been perfect, suited to her talents and interests. It was almost totally through her good sense that Guinevere had learned to live in her home.

One day, soon after the news about the hostages had arrived, Sidra climbed to Guinevere's room. Guinevere's cold was almost gone now and she was dressed and reading a new codex by lamplight. She smiled when Sidra called from the top step.

"You never need to ask to enter, Foster-mother. Please come and sit beside me. Look, this copy of the gospels has come all the way from Antioch. Each page is illuminated. Look here, they have even used gold leaf in the pictures. The priest lent it to me to read before he takes it to the copyist."

"Thank you dear, I haven't time now to look at it. I want to ask a favor of you. I'm not sure you will like it but I want you to hear me through. It doesn't seem fair to ask it of you with your brothers and all, but I really don't know what else to do with the poor child." She paused and glanced at Guinevere. Was she listening? Yes, her attention was caught. Sidra continued.

"You have heard that Arthur is sending some of his hostages to live with us?"

Guinevere nodded. A faint expression of distaste crossed her face.

"Yes, I know many people think we shouldn't house them at all. But, remember, these aren't common soldiers but the children of their kings. They have no more to do with battles and killing than you do. I wish Arthur would bring them himself but this message says that he can't possibly come here before spring and he wants them safely here at once. So he's sending them with Merlin. Thank the Lord there are only two of them."

She stopped again, apparently lost in her planning. Guinevere nudged her.

"What is it you want from me?" she asked.

"It's this way, my dear. I just don't know where to put them. One, I think, I'll put on the wall side of Gawain. He'll be out of the way there, but the other—I just don't know. It seems that these bloody Saxons think no more of their own flesh but to send their daughters to the enemy."

"Daughters!" Guinevere was finally surprised. "Do you mean one of them is a girl?"

"About your age, I'm told, maybe a little younger. Now do you think I could put her down there in the hall with all those people hating her so and me not always there to be sure that no one gets any ideas about her?"

"Sidra, you want me to take a heathen Saxon girl into my private room with me, don't you?"

"Now, Guinevere, did I say that? I know how you feel about them and who has more right? But I confess I did hope you would do it. You being so much better bred than most of the girls here, I thought you might be able to at least refrain from being actively cruel to the child. Think of how frightened she must be, sent away from her family for no crime of her own. But no, I see you are against it and I do understand. A pagan and a Saxon is certainly not fit to share a room with someone of your aristocratic background. I'll find a spot for her somewhere, in with the horses or the goats perhaps."

Guinevere knew when she was beaten. That, at least was something she had gained from her stay at Cador.

"Sidra, wait. She may stay with me. But you must bring in another bed. In my room, yes. But I'll not share my blanket with her."

"Of course not, dear. No one ever suggested such a thing. It's very fine and noble of you to do this much. I'm sure it will set a good example."

She gave Guinevere a motherly kiss and went back to her work with a satisfied smile.

When the day came that they were to arrive, the entire household assembled to meet them. Something made each person want to look their best, to let these heathens know what sort of people they were dealing with, so boots were scraped and fine robes shaken out and smoothed; hair was combed and some determined sorts even washed their faces and hands. They gathered in the main hall opposite the entry to await the Saxon foe.

Soon horses could be heard climbing the stone pathway. They stopped and someone could be heard calling that he would see to the animals and be in later. The voice was muffled but Guinevere thought it was one she knew. Then there was a long silence before the knocking came. Three heavy blows fell upon the great oaken door as if it were being pounded by a hammer. Sidra signaled the porter to let them in.

There was an audible intake of breath as everyone waited eagerly for the door to swing open.

Standing on the threshold was Merlin. Behind him on either side stood a young man and a girl. Guinevere gasped at them in astonishment and was glad to hear that she wasn't the only one.

They were both of a height and as tall as Merlin. They were dressed in leather and rough wool and the girl wore a cape that seemed to be made of feathers. They stood proudly erect and eyed their captors with disdain. But what had caused everyone to gape in astonishment was not their expression, but their trappings. Both of them were covered in gold. Each wore a filigree head-band, armbands, necklaces, bracelets of gold. They wore long golden earrings and their clothes were fastened by golden brooches. Even their shoes were decorated in gold leaf. It was more wealth than most of those present had ever seen. An angry murmur rustled through the hall. Sidra quelled it with a movement of her arm as she stepped forward.

"Welcome, Merlin, and welcome to your friends. May you each enjoy the hospitality of our home for as long as you desire. We have awaited your coming with pleasure and hope you will find our simple life acceptable."

Merlin bowed and entered without speaking. The other two followed him closely.

"I am honored to be again your guest, worthy Sidra, wife of Cador. I have brought with me two wayfarers who wish to bide with you a time. Their names are Ecgfrith and Alswytha, son and daughter to Aelle, king of the East Saxons." Ecgfrith stared straight before him, hardly blinking, but Alswytha bowed slightly at the mention of her name.

"We have prepared resting places for you all which I hope will be suited to your needs and rank," Sidra replied in the same formal tone. "I will send a servant to put your belongings in their proper places. Merlin, perhaps you and Ecgfrith would like to come with me so that I may explain to you the customs of our house."

A thought struck her and she dropped the ritual address to ask Merlin, "Do they speak our language?"

"Only a few words, but they will learn. I'm sure that with so many wellborn youths as you have here for fostering someone could be found who is capable of teaching his own language." Merlin raised his voice a little to be sure that those wellborn youths knew who he meant.

For a moment, Sidra was disconcerted. "Merlin, you didn't tell me that we couldn't make them understand us. How will we ever . . . ?"

"You will," Merlin smiled. He had known Sidra for many years. "That is why I brought them here."

Sidra grimaced but continued. "Guinevere, will you please take Alswytha to your room and show her where she is to sleep? Then bring her back here for the evening meal."

Guinevere glided forward. She was dressed in the last of her Egyptian silks and wore her hair unbound and fastened only with the jade pins given her by Geraldus' invisible alto. She had the pleasure of watching Ecgfrith's proud face widen in astonishment and admiration as she approached.

She first bowed to Merlin. "I hope you are well, Cousin," she said a little stiffly. She had never gotten over her discomfort near him.

He returned the bow. "I am quite well, thank you. I see that you have recovered from your recent illness. And your family? I have not seen them for some time."

"They were in excellent health, when I last heard from them, and enjoying a mild winter."

With mutual relief they ended the meaningless exchange that manners demanded. She hated the way Merlin glared at her as if she had committed an unpardonable sin. She turned almost gladly to Alswytha. The proud expression on the girl's face didn't falter, but Guinevere thought her eyes showed fear. She tried to smile reassuringly.

"Come with me and I will show you where you will live," she started. Then she remembered that the girl spoke only Saxon. She put her hand upon Alswytha's shoulder and pushed gently. "You, come," she said. "Up. Sleeping room."

The girl stared at her with no sign of comprehension. Guinevere glanced helplessly at Merlin, who spoke to his charge rapidly. Alswytha nodded and allowed Guinevere to take her up the stairs.

Sidra sighed in relief. "Well, at least you can understand them. Where did you learn Saxon?"

"That is of no importance," he warned her. "Someone had to be able to converse with them or no treaty could have been arranged. If you tell me what you want them to do and where they are to stay, I will explain it to them before I must leave."

"You might have told me that at once," she replied tartly. "Come along then. Bring Egfreeth or whatever he is called. All right, everyone. You can meet our guests later. Go back to your work and we will meet at dinner."

She waved them away but most of the people didn't go far. They broke into smaller groups whispering among themselves, and occasionally glancing covertly at the young man sitting stiffly between Sidra and Merlin.

"He doesn't even know that he's a prisoner," Cheldric sneered. "He thinks he's still a prince. A Saxon prince! We'll get those bracelets off him soon enough and teach him what he really is."

"I don't think that would be wise, Cheldric," Gawain said quietly. "You might not like to have to answer to Arthur for any harm that came to him. Or have you given up wanting to join his new corps?"

Cheldric subsided at this threat, but he and Mauron spent the rest of the afternoon in deep conversation in their corner of the hall.

Guinevere led Alswytha to her room, holding her hand and speaking to her much as she did to her three-year-old niece.

"Now, here we go, up the stairs and then a turn and here we are. This is your bed." She pointed to it. "Bed," she repeated. She patted the pillow. "You sleep here." She pretended to snore.

Alswytha stared at her in complete astonishment, then, to

Guinevere's indignation, she began laughing. Guinevere glared at her angrily. Alswytha laughed harder.

"I'm sorry," she gasped at last. "I can't help it. You look so ridiculous like that!"

"You can understand me!" Guinevere was too surprised to remain angry. "Why didn't you tell me so instead of letting me make a fool of myself?"

"I thought it would be safer if no one knew they could talk with me. I am rather afraid of some of those people down there. I think they would hurt me if they could. But you were so funny! Please don't let anyone know."

She looked so imploring and so truly frightened that Guinevere gave in.

"I won't say anything, if you behave well. But how did you learn it? You have a very good accent. Does your brother speak Latin, too?"

"No, Ecgfrith thinks everyone should learn our tongue, even the other tribes living near us, the Angles and the Jutes. Even other Saxon dialects are hard for him to understand. I learned from a slave at my father's hall. He was a captured soldier of your people. He was ill a long time from his wounds and then could do only very easy work in the hall. I was lonely then, with so many people gone to the fighting. When he learned enough to understand me, I asked him about his home. He didn't want to speak of that, so he taught me his language instead. You are angry because we have a slave of your people. I see it. Please, it is the way of things. We could have killed him or left him to die from his wounds. I tried to help him."

"He was a soldier?" Guinevere felt a sudden chill. "What was his name?"

"He never told me his name in his own speech. We called him Ceorl. It is not a proper name, but he didn't mind. I am not sure if I can describe him for you. His face was horribly scarred on the right side and one eye had been blinded in his last battle. There were burns, too, and even his mouth was twisted from them. His good eye was brown, very dark. I had never seen such dark eyes before. His hair was black, black as cloudy midnight. He stooped when he walked, so I am not sure if he was tall or not."

"The poor man!" Guinevere gave her a look of disgust. "Why didn't you let him go? Couldn't you have done something to help?"

"I gave him what special treatment I could and I smiled at him when we passed. I spent many long winters and springs talking with him. That was all I could do. Do you think my father would have praised me for letting him escape, even if he were strong enough to get away? At least I didn't despise him the way you do me."

Guinevere rose from the bed with dignity. "Since you understand my speech so well, I will not waste time. Be sure you remember all I say. You are to share this room with my maid, Risa, and myself. This is your bed. I expect nothing from you. You do not need to serve me in any way and I would rather not have to speak to you. Your people killed my brothers and are trying to conquer my country. I have no wish to love or understand you. You are a heathen and an enemy. Is that clear?"

The hopeful look in Alswytha's eyes died, to be replaced by a cold pride as great as Guinevere's own. "I understand perfectly. My brothers and cousins too have died. But I will tell you that I am not an invader. I was born on this island on the land given my grandfather by your king Vortigern. My home is as dear to me as yours is to you. I feel nothing but contempt for your army if it is not strong enough to protect itself. You are not what I expected from what Ceorl told me and I wish to have nothing to do with you either."

She sat down fiercely on her bed. Guinevere crossed the room and sat on hers. They each gazed resolutely at opposite walls. They might have stayed that way forever if they hadn't heard someone coming up the stairs.

"My love is like the su-uh-mer dawn," a voice caroled. "No, no! You don't come in until the next line. Do you want to learn this song or not?"

Both girls smiled and rushed for the entrance just as Geraldus entered.

"Guinevere!" he grinned as he hugged her. "It's been too long since I have seen you! You have almost grown up. And quite nicely too, I must say. How are you and Wytha doing? I was very glad to know that she was being sent here where you could get to know her and look after her."

He stopped when he saw their faces. "Oh, I see. You haven't started very well, I gather. Well, you really haven't had much time to get to know each other yet. It is odd. I somehow thought you would like each other."

He didn't know how to go on from there. Guinevere and Alswytha both stood in front of him, looking stubborn and a little ashamed. But neither of them made any attempt to answer him. Suddenly, the alto with the black hair peeked at them from behind Geraldus' shoulder. She nibbled at his ear a second and just then appeared to notice them. She grinned and stuck out her tongue. Both girls broke into laughter.

Geraldus rubbed his ear and looked gloomily from one to the other.

"Oh, no," he moaned. "Not both of you!"

CHAPTER TWELVE

Geraldus thought they looked like twilight and dawn. Alswytha's straight silver hair and pale-as-snow complexion oddly complemented Guinevere's rich gold tresses and tanned cheeks. He was correct, too, in supposing that they could grow to be friends. Warily at first and never with complete trust, the two girls developed a relationship that was as close to friendship as either had ever come with a girl of her own age. Guinevere had occupied her early years with her unicorn and had needed no one else. Alswytha was the only daughter of a warrior king and was not allowed much acquaintance with other girls. Her home was filled with swords and spears and leather caked with sea salt. She had spent much of her childhood in a world of dreams.

So they could understand each other and enjoy being together. But there was a last chasm that could not be bridged. To Guinevere, Alswytha was a friend. She was loving and gentle. Her Latin had improved to the point that she hardly ever made a mistake in grammar; her manners were refined and better than those of many of the people who sat down to dinner each night at the castle. But she was still a Saxon. She was the invader, the heathen. She was the symbolic villain of every horror story Guinevere had ever heard. Now and again Guinevere would forget, but a phrase, a gesture would bring it back to her, and she would pull away. Alswytha's pride felt this deeply and for this reason she too kept Guinevere from coming too close.

The others in the castle hardly bothered to find out about her. They assumed she didn't understand a word they said and made no attempt to teach her. The horror stories were good enough for them. When it was made clear that she was under Guinevere's protection as well as Sidra's, she was not treated as badly as she might have been. Men like Mauron and Cheldric considered Saxon women to be spoils of war and leered at her openly, making low-voiced comments that would have been clear to her from the tone even if she had not understood the muffled words. Alswytha knew that only a slender thread of respect and discipline kept them from paying more overt attention to her. In public, in the dining hall or courtyard, she was proud and aloof, but when she found it necessary to go alone from one part of the castle to another, through the long dank corridors or into rooms filled with shadowy cold alcoves, she frankly ran, looking from side to side constantly, like an animal pursued by a predator.

The women of the castle found her a ready subject of gossip, which they greeted eagerly, there not being much else to do in the winter. They sniffed at the cut of her clothes, which showed her ankles, her barbaric and ostentatious amount of jewelry, her disdainful way of looking at them, "for all the world as if she thinks we are the captives and she the mistress," someone would say.

"No doubt she is used to being somebody's mistress," another would slur softly over her embroidery. "We have heard about Saxon women and their free ways."

"It makes me ill to be under the same roof with her," a fosterling from a northern estate muttered. "And her brother! Have you seen the way he looks at us? I saw him ogling me openly the other day and I felt as if he could see completely through my clothes! I was so upset, I couldn't eat the whole day!"

She shivered in horrified delight.

"Someone should tell Sidra that he should be kept away from us," another fosterling suggested. But apparently no one wanted to be the "someone" to tell her, so the conversation circled on to other complaints and worries and back again to the Saxons in their midst.

Alswytha was Guinevere's shadow, except for an hour or two every day when she sat with Ecgfrith. She worried about him. He made no effort to learn about the Britons. He hardly ever moved from the corner in which Sidra had put him. The complaints, taunts, and insults rolled around and over him. They sounded to him like the growling of bears or the grunts of wild boars. He paid no attention. He had no desire to learn their language. It would please him greatly when they were forced to learn his. He knew the day would come. Look at them, he gloated. Prideful, stupid, clinging to their heritage as if stale history and the ashes of their ancestors could make them any greater than they were. Ecgfrith was sure that once they were gotten from their horses, these Britons who called themselves Romans would be too weak and clumsy to withstand the superior numbers and organization of his people. Everything he saw at the castle confirmed his opinions. Why, the clod who slept next to him could hardly stagger into his bed each night.

He cautioned Alswytha against letting anyone know how good her Latin had become. Guinevere and Geraldus didn't matter. He wanted her to listen to everything and repeat to him all the rumors, all the gossip, all the information he could get.

"But why?" Alswytha asked. "Even if we know how strong their army is and where they are going, we are still prisoners here. There is no way for us to warn our father. Even if we could, he has sworn a blood oath on our lives that he would remain in the territory granted him through the treaty with Vortigern."

Ecgfrith frowned at her. "Don't be absurd, little sister. Do you think an oath is binding when made to them? They were fools! Do you know that Aelle swore, not by our gods, but by that of these Christians! As if that were more threatening and of greater strength. Our father has planned to rule this entire island one day, and we will share it with him. He will not be stopped or intimidated by oaths and hostages. I will not be so bound, either. I have sworn a much more sacred oath to escape from this place at the first chance."

Alswytha was frightened by his talk. She was well aware of how shamed he had been to be turned over meekly to the enemy; to be unable to fight when all his life he had been trained for nothing else. She was afraid that he spoke the truth about his father and she knew then how little he valued her life.

"Ecgfrith," she begged. "You mustn't think of trying to

escape. How would you get away from here? This castle is stone upon stone with only a narrow passage back to the land. There are a dozen men who guard the gates and more who watch the ocean from the towers. How could you avoid being spotted and killed?"

"Perhaps there is a way. Your haughty friend Guinevere manages to go and return with no one the wiser. If I could find the path she takes to the shore, I could leave that way. It would be tricky for the first few minutes, but those guards are watching for ships far out at sea. They will not notice a man swimming right under their noses. If I swam only a few miles up the coast, I could make my way back to our encampment. Our father is not far from here. All I need is the chance to get to him."

"He has not returned to our hall? But then he has already broken trust. How could he do that?"

"Alswytha, haven't I explained it to you? There was nothing to break. I have thought of a way in which this Arthur can be defeated. Don't you want to be revenged for our defeat at Mons Badon last summer? I know where they are weak. I must return and report this."

"You would leave me here alone?" her voice trembled.

"Not for long. I promise to return for you. You won't be harmed. You are practically one of them already. You speak their language. You have friends. I would take you with me, but you are not a strong enough swimmer. You would never survive the icy water. Please my sister, *me leofre* Alswytha. Believe me. This is our only hope. You must help me. Follow Guinevere. Find out the path that she takes to the shore. That is all. I would dive from the cliffs but the rocks are all around. I must find a safe place to enter the water. Then soon, when the storms are not so fierce, I will go, and sooner than that, you will be returned to us."

Alswytha finally agreed. But she was troubled. In her own way, she was as naive as Guinevere. She believed in the sanctity of an oath. She could not see that it mattered what one swore by. All the old tales were full of solemn oaths. Everyone knew that an oath breaker was an outcast from all decent people. Ecgfrith said that it was invalid in this case because the oath was made by a god that was not theirs. She wanted to believe him, but it bothered her greatly. She wondered if the other thing he had said was true, that she was almost one of them. She didn't feel that she had changed. But if her father had done this terrible thing, how could she support him? Her head began to ache as she climbed the steps to her room.

She noticed through one of the chinks in the wall that Guinevere was returning. She was hurrying across the courtyard, wrapped against the mist in a long, woolen cloak. Although her face was hidden, an escaping gold braid proclaimed her identity.

"Where has she been on a day like this?" Alswytha wondered. "She hates to be out in the wet."

She shook her head. Guinevere had clearly been somewhere beyond the walls of the castle. The bottom of her robe was damp. This must be what Ecgfrith meant. But there was nothing there but the ocean beating upon the rocks. Why would Guinevere go down there?

"Perhaps she just needs to be alone, anywhere," Alswytha thought. "She has often said that she hates having all these people about her."

For some reason, Alswytha was reminded of Ceorl. She smiled and then sighed. She wished he were there to help her make a decision. He always managed to make her problems clearer and her decisions easier. And he had been so kind to her, even though he was so miserable, especially during those horrible months after her mother had left and the burden of being the hostess in the hall had fallen to her. He had kept her from despair when all the men were gone and the business of running the household was too much for her. He had hated the crush of people too, and told stories of times when he had traveled alone, just for the joy of solitude. It was strange that of all the people in her father's entourage, he was the one she missed the most. She blushed as a memory came to her of a comment she had overheard.

Two old serving women, distant aunts of hers, had been cackling over their soup by the fire. They hadn't noticed how near she was and didn't bother to lower their voices.

"I don't like the way she looks at him," one brayed to the other. "There'll be trouble from that, letting a slave in the hall at night."

The other agreed. "Aelle would flay him alive and beat her well. But now, I remember my own youth. There was this smith . . . There may be nothing to it anyway. Alswytha always did have a weakness for wounded things."

That had been over a year ago and Alswytha still cringed at the unbidden remembrance. She had tried to be more careful after that but those careless words had made her realize how much she did care for this wounded creature that had been brought into her house. Now that she knew what Ecgfrith was planning, she longed to return to him even more.

"I hope I may live to see him again," she whispered.

Guinevere came in then, radiant and breathless. Her own exultation was such a contrast to Alswytha's mood that for once she noticed and asked what was wrong.

"Has anyone been annoying you? I will see that they stop it at once."

"No, Lady Sidra has seen to it that no one ever speaks rudely to me," Alswytha hedged. She didn't want to tell Guinevere that she had been homesick for a slave. "You are very kind. I was only remembering my home. I miss my mother."

Guinevere sat down next to her and put her arm about her.

"I know. I miss my family, too. Soon, I am sure, you will be released and you will see her again."

"No, I won't. She's gone. I'll never see her again."

Guinevere was embarrassed by her clumsiness. "I'm sorry. I didn't think that she might have died. I . . . I . . . didn't mean to . . ."

Alswytha looked at her with a puzzled expression. "I must not understand your language well enough yet. I did not say she had died. I said she was gone. She went back to her own home-land, across the *hronrad*, the road the whales follow. She lives now in her brother's hall."

"How could she leave you and your brother?" Guinevere wished she had held her tongue.

"It's not that she didn't love us," Alswytha bridled. "She

wanted to pay the *weregeld,* for me at least. But there was no money left from her marriage portion, so my father paid her my price and she left without me. She could not abide here any longer. She hated it. My father is a good man. I am very fond of him. But he cares only for battle and would not allow my mother her work."

"Her work? I don't understand what you are saying."

"My mother is the finest crafter of gold in our clan. She made this for me, see? And this bracelet."

Guinevere had noticed the bracelet before. It was an intricate lacy piece of jewelry, made of dozens of separate coils all wound together, with spaces in between the joinings. They all seemed to be twining toward one place, and looking closely she realized that the coils were meant to be the necks of swans; their beaks and eyes appeared over and over in a line on one side. It was very fine work. Guinevere had never seen anything like it— but still, her mother?

"Why would your mother want to be a craftsman? It doesn't seem a suitable occupation for a woman of her rank."

"That is how my father felt, I don't know where he got the idea. Perhaps from your people. In the great halls of our homeland such a person is highly honored whatever their rank. It is a talent which only a few possess. Her brother was happy to accept her into his home. But here . . . So, after my other brothers were killed in the fighting and my little sister died of the winter fever, she said she would have no more of this place and she sailed back. I'm glad she went, for she was very unhappy, but I do miss her."

Guinevere was silent. She was trying to sort out this strange idea of a woman of rank who made jewelry and found it more important than her husband or her duties. It unsettled her, as if she feared that Guenlian might suddenly express a desire for blacksmithing. She turned it round and round in her mind but, since she could find no answer that appealed to her, she dismissed the whole idea and changed the subject.

"I think Geraldus has been hiding from us lately. We should go find him before he leaves again and make him teach us one of his new songs. He's been wanting you to translate some more of those riddles your people sing. He says that he'll make new melodies for them and no one will suspect they were Saxon first. It's just the thing for winter entertainment. Even those who can't sing can guess. I think they are very interesting but I don't understand them all. What was so funny about the one he told last night?"

"Which one, the bellows?"

"Was that what it was? I'm not good at guessing, but now that you tell me, it makes sense. But why were they all laughing?"

"Well, some people thought it might be something else and I suppose that it amused them to be wrong."

Guinevere gave her a penetrating stare. Alswytha blushed. Guinevere sighed and nodded her head.

"One of those. I thought so. People never want to tell me what they mean. I really think I'm old enough now to have some things explained."

Alswytha laughed at her annoyance. "I think you are, too. But I can't imagine who will have the courage to explain them."

Guinevere laughed with her, if a bit ruefully, and they went to look for Geraldus, who was not hiding but was being kept very busy informing Sidra of what was going on everywhere on the island. She was not a person who wanted a quick summary, and every day she had called him to sit with her or follow her around for hours explaining, in detail, every event, major or minor, that had happened in the last six months. He was glad when the girls pulled him away.

"Thank you," he gasped in gratitude when they were out of Sidra's hearing. "That woman would know when every tree blossoms and every horse foals from Land's End to Hadrian's Wall. And the most amazing thing is that she remembers everything I tell her!"

They walked up to one of the watchtowers and stood looking out to sea. It was a gray world, starting with the rocks, almost black, to the silver and polished waves of the sea and up into the rising fog and clouds. Guinevere thought it was rather boring, but Alswytha loved it. She never tired of watching the subtle shifts in light and shadow. Perhaps, in another time, she would have been an artist, too. Perhaps it was only that the dull colors soothed her by not conflicting with her moods.

While Alswytha watched, Guinevere teased Geraldus.

"I see you didn't bring the whole troupe this time. Have they grown tired of your shouting and criticisms?"

"I only wish they had. No, they don't care for the sea air. It gives them chills or something. You should hear them when we get into the mountains and, of course, they are always in full force when I visit your parents. They are very fond of hot baths."

The dark-haired woman appeared beside him and began aimlessly twisting his long curls about her finger. He brushed his hand across them to stop her, but not as fiercely as he used to, more with a casual tenderness. Guinevere noticed it.

"You have changed in the last few years, Geraldus. You seem happier now, somehow.

Automatically, he glanced over his shoulder although he knew he would see nothing. Then, he smiled. "Yes, I am very content with my life. I know now what lies before me."

The woman nuzzled against him and rested her head on his shoulder. He put his arm around her.

"I'm going to live with them someday. Not soon, I don't think. I have too much to do here. But I can wait. I have made my choice and I am at peace."

Guinevere felt wistfully that he was slipping away from her. He didn't need her friendship in the way that he had before. It made her very lonely until she remembered her unicorn. After all, she needed no one else as long as she had him.

Spring was slow in coming that year, but gradually the days lengthened. Gawain began to move around more actively instead of wandering about half asleep all the time. He and Geraldus could often be heard out in the courtyard, Geraldus harping and Gawain exercising, and both of them singing ribald drinking songs at the top of their lungs.

With Gawain out more and not in his bed next to Ecgfrith, the Saxon had more opportunity to get out unnoticed. Alswytha had shown him the path to the beach that Guinevere took but refused to do anything more. Ecgfrith followed it and found the tiny beach, large enough for his needs. Now he only awaited a clear night with little wind. Ecgfrith drew even further into his corner, looking like a pale shadow against the dark wall. While everyone thought he was sleeping he lay constantly tensing and releasing his muscles, determined to remain strong enough for the swim, and even more, to return to defeat these arrogant idiots.

Risa spoke no more to Guinevere about Gawain, but one evening Guinevere noticed him smiling sleepily at the maid as he finished a cup of wine before bed and the next day she saw them strolling across the courtyard hand in hand.

Finally the sun broke through and everyone really began to believe that spring was near. In a few sheltered areas where the ground was not covered by rock, small flowers were sprouting.

On a particularly fine day Guinevere and Alswytha went to the hall for the noon meal. The company was lively and cheerful, for many of the men would soon be leaving to join their units or at last to apply for admission to one. After a winter of inactivity, they were eager to be off. There was a lot of mock skirmishing that got slightly out of hand as the thick round loaf of bread was tossed from knife point to knife point about the table. The man beside Guinevere, Belinus, grew overexcited and reached out for an impossible catch, just as Guinevere put out her hand for a piece of meat. The knife flashed across the table, ripping her sleeve and grazing her hand. She cried out, more in surprise than pain. Belinus dropped the knife and went white.

"Oh my lady. Forgive me! Please, I didn't see you! What can I do? I am so sorry! Here, let me help you. Oh, forgive me!" he babbled almost hysterically.

Guinevere looked around the table and saw horror on everyone's face. She checked her arm. The fabric was torn and the sleeve dangled so that it would fall in her dish and be in the way, but the scratch on her arm was nothing. It had already stopped bleeding. What were they all so upset about? She smiled reassurance to Belinus.

"No, no, don't worry. It was an accident. I'm not hurt at all. The cloth can be mended. There's nothing to forgive. I simply got in the way of the game. Finish your meal. If our hostess will excuse me, I will change into another gown and return." She

gestured to a startled Alswytha. "Don't get up, I can manage."
She nodded to Sidra, who had not intervened in the matter
and nodded back at her with amused approval. Sidra spoke.
"Perhaps, Belinus, you could pass me the bread on the plat-
ter?" Sidra suggested in an ironic tone that made Belinus wish he
were surrounded by bloodthirsty Picts instead of the group staring
at him now.

Guinevere hurried up the stairs, her slippered feet making
no noise on the stone. She lifted the curtain to enter her room
and then dropped it with a startled gasp. She retreated a few steps
and then sat, unable to go further. She felt weak and her hands
were trembling. Had they seen her? She thought not. Gawain's
face had been turned away and Risa—her eyes had been open but
Guinevere didn't think she was seeing the room around her.

She tried to control herself, to reason out her feelings. If only
they had covered themselves with something! But after all, she
had encouraged them. It was what Risa and Gawain had both
wanted. Gawain certainly couldn't keep a midnight rendezvous.
Then why did she feel so sick? Her mind kept going back to the
glistening of their skin, the undulation. She shut her eyes, trying
to force it out. It's just, she thought, that it's so *intimate,* so
complete. She couldn't find the words for her feelings. They
frightened her. Deep within her mind she was afraid that the
repulsion she felt might also be attraction or even envy. The
thought of sharing herself that much with another, vague, unknown human being was terrifying, and yet, she couldn't forget
the rapture on Risa's face.

There was someone at the top of the stairs moving around
now. She could hear voices, low and caressing. In a panic, lest they
catch her, she raced down the steps and right into Geraldus. She
looked so upset that he was startled.

"What is it, Guinevere? What's wrong?"

"Let me go, Geraldus. Hurry! Gawain . . ." She peered back
up the dark stairs.

"Gawain? What did he do to you? Are you hurt?" Geraldus
was more puzzled than anything else. He knew Gawain well
enough to know that he wouldn't make advances to Guinevere.

"No, of course not," Guinevere made an effort to calm

down. "I went up to fix my sleeve," she held up her arm, "but Risa and Gawain were there. I don't want him to see me."

Geraldus nodded. That would be a simple statement from anyone else, but he could tell she was still shaking. He heard Gawain whistling as he descended. She must have had quite a sight, from the exultant tone.

"Come with me, dear. Have a cup of wine here in the corner and then go change your robe. You needn't be embarrassed. I don't believe they saw you."

That wasn't the real problem, he knew, but it was beyond him to give advice on such matters. Better leave it to Sidra or Guenlian. That was their job.

He calmed her down and, when she was sure Gawain was well away, she went back up. Risa was still there, belting her robe. Her hair needed combing. She was humming. When she saw Guinevere, she gave her a radiant, secret, smile.

"You were right! I can't believe it! I never met a man before who lived up to his own boasting. If only—" she stopped, noticing the look of distaste Guinevere had given her.

"I know it's not what you would do," she defended herself. "You can't. Someday your family will expect you to marry someone important; to make an alliance. You can't just have a man any time you want him. But it's different with me. My father is just a small farmer, hardly more than a boundman. If I brought home a lord's child he wouldn't care. Another mouth to feed means another person to help with the work. He might even think it an honor. I have no great connections that would make me appealing as a bride, and I certainly have no interest in those rough-fingered workmen more suited to my station. I'm happy. Gawain is happy. Don't scold me with your eyes. I can't stand it!"

Guinevere closed her offending eyes and sat down on the bed. "I didn't mean to. I don't blame you at all. It just makes me uncomfortable. I wish you wouldn't speak of it."

Risa shrugged. "If you wish," but her tone was more of pity than of shame.

This event, more than any other, typified the reason Guinevere was often discomfited at Cador. It wasn't just the shock of watching others engaging in what should be private activities, but the constant necessity of being around other people and having to deal with their emotions and desires, however she might try to avoid them. Strong feelings frightened her. At the villa there had always been a way to shield herself from the others; a room to go to, a clearing in the forest. She could lie in the baths for hours and hear nothing but the rustle of the water. Loud voices, rude noises were not allowed in a cultured household. In Cador's castle they echoed off the bare stone walls and rang through the corridors. Even in the middle of the night there was always the sound of the watchmen calling to each other, dogs howling, clanks and grindings that seemed to come from the earth and rocks themselves. They battered at her constantly until she felt her very soul was bruised.

Early the next day, before the dawn had dispelled the gray crust of fog, Guinevere gratefully buried her face in the cool silver of the unicorn's mane.

"We must go home," she whimpered. "I am so lonely for you here. Would you not like to live in the forest again?"

She felt a soft rumble of disquiet in his mind. He pawed the sand with a cloven hoof.

"I do not see myself returning there," he sighed at last. "I believe I would be happy to lie in the grass and flowers again, but I do not think it will be."

Guinevere did not wish to question him about this. It was too ominous a warning; if she didn't hear it, it might not happen. She gently stroked his back.

"You haven't found the others yet?"

"No, but I have found my answer. There are no others. I don't know what voices called to me, but they were not what they claimed. I am the unicorn. Whatever that should be, I must somehow discover for myself. I begin to believe that the answer does not lie in this life."

Guinevere clutched his neck and forced his eyes to hers. "We have spoken of this before. You mustn't leave me!"

His tears spilled over her hands, so hot that they left red streaks as they fell. But she would not release him.

"You are all that keeps me from despair in this miserable place, all I have ever wanted in my life. If you die, I promise to accompany you."

"No, you are not allowed to do that," he paused, confused. "I don't understand why. Humans are still the most mysterious of creatures to me. But that is not the way you are allowed to follow. If I do not die, there will never be another unicorn. I will be eternal, but eternally alone. Perhaps in this place we call Death I will find what I seek. But it is different for you. I sense somehow that by my presence I am keeping you from being truly human. Do not cry, my other self. I will not leave yet and you will know when and why I do. Perhaps it will not be what either of us imagines."

That had to be Guinevere's comfort.

A few days later she asked Sidra if she could go home for a few weeks.

"At this time of year? It's hardly safe. The seas are clear now and if the Saxons bring new armies now is when they will come. The road between here and your home is right in the path from the sea to the Saxon-held lands."

"Please, Sidra. I am so homesick. I cannot bear it any longer. There are over a dozen men here who are going that way soon, to join Lord Cador and Arthur. Couldn't I travel with them? That would be safe, like having my own army. I'm sure they would be willing to take a short detour and stay a night with my parents before they face the wars. Sidra, I must go home for a while!"

Sidra gave in. "I see that," she said. "I don't approve, for many reasons, but it is clear to me that you need to be away from us for a time. You lasted almost a year this visit. Perhaps someday you will not need to go home but only wish to. I will make the arrangements. The men were planning to set out sometime next week. I assume you can be ready by then?"

"Of course I can. Thank you, Sidra." Guinevere hugged her joyfully, ignoring the disapproval of the older woman. "I will come back again very soon. I promise. Just a few weeks with my parents, time to play with my niece. That's all I need. Truly!"

She was not so blind to the terrified expression Alswytha

gave her when she explained where she was going and how long she would be gone. But all the Saxon girl said was, "Let me help you decide what things you will take. I hope you have good weather for your visit."

"Alswytha, I'm not leaving forever, just for a little while. Risa will stay with you and Geraldus has promised to remain here until I return. They won't let anyone hurt you and Sidra will . . . Alswytha, I can't stand it here any longer."

Something that was almost anger crossed Alswytha's face. "*You* can't stand it? Then of course you must go!"

She turned away quickly and began folding robes and sorting perfumes. But even the set of her spine told Guinevere what she was thinking. How could anyone be so spoiled, so self-centered?

Guinevere stood uncertainly, not knowing what to do. She stretched her hand out, and spoke softly, begging forgiveness. "I will be back, very soon. Only give me a little time."

Alswytha's shoulders dropped. She took the offered hand and clasped it tightly. She spun around and hugged her, holding her wet cheek against Guinevere's.

"It's not your fault," she wept. "Of course you must go."

That night she told Ecgfrith all about how Guinevere was leaving and how lonely she would be. She was so miserable that she didn't notice the gleam of triumph in his eyes.

The next morning his bed was empty.

Even the resulting uproar didn't convince Guinevere to stay. The general opinion was that he had tried to escape but had been crushed on the rocks or drowned and washed out to sea. So few of the Britons could swim that it never occurred to them that anyone was strong enough to enter the sea and survive. If Alswytha was afraid that they would treat her more harshly because of Ecgfrith's escape, she soon realized that she was wrong. If anything, it improved her position. People felt sorry for her. She was not so threatening now that her brother was not there, glaring sullenly from his corner of the wall.

The air was clear and the wind smelled of damp earth the day they left. Guinevere hated riding pillion behind someone but she had conceded this point and held tightly to Belinus. She had chosen him to show that she held no ill feeling against him in the matter of the bread game. As she had suspected, no one objected to being her guard of honor to the villa.

She kissed everyone good-bye indiscriminately, she was so happy. And she resolutely failed to notice the look in Alswytha's eyes. As she left, she twisted back to wave. Her last sight was of Geraldus standing behind Alswytha who was, oddly enough, leaning on the shoulder of the raven-haired alto.

ChAPTER ThIRTEEN

Guenlian knelt in her garden plucking miniscule weeds from among the herbs. The earth was cool and moist under her hands and the sun warm across her back. Laughter dappled the air as Rhianna chased her daughter, Letitia, around the courtyard. Guenlian raised her face and absorbed the peace of the day, the infant plants in the fields and the deep green of the forest blending, far off, into the mountains. It was a morning culled from Eden. The impermanence of it cut into her heart.

She sighed and wiped her forehead with a soil-stained hand as she heard Leodegrance approaching from the villa. His shadow blocked the sun as he stood over her. Guenlian reached out her hand to be helped to her feet.

"Where are you going today? Who among our friends has need of you now?"

"No one," he grinned. "It seems that I have solved all the problems of our tenants and neighbors." He swept his arm across the view before them. "You see how smoothly the world functions? I have even arranged for a few gentle clouds to touch up the sky a bit. See them, floating in from the west, just as ordered."

Guenlian stood next to him for some time, watching. The world was indeed beautiful today. Then she turned away from it. "Why is it then, that I am so sorrowful, so afraid?"

The torture she saw in his face shamed her.

"We have good reason, my dear, to suffer. But while we live we must search for tranquillity at least."

"It isn't that. My grief for our sons is a part of my bones now,

177

and I almost believe that I would feel something missing if I woke one morning and it was not with me. This is a different feeling. I can't understand it. All our lives we have fought, we have given everything to preserve our way of life. When it was certain that we and all our work would become ruins and ashes, I still believed; I still hoped. Now it seems as if Arthur has won this battle for us. The Saxons are truly being pushed back into their holes along the coast. He has dreams of rebuilding the towns and reinstating central government, all the things we planned. Why, when everything is coming right at last, so I feel the threat of certain doom?"

Leodegrance was silent for so long, she feared that he wouldn't answer. She needed to have an answer, even if he only told her that he didn't know.

"I have pondered this for many months," he finally replied. "Yes, I have felt it, too. And I believe that I have found an answer although I hope that I may be proven wrong. It is as I said before. Rome is dead. A togaed king of the Goths sits on the throne of the emperors. Gaul is in flames and is controlled by Germanic tribes. Britain was always the most removed of the outposts. We preserved a life we only knew about from books and proclamations and the rosy memories of our grandparents. Guenlian, our goals were those of the perfect world, a society that never was! Arthur is trying to create a new Rome. But we see what he has to work with. We know the corrupt men who would be senators or proconsuls. They are not Cicero or Pliny. They are only soldiers and badly educated lords with a few acres of land and a dozen or so tenants or slaves. How could they know of the grandeur of a great oration or the glory of a unified world? They are only impressed by an abundance of hot water."

"This can't be true," Guenlian moaned, although she feared he was right. "The world is supposed to be getting better. We are preparing for the millennium, when earth and heaven become one. But you can see that we are drifting away from everything that should bring man closer to God."

"I will not believe that, my love. I have held my faith too long. We are just blinded by our visions so that we do not see the new order. We think that the end of Roman life is the end of the world. . . ."

"It is. It's the end of my world."

"And of mine. I confess that I cannot see how joining hands with barbarians will improve the state of things, and the prospect of my grandchildren living in a land ruled by heathens, who don't even read their own language, much less ours, terrifies me. But I cannot stop believing that civilized man, in some form, will eventually triumph, even if no one I have loved will live to see it. There is no reason for my certainty. I know it is foolish. But haven't we learned, my dearest love, that when nothing is left but faith, it is that which we cling to?"

Guenlian sighed and touched his cheek. "I find little comfort in your words or in the hope of a victory which none of our blood may see. But I also find that somehow I can be strong again. It is a large world and I suppose we have done little to change it, for good or for ill. But that little we have done in our lives may have been what was needed to keep the night from overwhelming us. Perhaps, like you, I cling to that belief because I am growing old and there is little more I can do. Isn't it ridiculous? I always felt like Lavinia, mother of Rome, waiting in regal certainty for Aeneas to arrive. I never feared for you as I did for our children. We were legend, part of the epic. What has it come to? Here we are, an aging man and woman, not very well educated, influencing a few acres of land and few dozen people and we find we are not able to read the future at all."

At the same time, in a semi-ruined house in Chichester, Arthur was explaining to Merlin his plans for a new society. Merlin was listening patiently to the rebirth of the ideas that he had planted twenty years before. As he made appropriate noises, he was really thinking of Arthur and how he had grown and developed over that time.

In the past three years, Arthur had changed. His body had finally filled out his height and he was an awe-inspiring figure to his men, well over six feet tall with flaming red hair and a roaring voice. He had completely mastered the art of claiming obedience not by violence but through the belief of his fellow men in his authority. His men respected him, even though most of his war leaders were senior to him in years. But it was easy, he was learning, to command in time of war, if one continued to win. The next step, much more difficult, was to govern a country in time of peace. Arthur had never lived in a Britain free of fighting, but he had wonderful plans.

"First, we must reestablish the old governmental offices. We need to appoint local officials and make clear divisions between the provinces. Then we must rebuild the roads and convince people to move back to the towns."

"A day's work," Merlin scoffed. "For one thing, our population will not fill even a few towns. Too many have died or fled."

Arthur waved that problem aside. "Never mind. We'll rebuild the population, too. There should be little resistance to that suggestion."

"Besides," he added, "once it is known that the old order has returned, those who fled the chaos will return, too."

"Do you believe that those who have spent two generations building estates in Armorica will bother to return to the ruins that they left here? You are not looking at this situation clearly."

"Merlin," Arthur said sternly. "You are trying to discourage me. But I have an even better idea, one I didn't get from you. I want to build a new city, a great, towering, shining town high on a hilltop, so that travelers approaching will see it long before they arrive, glistening in the sun like the Holy City. It will be more beautiful than any spot in the world, and I will call crafts-men, artisans, scribes, teachers, even philosophers to live there with me. Among us we can create a new world where every man can read and learn as he wills. It will be greater than Rome in all its glory. For my city will have a mind and a soul. It will be—why are you staring at me like that?"

Merlin brushed his hand over his eyes. "It is nothing, Arthur. I was only thinking that perhaps I didn't teach you as well as I should have, or too well. And I was wishing that I was young again, before my visions came to me. I was also marveling that you could have such hope for man with all you have seen of war."

"I have seen other things, Merlin. You have shown me some of them. And I know you never believed me, but I am certain that my cause is blessed by the Virgin herself. With her face always in my memory it is not so difficult to wash out the horrors I have seen, the deaths I have witnessed. I do not love to fight! Of all people, you must know how I curse this talent I have for battle. My sword and spear may become plow and pruning hook this moment for all I care! Yes, I know I am not a Marcus Aurelius. I can barely read and a stylus seems to slip through my fingers when I try to write. But I am the one who is here, the one who is left to try and salvage what remains of our people. Merlin, why must you always ridicule my plans for the future? Can't you even allow me my dream?"

The older man leaned back in his chair. He stared at the wall behind Arthur with its once beautiful fresco, now faded and peeling. Even in his memory, the town had been almost empty. What must it have been like full of people, coming and going in such security that there was no wall about the town, no lock upon the gates. The town even had a theater! Even he could not imagine that. Poor Arthur! What chance did he really have?

"My dear son, you cannot afford such dreams. If anyone in this land must be hard and cynical, it is you. When you lead an army, they follow you or they die. Every man knows that. But when the army is disbanded, there are no more soldiers, no more fighting units. There are only a thousand men with a thousand different ways of looking at things using all the emotions that are ignored in war. They will want land of their own and for their children. They will want comfort and security, and those who have served you well will expect preferment even at the expense of one another. They will not care about philosophy but they will remember again all the petty feuds and land disputes they have put aside to fight with you. That is what they will want you to do for them. There are days when I almost wish that we could go on fighting forever. For the moment the war ends there will be such chaos and anarchy! You can't count on dreams to put that in order. Poetry will not amuse men who want power. And the saddest part is that I do believe in you. All my hopes for the past twenty-five years have been set on you and your dreams. You are the only man alive today who has a chance of uniting Britain and making her live again. But even I can't see the possibility of building a new city, a refuge of the arts in the midst of this destruction."

His gesture encompassed not only the room they sat in, but all the world outside. The men and women out there were bred to fear, had never known a summer without the danger of raids, the threat of total annihilation; they huddled now, in the shadows of stone forts, creeping into the fields to plant and reap enough to keep themselves alive one more year. The rough, belching lords and petty tyrants won the people's allegiance because they were strong enough to protect them. What would these men say to a consul, come to establish Roman law in their holdings? And the Saxons, they were not going to vanish. They were settled in their massive halls of wood. The people of London had gone so far as to establish trade with the Saxon villages south of them, gold and leather for grain and protection. Would the Saxons submit to Arthur's laws? There were just too many changes, too many differences to bring the old ways back. Yet Arthur wanted to go even beyond that. He wanted to make a kingdom of philosophers, a perfect realm. Merlin studied his own hands. They had never held a sword or an ax. They had never learned a trade beyond writing. And yet his own life had been hard enough so that they were brown and calloused like any farmer's or soldier's. He idly wondered if even he could fit into this ideal society. Could Arthur?

"There is one other thing, Merlin," Arthur broke into his reverie. "I want you to help me with something else. I am growing older. It is time we should think of my marrying."

Merlin started in alarm. He had been hoping to put this talk off, for he had always felt a sense of dread whenever he thought of the matter, although he didn't know why. He tried to assume a jocular attitude: "So, you have met some local girl who appeals to you? There are a few of the old families still living around here. Would you like me to speak to her father?"

Arthur blushed and his years and self-assurance slid from him. "No, Merlin. I have not met her. But I have thought long upon this subject. If I am destined in some way to rule Britain, I must have a wife who is worthy of that, even more than I am.

Also, if she could bring something, a dowry, which would be a sort of symbol . . . that is . . . I have heard of something . . . she is said to be very . . . Merlin, you must guess whom I mean. Help me!"

Merlin guessed. The last thing he wanted to do was help.

"Do you mean that empty-headed child of my cousin? She is hardly the type I thought you would consider. I don't know what you have heard of her, but you mustn't believe it at all. It is true that she is rather pretty, but hardly worthy of her family. She is spoiled and heedless, with no more feelings than an insect. There isn't a man in the world with luxuries enough to satisfy that one."

"That isn't what her brothers said of her. And why would Lady Guenlian long for her so if she had no heart? Even Lady Sidra praises her. Others tell me that she may be the most beautiful woman in all Britain. They say she smiles kindly on everyone, regardless of their station. That speaks well of her feelings. I would like, at least, a chance to meet her. Won't you arrange that much, Merlin?"

Merlin felt a chill wind at his back. He knew that he must not do this thing. There was something terribly wrong. But he did not know why. And he could think of no excuse that would satisfy Arthur.

"I think it will be a mistake. But if nothing else will make you happy, I will ask Leodegrance if you can visit Guinevere at Cador." Merlin hoped devoutly that she would have a cold.

"Thank you, thank you! You won't try to prejudice her against me, will you? I know I am clumsy and loud and not well-bred, as she is, but I would give her everything I had and be very kind to her. You know that."

"Of course I do, you young idiot! Don't you see that I am trying to tell you that I don't believe she would be kind to you!"

"That is my concern. Let me at least meet her." Arthur's jaw was as set now as when he planned his famous strategies of war. Merlin knew there would be no more argument.

"If that is your desire, lord of Britain, that is what shall be done."

Guinevere rode through the forest joyfully. The day was beautiful, soft, and moist with growth. A thousand shades of green crept across the trees, the stones, and the earth. She was still riding pillion behind Belinus, as a proper lady should, but she wished for her own horse and the freedom of riding astride. It could be very uncomfortable to have to twist like that, sitting sideways but turned forward to hold on to the rider. But today they were traveling slowly, so that she did not need to hold on. Everyone was relaxed. The men sang or told stories or speculated on their chances of being accepted to serve in the mysterious new legion Arthur was forming.

Gawain led the group. Once this had been a good-sized road, wide enough for at least three men to ride abreast. But it had been abandoned to the forest some years ago and now young trees burst from between the stones, and moss and tangly vines covered most of the rest of it. Still, the trees were not yet full grown and the pathway was still visible. It was a good road to take if one was in no hurry, cool and inviting. It was not much trouble to pick a way around broken rocks and saplings. Gawain yawned. It was late afternoon and time to be looking for a place to camp. He glanced back to see that everyone was keeping up. Guinevere seemed to have drifted into a half sleep herself, he noticed. She leaned against Belinus' back with her eyes closed. He could tell that Belinus was nearly rigid in his attempt to keep straight and still so as not to jostle her. Gawain chuckled. She would have to ride with someone else tomorrow. The honor of carrying her was clearly more than Belinus could bear. Every muscle in his body would be sore by morning if he kept that posture long.

Suddenly there was a crashing sound in the forest, and, before they could realize what was happening, the road on both sides and before them was full of men. They were shouting and waving long knives and axes. The horses reared and tried to plunge through them, but the men held firm and their axes glittered in the setting sun as they slashed at the horses' legs and necks.

"Treachery!" Gawain cried, drawing his sword. "Belinus, get Guinevere away from here!"

With a wild cry he drove the sword into the attacker nearest him. Then he circled around, trying to cut his way to Belinus, who was trapped. He was glad to see that everyone had kept their heads and had tried to form a tight circle around Guinevere. She was clutching Belinus' waist tightly, and sensibly leaning to the left so that his sword arm would be free. But there were only a few of them and there must have been over fifty Saxons. Where had they all come from? How long had they been waiting? How did they even know that the caravan would come this way? Gawain hacked at another man in his path, and was frightened to feel how heavy his sword was becoming. He realized with a wave of panic how low the sun was. In desperation, he swung wildly at the glinting knives that were trying to chop his horse from under him, to drag him to the ground. He could tell that he was being cut off from the others and that they were all being separated. Belinus was making a valiant effort to get through and away, but it was no use. Someone had planned this too well, he thought bitterly. But who could have known?

He could feel the energy flowing from him as the sun sank behind the trees. As if in answer to his question, his last sight before he lost consciousness was of Ecgfrith, watching from the side of the road, a satisfied smirk on his face.

For a moment, Guinevere was hardly aware of what was happening. Her first thought was that she must keep her seat or risk being trampled. Soon it was clear to her that the other men were being surrounded and pulled from their mounts. She could hear their cries of anger and pain. She saw Cheldric frantically switching his sword to his left hand, his right arm hanging limp and bleeding at his side. Then they were around her and she was too frightened and confused to notice what was happening to the others. The attackers were pulling at her, despite Belinus' brave attempts to ward them off. He was hampered by the fact that he couldn't use his weapon well without hitting her, too. His horse reared and plunged and Guinevere slipped. She hung from the folds of his cloak and tried to scramble up again. But someone grabbed her leg and another got her about the waist. She screamed and dug her nails into the cloth. Belinus frantically tried to twist himself around and hold her, but another man slashed at the horse's hindquarters so that it reared again. Belinus was caught off balance and thrown off, taking Guinevere with him. Her fingers were still so tightly attached to the cloak that when they pulled her loose, the material ripped and stayed in her bent hands. She screamed hysterically and struck out in blind terror at those holding her. She heard raucous laughter and smelled a nauseating combination of human sweat and rancid animal oil. Then something hit her and she slumped across her captor's shoulder, unconscious. Her last thought was of her unicorn.

Once Ecgfrith saw that she was taken he called to the other warriors to come away quickly.

"But some of them are still alive!" one protested.

"Leave them!" Ecgfrith ordered. "Especially that one!" He pointed at the snoring Gawain. "I want them to know how we have beaten them and what we have taken from them. Lame the horses so that we cannot be followed. We have no need of them to defeat these dotard peacocks. Hurry! We must be back to our camp by tomorrow at dawn."

The men disappeared into the dark woods. Most of those in the company that had ridden out from Cador were dead or severely wounded. The horses went mad in their pain and wandered wildly among trees and sharp-edged rocks. They stumbled on far from the place where the men lay in their agony. Only Gawain slept peacefully through the night.

CHAPTER FOURTEEN

Gawain had awakened at the first light of dawn to the screams of the downed horses and the moans of the wounded men. He saw that apart from a cut on his leg, he had not been harmed. He felt sick with self-hatred. They hadn't even thought him dangerous enough to kill. At this time, he considered, a proper Roman soldier would fall on his sword and so assuage his shame. Luckily, Gawain had little Roman blood, and it occurred to him that his death would not help those of his friends who were still alive. Of the twelve men who had been the escort, four were slain, three more were probably near death, including Cheldric, and the others, excluding himself, were wounded badly enough that they could not be expected to travel far on foot.

Gawain cursed himself again as he realized that in the new morning he had strength enough to bury the men that he had been too weak to save the night before. He tended first to the wounded and then started preparing the graves. He had just finished his task when he heard a horse trotting through the forest.

A messenger on his way from Lord Cador to Sidra halted and gaped in disbelief at the carnage before him.

"Stop gawking and race for your life to Leodegrance. Have him send help; horses and litters. Tell them the Saxons have captured his daughter. Go!" Gawain shouted. The man never bothered to speak. He simply turned his horse and went back as fast as the road would let him.

Gawain placed the men who still lived on a pallet of blankets and clothing under the trees. He did his best to bind the cuts and gashes, but two more men bled to death before noon. Cheldric was delirious with fever and the pain of his mangled arm, but he would not submit to death. He was furious at being trapped so ignominiously and shrieked over and over again what he would do to the Saxon swine, until Gawain felt almost grateful when he finally fell unconscious and subsided to an incoherent mumble. Gawain had managed to slow the bleeding, but it seemed impossible to him that the arm could be saved. Knowing Cheldric, he thought it might be better if the man did not survive.

Belinus had only hit his head when he fell from his horse and had been knocked out for the night. He had a terrible headache and was having a difficult time focusing, but otherwise he was whole and feeling more guilt than pain.

"I couldn't protect her, Gawain. I let them trick me. What will they do to her?" he repeated, despite Gawain's insincere reassurances that they probably only intended to hold Guinevere for ransom.

The other two men, Lothra and Morcant, had deep cuts on their legs from the knives. Although they would be unable to walk for some time, they had received no permanent harm.

Gawain tended them as best he could all day, and Belinus was well enough to take over for the night. Early the next day Leodegrance galloped in, accompanied by half the men from his estate. He didn't bother with formalities, but took in the situation at once and set his men to preparing litters and administering medicines. His eyes swept across Gawain, who was so obviously unhurt, and turned from him in contempt. He knelt beside Morcant and asked him gently what had happened.

Morcant glanced questioningly at Gawain, who gestured for him to answer.

"It was that Ecgfrith, sir, that hostage that escaped. We thought him dead or we never would have come this way. He knew where we would be! He knew our weaknesses. That sister of his! She made out that she was Lady Guinevere's friend, so shy and frightened! She must have told him everything. He didn't understand two words we said. Pigs!" The word spat itself upon the ground.

"Is the Saxon girl still at Cador?" Leodegrance wanted to know.

"Yes, she's safe enough there."

"Then we will deal with her soon, when there is time. The first thing we must do is to get my daughter back. We are taking you all to my villa. None of you is in any condition to fight. You acquitted yourselves well in her defense, but your work is finished. I've sent for Arthur."

Without a word to Gawain, he arranged for everyone to be taken with them. Gawain was given a horse and followed the procession, loitering behind, ashamed to stay with them but too proud to run away. He cursed his unknown father passionately.

They traveled all day, keeping a fast pace despite the care needed for the wounded. But Gawain's heart sank when he realized that it would be nearly night again when they arrived. He lashed himself to the horse with his reins, determined not to make a fool of himself by sliding from the beast and being lost in the woods.

Guenlian met them at the gate, her face drawn and empty. Merlin and Arthur, she told them, were already there and Cador had been reached and would arrive soon. Arthur had brought a large force if needed, to attack the Saxons. The legion was camped in the field behind the villa. She sent the wounded men to rooms made ready for them, but paused when Gawain slid clumsily to the ground before her.

"Bring that one with you," Leodegrance ordered sharply. "There's nothing wrong with him and he has many questions to answer."

With a mighty effort, Gawain managed to stumble after Guenlian into the atrium. It was half an hour past sundown. All the strength he could muster was not enough to keep his eyelids from falling and, as soon as they had entered the building, he slumped limply to the floor.

"Leodegrance! I thought you said he was not hurt!" Guenlian cried in alarm. "What is wrong with him, then? I can't rouse him."

Merlin hurried over from his place and gazed with pity at the collapsed form.

"His name is Gawain," he explained. "He is one of Morgan's boys, remember? The summer Lot was away and she declared that the child had been fathered by a ray of light that had forced its way into her sleeping chamber."

"Oh, yes," Guenlian nodded. "That remained a conversation staple for about two years. So this is the child. I had heard that there was something strange about him. What should we do with him?"

"Have someone carry him to bed. He cannot be awakened until sunrise. We can speak to him then."

When Gawain awoke the next morning in a strange, soft bed in a clean, dry room, he thought for a moment that he had died in the night and was now in paradise, but upon reflection he realized that heaven was not likely to be his fate, and the sound of voices outside the window reminded him of where he was. His heart sank as he remembered Leodegrance's stern accusations, and knew that he would now have to face him and Guenlian and explain how he had let their daughter be captured. He lay in bed for a long while, hoping that everyone would forget about him. Then he grew angry at his own cowardice and got up, dressed, and went out in search of his host.

He found them all in the dining hall, sitting much as he vaguely remembered from the night before. Leodegrance, Guenlian, Cador, Merlin and, oh no, Arthur, too! It could not be anyone else. Gawain saw all his dreams of glory flutter away.

The table before them was set with food which had obviously been there some time, for pools of grease had congealed upon the plates. The candles from the previous night were burning low or had already guttered out, unnoticed. Gawain entered as unobtrusively as he could, but he came in just as a lull occurred in the conversation and all eyes turned on him. He didn't know what to do. He felt like an intruder and a fool. He didn't know that in the early morning sunlight he looked like a god, valiant and strong. Guenlian thought in surprise how much he resembled the portrait of Christ in their chapel, which, as was well known, was simply a portrait of Apollo with a nimbus added.

For a moment, no one addressed him. Then Guenlian gave him a tired smile and beckoned him closer.

"Merlin has explained your problem to us, Gawain," she comforted him. "We know that you could do nothing more than you did for Guinevere. Now we must try to find a way to get her back. Come sit with us. Perhaps you can suggest something that we haven't thought of."

"Guenlian," Cador sounded exasperated. "We have chased this around and around like a dog after its tail. We must recover Guinevere before the Saxons get her back into their territory. The only way to do this is with a large army and a sudden attack. The longer we delay, the less hope we have of catching them."

"And I have said that is madness!" Guenlian retorted. Her voice was growing hoarse. "That is the one sure way we have of getting my daughter killed. The first thing the Saxons will do is slay her."

"I think we should try to bargain with them," Arthur added. "I've had enough of killing. Perhaps they are sick of it, too. They may only want a simple exchange, Aelle's daughter, Alswytha, for your daughter. I would go myself, to treat with them."

"They have already broken their bond," Leodegrance broke in. "We cannot trust them to return her unharmed in any case."

Gawain realized then that they were only reiterating arguments they had made over and over throughout the night. Each gave an opinion and then waited for a rebuttal. But no one was sure enough for them all to agree.

Merlin knew it too, and was tired of pointless wrangling.

"Stop," he commanded in a thunderous roar. "We can't wait for Guinevere to be imprisoned in their land. They are too powerful there and the conditions for her release would be even harsher. They have already shown how little they care for Alswytha, for her safety was forfeit when they broke the truce. We cannot attack them openly for they would slay her at once, having nothing to lose. We have considered everything tonight but a Trojan horse. And for all we have argued, the time is quickly fading for us to catch them. If we do nothing, she will certainly be lost to you forever. Now, let us decide on some plan. Anything."

Merlin was furious, half because he was tired of the arguing and half because he was irrationally angry with Guinevere for causing him yet another problem. Why couldn't she have stayed at the castle! It seemed that every time that child did anything, she upset the entire country. And Arthur had it in his head to marry her. Merlin knew that it would be a disaster. Damn these forebodings! Why couldn't he either see the future clearly or not at all? He sometimes felt that God was mocking him, reminding him that he was only a man after all, despite what people might believe. He almost wished that Guinevere would be killed. It would be a clear rallying point for amassing an army, and then they might be strong enough to rid the island of Saxons once and for all. Also, it would leave Arthur's mind free to consider a more sensible alliance. If she were anyone's daughter but Guenlian's, he might even try to arrange an accidental death to be blamed on the Saxons. However, he sighed and reached for the flask of wine.

Gawain only half listened to the discussion. He was still reeling from the relief he felt at being understood and forgiven. Anyway, he didn't think he could come up with anything better than Merlin could. Then his ears pricked up at one of the phrases that connected with something he remembered.

"A Trojan horse?"

Leodegrance stopped what he had been saying and stared at Gawain.

"Do you know what that was?"

Gawain nodded.

"Well, then, I don't suppose you take such an idea seriously? It would take months to build such a thing. It was very useful to the Greeks but somehow I doubt that even the Saxons would be taken in by a hollow wooden horse. There always seemed to be a number of flaws in that story, anyway. How did the soldiers keep their armor from clanking? Why didn't the Trojans hear them breathing? How many men could really fit inside a wooden horse? How would they get out without being noticed? Perhaps the Greeks knew the answers, but it won't help us now."

He dismissed the idea.

"That's not exactly what I meant, sir," Gawain said eagerly. An idea was growing in his mind and the words spilled out. "What I meant was, must we attack them honorably? Do we have to send warning or follow the usual plan of attack?"

Leodegrance looked at him as if he had gone mad. "Honor? What has that to do with the situation? Guinevere has been kidnapped in a vicious trap sprung on you quite without warning. The Saxons have broken every binding solemn vow they have given. We will get her back by any trick we can think of."

"Only," Guenlian added sadly, "we can't think of any."

"Well," Gawain hesitated. He felt rather outclassed by his company. "I did have a thought. Alswytha told us many of the stories of her people. Geraldus is helping her translate them. One thread that seems to be in all of them is a great fear of monsters and ghosts."

"Monsters?" Cador snorted. "What child's tale is this?"

"It's true," Gawain insisted. "You have seen that they won't live in our abandoned towns. Alswytha says that's because of the ghosts. And one of their kings across the sea apparently won his crown as a result of his defeat of some horrible monster that was ravaging their land."

"Legends! Minstrels' tales! No one really believes them." Leodegrance waved him away.

"No," Gawain repeated. "The man is still alive! Aelle knew him. The Saxons believe that the forests and meres are full of monstrous beasts and they fear them when they shrink from nothing else."

"That is very interesting, if true," Merlin said calmly over the derision of the others, "but I do not see how it will help us."

Gawain looking pleadingly at the group before him said, "I

know it seems impossible, but everything else you suggest sounds even more so. Couldn't we create a monster? Maybe have it carried within view of their camp on horseback so that it would seem even larger? Take along kettles or horns to make a noise with. Then, when they are engaged in fleeing from this creature, another group, perhaps only a few strong warriors and horsemen, could race in from another direction and rescue Guinevere. The horsemen might even paint their faces like the Picts in the north and wear horns or masks to be more fearful? It could work . . . couldn't it?"

He saw that they were considering. Perhaps it sounded too theatrical to work. His shoulders drooped. What hope did Guinevere have?

Arthur spoke first, slowly, as if still revolving the plan in his head. "There are problems. It would have to be done carefully and swiftly, with no mistakes. Still, it appears to present the smallest amount of risk, both to the Lady Guinevere and to the rescuers. I would be willing to lead the group that attacked. The greatest danger would be to those who played the 'monster.' Finding the camp will be the least of the worry. They are making a direct line for their own territory. I think we should try it. But it is your daughter. I will not go without your approval."

Leodegrance and Guenlian looked at each other. They were silent a long time. Finally, Guenlian laid a trembling hand upon her husband's. Without looking away from her face, he nodded.

"There is no plan without danger," he said. "If you will take the risk for Guinevere's sake, we will give it our blessing."

"Gawain, would you be one of the rescue party?" Arthur asked. Gawain ground his teeth in frustration. "I cannot, Lord. I would give anything in life to do this, for Guinevere is as dear to me as a sister. But this must be done late at night, when most of Aelle's men are asleep and easily surprised. I . . . am unable to be of use then, you see. . . ."

"I'm sorry, lad. I forgot," Arthur apologized. "Don't be ashamed. I have had excellent reports of your valor and courage and, when I return, we will try to find a place for you in my cadre, if that would please you."

"Oh, yes, my lord," Gawain breathed, almost forgetting Guinevere in his good fortune. "It would please me greatly."

Guinevere finally woke to find herself lying on a pile of dusty furs. Her head hurt and her back and stomach were sore. She couldn't imagine what had happened to her. There were Saxon guards all around her and at a campfire a few yards away were more men in Saxon dress. Her hands were not bound and she wondered how they had missed this, until she realized that the guards would surely be able to catch her if she tried to escape. She was hardly a match for them. The night was chilly and she was still clad in her thin woolen gown. Her braids had become unpinned and hung across her shoulders and almost to her knees in disheveled plaits. She was frightened, but also curious. So these were Alswytha's people. There were resemblances. They all had the pale, almost silver hair, which the men wore in thick braids held in place by gold buckles. They wore short tunics over leggings and boots, and every man she could see was festooned with gold jewelry: arm bands, brooches, pins, earrings, belts, all of it intricately shaped and finely wrought. She wondered if all of them were noblemen or if everyone among the Saxons was so rich.

One of her guards noticed that she was awake and called to the men about the fire. One hurried over and stood above her, staring thoughtfully. Guinevere stared back in pride and fear.

"Yehwineferah!" he said. It made no sense to her and she continued her blank gaze. He repeated it. "Yehwineferah" and pointed at her.

Suddenly, she realized that he was trying to say her name. She lifted her chin in disdain and pronounced it correctly. Now the man looked puzzled. He switched his stare to her braids and, with a strange look, reached down and lifted one. Guinevere shrank from him. He laughed, not unkindly, but she was too afraid to tell.

"*Ic haebe an dohtor with swa gold,*" he murmured. It wasn't true, of course. His daughter was lovely, but her hair was not as rich and living as Guinevere's. Still, in his eyes, Alswytha was beautiful too. However, Guinevere had no idea of what he was saying and only grew more terrified as he tried to speak to her. Finally, he put down the braid and went back to the campfire. There he seemed to be giving orders about something. Guinevere peered into the dark. Someone was being dragged from the other side of the camp. The person was protesting and struggling all the way. The fire was too bright between her and whomever it was, so she couldn't tell if it was a man or a woman. She saw the light gleam upon the neck band of a slave, and wondered why the poor thing was so determined not to be brought to its master.

Aelle was not interested in hearing the complaints of his slave. "We brought you with us because you speak her language. Now go over there with us and translate. I will hear not a word more. And if I discover that you have said one word other than what I tell you, I will have your tongue for my breakfast!"

Guinevere heard the shouting and angry words and shrank as far as she could into the furs. Aelle was coming back now. Two other men were dragging the slave between them. She could see that his clothes were ragged and that the collar was his only ornament. Even though Guinevere had no imagination, she felt a nameless dread slip over her and she remembered half-heard stories about strange, horrible things Saxons did with women captives. She felt her hands grow icy and her heart pound in her throat as the men brought their struggling burden nearer. The slave kept his face averted all the while so she could not see him. No matter how he fought, he didn't move his head. She could tell that the side toward her was hideously scarred and feared that the side he was hiding might be even worse. Her stomach started to recoil when a slap made the slave turn and face her fully.

For a second Guinevere just stood there, unable to believe what she saw. Then she screamed. Over and over in choking gasps she cried out. Finally she managed to push forth one lone word.

"Mark! Mark!" she sobbed and fell into his arms.

"Hush, Guinevere, hush. You mustn't let them know who I am! Try to control yourself," he begged. But she couldn't stop shaking and sobbing.

"What's wrong with her?" Aelle demanded. "What does *mark* mean?"

"It means 'mercy,' " Mark replied angrily. "You have terrified the poor girl. She recognized that I was one of her own people and wants me to plead with you to save her."

"Well, calm her down. Tell her that we won't do a thing to her if she stops that shrieking. What a noise! I thought she was bewitched!" Aelle complained. "Go on. Tell her!"

Mark disentangled her arms from him. He smoothed her hair and wiped her eyes and nose with his shirt as he had when she was a child. "Guinevere, it is all right. Never mind why I am here. Just listen to me. This is Aelle. He doesn't want to hurt you. He only plans to trade you for Alswytha. The Saxons are a strange people, but they have their own ideas of honor and he won't harm you, I believe, unless they refuse to return his daughter. Do you understand?"

"Alswytha?" Guinevere questioned.

Aelle was watching her closely. He nodded emphatically.

"They know you are her friend. Ecgfrith told them all about his stay at Cador."

"Ecgfrith? We thought he had drowned."

Mark frowned. "I wish he had. It was his idea to capture you. Aelle never would have thought of it. He is more the type to storm the castle."

"But what can we do, Mark?"

"Nothing. Just hope that Arthur agrees to release Alswytha. And when they do, Guinevere, you must promise you will never tell anyone that you saw me here. Do you understand?"

"What! What are you talking about?"

"That is enough!" Aelle thundered. "Does she understand?"

Mark refused to face her again. "She does," he answered.

"Then return to your work, Ceorl, and next time you receive an order, don't ignore it, or you will wish we had killed you with the rest of your army."

Mark only gave him a mocking smile that was particularly horrible on his stricken face.

In the following days, Guinevere grew less concerned about her own fate and more worried about Mark. It made no sense to her. She was alone in this strange place and she wanted him now more than she had ever wanted anyone before. Finding him here was a miracle and she supposed that he would be as overjoyed as she. But he shrank from her. When he wasn't being used as an interpreter, he kept as far from her as possible. She couldn't understand why. The scars on his face meant nothing to her. Was it something she had done? His rejection of her hurt her terribly.

Each day they broke camp and started her walking again further to the east. She hated this. If only they had given her a horse! Her shoes were for riding and not strong in the soles. But she had learned that if she lagged or stumbled, someone would pick her up and carry her, and this was even more offensive. So she marched on with set lips. She saw that Mark was not forced to stay in any one place and yet he always managed to be as far from her as possible. Finally she decided that he was completely indifferent to her and for some reason liked living as a slave. This made her angry and her anger carried her on for several miles.

She had started calling her unicorn almost at once, but he had taken a long time to respond. Finally she became aware of the touch of his mind, but his answer was very faint.

"I am far from you," he told her, "but do not fear. I am coming for you."

That satisfied her and Guinevere ceased to worry that she might not be rescued. It would happen. That was enough to know. The only problem now was in reaching Mark, who was further away from her than a mythical creature could ever be.

For Mark, these days were the worst of any since that murky afternoon of his last battle. He thought he had drawn a boundary line carefully through his memory. His life before was neatly kept deep in some dark place where he need not look at it. Any thought of his home, his childhood, his family always brought him to that last moment, to the death screams of his brothers, to his own insane rage and the searing pain across his face and, finally, to the knowledge that he had lived. It was better to imagine that he had always been a slave, following the rounds of labor and subservience with the dull numbness of the hopeless.

But there was Guinevere, resting serenely upon her cushions, as unconsciously arrogant as only the pampered child of the wealthy could be. She showed no more fear of her captors. She didn't even seem to be interested in them. Mark had forgotten that calm, assured tilt to her chin, the air of being sublimely certain of her place at the top of the orders of society. Had he ever been like that? Alswytha had always called him, "my lord Ceorl." He had thought she mocked him. But that was another memory to subdue. Her cool hands reaching through the pain. She had never shown disgust at his looks. She had kept him alive for weeks when he longed for death. How he had hated her for that gift. Poor little Alswytha, so timid, so lonely. Blast and shrivel that Ecgfrith! What kind of man would leave her alone like that, among enemies? Mark's brain followed the treadmill of all he would forget. He wanted to ask about home and if his parents were well, but that would only start the cycle again. The only thing was to avoid Guinevere and hope she would respect his desire and keep silent about his fate.

Aelle and Ecgfrith had been watching Guinevere, too.

"She would make a fine queen," Ecgfrith mused. "She would be an ornament to any hall. Why should we return her to her people? What if we gave her a greater honor? We gave Vortigern one of our women to wed. It is time that they returned the gesture. What better way to affirm our right to Britain than by forming an alliance with one of their great houses?"

"I am glad you feel that way, my son," Aelle smiled craftily. "I have been thinking the same thing. I have been very lonely since your mother left and things have not been managed well. Alswytha never had any authority in the hall. This woman will do for me very well indeed."

Ecgfrith glared at his father, who laughed in his face.

"Get your own bride, my son. This one is for me. Remember, I have many sister-sons with the same right as you to my lands. Why should she marry a man whose landhold is uncertain?"

"And what of Alswytha? You have said how much you care

for her. She will not be returned unless we can bargain for her."

"You didn't think of that when you wanted this woman for yourself. But we can arrange something. Perhaps one of their lords will take her to wife. That will solve the matter."

Ecgfrith swallowed his words and bowed from his father's presence. But he vowed that he would rather see Guinevere and Alswytha both killed than know that his father had taken his prize from him.

CHAPTER FIFTEEN

Guinevere was sharply awakened late one night by a strange noise in the woods on the opposite side of the camp from her. Her first impulse was to pull the furs over her head and go back to sleep. She had walked all day over scarcely visible paths in worn-out shoes and was tired to the marrow of her bones. The guards around her were silent but alert, and were staring anxiously in the direction of the noise. She heard people moving about the camp as the rustling in the trees grew louder. Finally she forced herself to open her eyes and find out what was going on.

The fires had died out. It was about an hour before dawn: the sky was that gray color between stars and sun that is more difficult to see in than dark night. The earth was smothered in fog. Guinevere could hear the guard muttering nervously. What was that noise? It sounded like a large animal pushing its way through the undergrowth, but there was also a noise of wood being snapped and gnashed and perhaps metal being pounded. She peered into the darkness, but the fog shifted and spun so that she could make nothing out.

The clanging and gnashing sounds were getting louder and closer. Trees swayed and branches crackled as the thing passed by. A red glow bobbed through the darkness, twice the height of a man. By now, everyone was awake, standing, gaping in awe or terror as the noise and the light came closer to the camp. Suddenly there was a tremendous roar and a hideous monster came raging into the midst of the men. It was huge, as tall as a watch-tower and covered with fur and tough hide. Long strings of moss dangled from its shoulders and several arms. Its single eye glared in crimson fury and its cavernous mouth glinted with steel-sharp teeth. Blood dribbled down its chin. A constant cacaphony of groans and whines came forth from its midsection and, as they watched, frozen, it charged the nearest man and trampled him underfoot before the terrified Saxon could even draw his sword.

A few soldiers made a feeble attempt to stand against the thing, but most of them ran screaming into the forest. Many returned in a gibbering streak of panic, pursued by a second beast that appeared from the opposite side, just to the left of Guinevere.

She watched in bewilderment as her fierce captors fell in a babbling heap on the ground or grabbed what they could and sped to the safety of the dark woods. Aelle, Ecgfrith, and a few of their eorls were making an effort to fight the things when, all at once, a mass of horsemen, all wearing horns and with their faces painted scarlet and blue, forced their way into the clearing. At the sight of them, Aelle understood how he had been tricked and, with a savage scream, he attacked.

One of the riders galloped to where Guinevere stood, too stunned to move. He swooped down and tried to pull her into the saddle with him. She writhed furiously in his grasp and at first could not make out what he was yelling.

"My lady, stop! We're here to save you! Please, you're pull-ing my costume off!"

Guinevere relaxed her kicking and looked up into the face of the man holding her. She saw a Roman nose and a strong chin streaked with paint and dirt.

"Who are you?" she shrieked over the tumult.

"Arthur. Your parents sent me to find you. Hurry! We mustn't give them time to reorganize!"

She swung up behind him and screamed in his ear.

"We can't go without Mark! You have to find him!"

"Mark?"

"My brother! He's here somewhere. We can't leave him!"

"Guinevere, Mark is dead! We saw him go down!"

"No. He's here, I tell you! Help me find him!"

She slid from the horse again, despite his attempts to catch her. Then she waded right through the jungle of riders and monsters and frantic Saxons, totally oblivious to the swords and hooves and the shouts of those she passed. Arthur yanked his horse around and tried to follow her. He hacked his way through the mess, hoping that he hadn't hit any of his own men. He found Guinevere on the other side, tugging at a slave who was resisting her ferociously.

"I told you to leave me alone!" he cried. "I'm not going back! I won't let them see me like this. Guinevere, get away from here!"

Arthur could never have recognized his battered face, but the voice was past mistaking. For a second, he could only sit in disbelief, tears blurring his eyes.

He shook himself quickly. This was no time for questions. "Lieutenant!" he barked. "You are coming with us. Take this horse and your sister and get out of here. That is an order!"

Mark squinted at him and then his eyes widened as he recognized his commander and friend.

"Arthur . . . I can't!" he began.

"You will!" Arthur roared, and leapt to the ground. "Guinevere, take my horse and get up behind him. Be sure he stays with us. Her safety is on you, Mark!"

One of the men was wounded and hanging from his horse. Arthur scooped him up and mounted behind the injured man. Guinevere caught at the bridle Arthur threw her and pushed Mark until he was on the animal's back. Then she clambered up herself. The sky was growing lighter and the "monsters" had wisely stomped back into the forest. A knot of horsemen were still fighting Aelle and his companions. Seeing that Guinevere had been recovered, the horsemen tried to disengage themselves but were having trouble getting away. Arthur dove his horse through the center, his wounded partner gripping the mane for dear life. Aelle faltered and fell back onto his son, his shoulder gashed and spurting blood. Ecgfrith saw that the Britons were getting away and tried to throw Aelle off. But it was too late. In another moment, the remnant of the rescue party was gone, Arthur at their heels.

There was nothing more to be done. Arthur had won again. Ecgfrith surveyed the destruction caused by the monsters and the Britons. He rained all the curses of the goddess Hel upon the cowards who had run. Some of them would never know a roof over their heads again, if he had his way. Outcasts from their clan they would be for this, and he would be sure that they wandered unaided by any lord until they died. But even that revenge could not console him for this outrage. With smoldering hatred, he returned to the side of his father. Perhaps the old man would die and then the land right would be his. The thought was grimly cheering.

As Guinevere rode through the growing dawn, her arms wrapped tightly around her brother, she thought she heard laughter. She looked all around in her astonishment for the source. No one near her appeared in a mood for levity. The men around her were exhausted, each painted face bowed over his horse's mane as they tried to stay awake. The monsters, towers of wood overlaid with leather, fur, and branches, had been cast off and left to rot among the trees. The men who had carried them, perched dangerously on platforms over their saddles, were making no pretence of staying alert. They were slumped on the horses' necks, swaying a little as they passed from sleep to drowse and back again. Their animals looked as tired as the men, for they had been ridden hard since the previous morning to reach her before it was too late. The tired beasts kept moving from habit and in the hope, no doubt, that somewhere soon there would be some soft grass and clover. So who was laughing? There was such delight in the sound that Guinevere smiled, too, in anticipation of the joke.

Then she became aware that no one else had heard the merriment. The sound was in her mind alone. She sent out a question.

"Yes," the unicorn answered. "I was here all night, but you didn't need me. I have never seen such amazing creatures! It was really astonishing the way they put those monsters together! Some of those men who captured you ran directly into me in their flight. They cried out in horror and flew in the other direction. I was somewhat offended. I have always gathered from you that I was a rather handsome beast."

"Of course you are," Guinevere soothed. "But what do you find so amusing?"

"Humanity," he replied, and she could get no more explanation than that.

"I must return to the shore," he continued. "I will wait for you there. You should come soon, I think. I have a feeling that someone needs you there."

Then he was gone.

Mark sat stiffly before her, his head and face hidden in a cloak someone had tossed him. She leaned her cheek against his back and tried to feel a softening in him, a response to her concern. But his spine remained straight and he showed no interest in her. He was lost in his own anger and fear.

Arthur watched him and worried. He thought he knew what Mark was feeling. How could he face his parents after allowing his brothers to die and himself to be so degraded by his captors? Arthur could sense the pride and the shame, even though he couldn't completely agree with it. He hoped Mark would change when he had been home for a time. Perhaps he would fit back into his old life when he realized that no one would blame him for what had happened, that they would only rejoice that he was alive. And, Arthur considered a little guiltily, I need him. I must have a man like that in my government; one who knows both worlds and can bring them together. But Arthur had no idea how to convince this sullen stranger of that. He fervently hoped that Leodegrance would know what to do.

He had pushed all his men well beyond their strength, and finally it was clear that they would have to rest, himself included. So he signaled a stop. Most of the men were so tired that they simply fell to the ground, dragging their saddles and blankets with them and trusting that their horses would be nearby when they awoke. No one suggested setting a watch. Arthur wanted more than anything to be able to join them, but being the commander had its curses. He carefully tethered his horse and then strolled over to where Mark and Guinevere had settled themselves. Guinevere still had one arm around her brother and was speaking to him in a low, urgent tone. As he approached, she turned her face up to him with a look of supplication. He stopped cold in his tracks. Until this moment, he hadn't had time to look at her directly.

"Oh Holy Mother!" he exclaimed.

Her expression changed. She put one hand to her cheek. "Is my face smudged?"

He simply stared, his mouth open. She was the living image of his vision. And yet human. She must be human. What if she vanished when he tried to touch her?

The distance between them seemed to lengthen, and Arthur wondered if it would ever be possible for him to cross the space to where she knelt.

Guinevere smiled nervously and held our her hand to him. It was a sign, a miracle.

He took a step toward her.

Guinevere tried to give him a grateful smile. She was very glad that he had saved her and was respectful of the authority he had showed when he made Mark accompany them. Even now, covered with grime, he appeared impressive. She watched him come toward them, unaware that her gaze made it difficult for him to move. He was the biggest man she had ever seen, next to Timon. And while Timon seemed to be part of the forest he lived in, brown and sturdy as an oak, Arthur was different, like some force which has come to tame the wild things, yet is still half wild itself. His short hair was a rich auburn and his fine chin, normally cleanshaven, was now shaded by a stubble oddly darker than his hair. Although he felt clumsy and foolish, to her he appeared powerful, imposing, strangely exciting. Guinevere decided she liked him. There was something about him that reminded her of Gawain, only fiercer.

Arthur was amazed to find that it was still daylight when he reached them. He knew he had been walking those few steps for hours. Mark sat with his head buried on his bent knees, determined not to notice either one of them. Guinevere put her hand out to Arthur with a glance that made his head spin, so that he didn't catch what she was saying.

"... and I don't know what else to tell him to convince him," she concluded, as Arthur tried to focus on the conversation. Who was she talking about? Oh yes, Mark. He sighed. He was more tired than he realized. What could he say to Mark? If only Mark would say something for himself.

He bent and touched Mark's shoulder. There was a shrug as if to throw him off, but it was checked. Arthur thought it was a good sign. He wished that he had Merlin's talent with words.

"Mark, you must listen," he began roughly, surprised at the choke in his own voice. "I don't know what they did to you. I don't know why you won't greet your sister or your old friends. We could not have rescued you sooner. We thought you were dead. You have a right to be bitter, spending three years and more in captivity like that. Please forgive me for not finding you before."

That set Mark off. He sat up at once, his good eye blinking away tears.

"Forgive you?" he rasped. "Arthur, you always were an idiot off the field! I allowed myself to be captured. I made no attempt to escape, to send word that I still lived. I wanted to see no more of anyone! Do you understand? I'm sick of it all. I don't want to go back. If I can't be dead to myself, at least let me be so to the rest of the world. Look at my face! I'm half a corpse already!"

"Mark, your scars were honorably earned in battle. You have no cause to be ashamed of them. Listen to me, please! You needn't fight again. You needn't go near a battlefield. You are more important to me than that. So much has happened. I must have someone to help me build my city, someone who can read, who knows the old ways and who can call back the exiles. It is not enough to push back the invaders; we must create a new society for those who have survived. It doesn't have to be Rome again. It can be better. A city of God and a city of Man combined. I have such plans, such dreams . . . but I need you to help."

Mark looked at him with a kind of wonder. His answer was softer than before, but no less firm.

"You will build a new order, if anyone can. But not with me. It is too late for me. I have gone far beyond caring about what happens to the world. The stench of the dying, the dead, the rotting clings to me. I can't look at anything now without wondering how long it has before it joins the refuse pile, and almost wishing that the time would come soon. I can no longer even desire the delights of heaven, but only to lay my body in the earth and shrivel into oblivion."

Guinevere shrank from him. She could only see the ravaged profile of his face and his words, his voice were not of the brother she had loved. She wondered vaguely if Mark had died after all, and she had been tricked by some roving demon into releasing him into the world.

Arthur regarded his friend with pity. "You sound like the mad Irish saints, howling that we live in a world filled with sin and decay, but they at least look forward to the purity of the next life. I have seen and smelled the same foulness as you have. I have wept over the bodies of men I sent to their doom. But it has only determined me to try, at least *to try*, to make something better! What good are you to the world like that? What will anyone gain by your death?"

Mark spoke slowly and with bitter defiance, "What do I care?"

Arthur sank back on his heels, defeated. His friend Mark was gone. He could not communicate with this man. All his pleasure in the accomplishment of a successful mission evaporated. Guinevere laid her hand on his shoulder.

"It's not your fault. You tried. He's not Mark anymore. I don't know him. If we could only get him home!"

"No," Mark dropped the word into the abyss between them. "I will not go back. I don't wish to see them. You have Guinevere safe. Leave me behind."

"Ride with us for one more day, Mark," Arthur begged. "Just until tomorrow night. Then you may go where you wish. I will even give you a horse."

Even as he said it he realized how foolish it was. Why would tomorrow make his feeling any different?"

"I don't care," Mark answered. "If you insist. Now let me be."

His head returned to his knees.

Guinevere and Arthur rose. She was tall, only a few inches less than he, but so finely built that he felt like an oaf beside her.

She moved away from her brother with casual grace, and he struggled to stay next to her without tripping on roots or the hem of her robe.

"My Lord Arthur," she was saying. "I thank you very much for trying to help Mark and for coming to my aid. It was very kind and courageous of you to take so much trouble for me."

He wanted to tell her that a trifling few days of his life, the danger of death, a lost night's sleep were hardly worth her gratitude, that he would cheerfully have stormed the walls of Constantinople for the honor of having her beside him. But he could only stare at her like a homeless puppy, begging for notice.

She was puzzled that he didn't reply. Then it occurred to her that he had probably had no rest at all in the last two nights. How rude of her to stand like this making conversation with the man, when all he wanted was a few hours' sleep.

"But I am sure my father will better express our gratitude when we arrive at my home. Please excuse me now. I will stay with Mark, in case he . . . in case he wants something."

She backed away, making a mental note to ask Sidra how one politely left a conversation like that. Arthur was still staring at her, and she felt she had not acquitted herself well.

He finally came to himself and returned to the place where he had left his saddle and blanket. "What a dolt I am!" he mourned. "She must have thought me a country clod, standing there, gaping at her, slack-jawed, unable to reply to the simplest sentence."

He gave a quick glance around the camp, saw that everyone seemed to be taken care of, and dropped at once into a sound sleep.

He woke up suddenly to realize that it was already night. He jumped to his feet, conscious that he had neglected his men and failed to set a watch, but to his relief, everything was in good order. Some of the men were still snoring, but others had wakened and started a campfire, over which a whole pig was roasting. He called to his foster brother, Cei, who was watching the spit with hungry eyes.

"Where did that meat come from?" he demanded.

Cei chuckled. "It just wandered through the camp about

dusk, thinking we were all asleep, and began rummaging in the packs. When it got to mine, I just lay there, my hand on my long knife—a swipe, a squeal, and roast pork! It's only a small one, or I might not have been able to hold it," he added modestly. "But it will feed us all tonight!"

Already the men were rousing to the smell of fresh meat. In spring it wasn't often that they had anything but smoked or salted remains from the slaughter in the fall. This was a reward in itself.

Arthur noted that Guinevere was also asleep, next to Mark. His back was to her, but he had overcome his apathy enough to cover her with his cloak. Arthur wondered if he should wake her, but thought it might be indelicate. He saw to it, however, that the best cut of pork was saved for her.

Despite the desire of Guinevere to return quickly to her family, Arthur decided that it would be wisest to remain there for the rest of the night and finish the journey the next day. Now that most of the men were rested and their few cuts attended to, there would be no problem finding someone to keep watch. He doubted that the Saxons had tried to follow them, but it was just as well to be careful. All the men were in high spirits. They were immensely pleased with themselves. It boosted their morale wonderfully to know that the Saxons, who were so ferocious in battle, would run like frightened children from a ridiculous contraption such as the one they had created. Consequently, the banter that evening was light and cheerful. Most of the soldiers were too busy or too tired to be aware that the other person rescued was Mark. Arthur decided not to tell them. It wasn't likely that Mark would let them know. He stayed away from them all and as far from the firelight as possible. Guinevere refused to leave him. She only got up for a moment to give a short speech of thanks for their daring and resourcefulness and then retired. They all agreed her words were appropriate and well-deserved.

The sun had barely risen when they left the next morning. Even traveling by the better roads, it would take almost all day to reach the villa, and Arthur guessed how eager Leodegrance and Guenlian would be for their return.

But he underestimated them. That same morning, Leodegrance had become disgruntled by the ordeal of waiting and decided to ride in the direction from which the party should return. Guenlian, seeing his intent, insisted on going with him.

"But my dear," he argued. "You are needed here. Who will entertain Merlin? Who will arrange dinner for everyone?"

"Pincerna will see to the dinner and Merlin can see to himself. I am going with you."

"But what if they were not successful?" Leodegrance cautioned.

Guenlian's hands clenched. "All the more reason for me to be with you."

He saw there would be no more discussion. The two of them set out, alone, together.

Leodegrance heard them singing before he saw them. His heart lifted. He urged his horse ahead and soon the whole company came into view. Arthur rode at the head and not far behind came Guinevere, riding behind some heavily cloaked man. As soon as she spotted them, she waved excitedly. Leodegrance and Guenlian hurried to her. Neither would be truly sure she was safe until they had their arms around her.

What was the matter with that man? He was trying to pull her away from them. Now he was pushing Guinevere from the horse and trying to escape. She was fighting him and yelling something they couldn't make out. Then, Guinevere gave a sharp tug and managed to pull off the cloak.

Leodegrance heard Guenlian's cry, a scream turned inward to a gasp. He suddenly felt as if someone had hit him hard directly below his ribs. He couldn't breathe. Guinevere was hanging onto the man's arm now, calling.

"Help me! He doesn't want to come home! Hold him!"

They were with her at once. Mark knew there would be no escape now and found that he was sobbing too as his mother held him again, her hands searching him, touching, arms, legs, there and whole. "Oh my darling! Your poor face!" Kissing those hideous scars as if they could be charmed away like a childhood bump. Leodegrance, hands trembling, reaching out for him. How old his father had become! And Guinevere smiling as proudly as if she had invented him. For a sudden flash of time Mark felt that it might, after all, be possible to come home.

The rest of the journey took longer than anticipated, because neither parent wanted to be more than a hand's reach away from their son. Guinevere happily traded places and rode behind her father, so that she could hug him and explain everything that had happened. It was well that Guenlian's horse knew how to find its own way home, for she gave it little guidance. It was late afternoon before they were spotted by the guard, and as they rode in the entire household was at the gate, cheering.

"God Almighty!" Pincerna exclaimed. "It's Lord Mark!"

"Can't be, you old fool," someone muttered, then, "I'm damned if you aren't right!"

There was silence, as everyone tried to comprehend this miracle, and then the cheering became hysterical. Mark lifted his head and looked at them. He tried to pick out faces, to find one that meant something to him. But they were just faces, blurred and anonymous. The glow in the morning that for a time had convinced him it could be the same again had meanwhile vanished. He felt a fool to have believed that he could go home and be cosseted by his family and spoiled by the servants, and that the last few years would melt into nightmare, something misty and unreal. But with the first sight of the fields and brooks, the memory came back to him.

"Matthew and John aren't here," he thought with a jolt. "I am the only one left. Their ghosts will hound me, taunt me, every second I stay."

As soon as he rode into the courtyard, Arthur felt a return of the sense of inferiority he had known before as he changed from his role of leader to that of guest. He could tell that this was Guinevere's natural setting. As she dismounted and casually handed the reins to the stableman, Arthur noticed Gawain standing, leaning on the doorway. He grinned at Guinevere, who ran to him laughing and let him swing her around as he hugged her.

"I knew it was your idea!" she cried. "And I'm so glad that the days are getting longer so that you are awake to greet me! You won't believe this, but we found my brother, Mark. He's alive after all! Isn't that wonderful?" and she hugged him again.

Arthur watched them in amazement. How could he treat her so casually? There he stood, one arm across her shoulder, not even looking at her, but chatting with some of the other rescuers. He had said she was like a sister, but a thought struck him with a suddenness that made him sick: She must be more than that. She must already be engaged to him. They looked well together, he had to admit. Suddenly all his heroics seemed a little flat. He looked around for Merlin.

Merlin wasn't far. He had been watching Arthur as he observed Gawain and Guinevere and had guessed what Arthur was thinking. He would certainly do nothing to disabuse Arthur of the idea. Merlin had not really looked at Guinevere for some time. He knew she had grown but was startled and worried by how mature her beauty was. He had hoped somehow that it would fade as she grew older. He shook his head. It was clear from one sight of her that she was as naive as ever. It would never do to let that one around his Arthur too much. She didn't belong. This idiocy of his about a marriage could only mean trouble.

Mark was hurried off to his old room and his own clothes were pulled from cedar chests for him to change into. Guenlian hated to have him out of her sight for an instant but resigned herself to it, only making him promise to bathe *quickly,* change, and come to her room before eating.

It was hard to bathe quickly with three years of filth to be scrubbed from one's body, but Mark dressed as fast as possible and, his heart constricting at the thought of having to face everyone, to explain, to retell all the horror, he left his room.

He nearly ran into Rhianna. She stepped back from him with a little gasp, then gave him her hand. The other hand was holding a small girlchild who stared at him with wide, familiar eyes.

It took Mark a moment to remember who she was. Then he gave the child a searching look, which caused her to hide her face in her mother's skirts. Then he held Rhianna's hand very gently. There was something about her that made people want to be gentle.

"I remember now. When Matthew came back from his leave, just before . . . He told me then. He said, 'I have given Rhianna Grandmother's ring. I never thought I would give it to anyone.' He told us to take care of you, if . . . anything happened. But he was happier then than I had ever seen him."

Rhianna smiled at him, a smile full of compassion and tenderness.

"Thank you," she said. "I'm glad you've come home."

They went together to Guenlian's sitting room, where, to Mark's relief, only a few people were gathered. After a few hearty slaps on the back and comments of pleasure on his return, Mark was even more relieved to know that no one planned on questioning him. Their minds were taken up by a message that had just come to Cador from Sidra. Guenlian only insisted that Mark sit on the same cushions with her so that she could have him always close enough to touch, should she need reassurance that he was truly alive.

Mark didn't pay any attention at first. He was back in the mire of his own misery. Then a name caught him by surprise and jolted him to awareness.

"Alswytha, what about her?"

"Oh, I'm sorry dear," Guenlian smoothed her hand through his hair. "I didn't mean to remind you of them. Sidra has just sent us a note. It seems that since Aelle broke his word and attacked us again, not to mention kidnapping your sister, it is now necessary that some sort of decision be made about what to do with this girl we have as hostage."

"Don't worry, son," Leodegrance patted his shoulder. "It's nothing to do with you. I suppose I must go to the council to keep them from being too vengeful."

"What do you mean?" Mark's voice was hard, but his father didn't notice.

"Well, now that the vow is broken, her life is certainly forfeit. I imagine we will have to execute her, but I will do my best to see that it is as painless as possible and that she isn't tortured first."

"What!" Guinevere and Mark spoke at once, but Mark's voice was louder.

"How can you talk so calmly of murdering her?"

Leodegrance tried to pacify him. "I don't want you to bother about such things on your first night home. It is unfortunate that this happened now. I will go with Cador and do what I can for the girl. You must not let yourself be concerned."

Mark gazed around the room as if everyone had suddenly gone mad. Arthur squirmed uncomfortably. Merlin and Cador just looked worried. Guinevere was the only one who seemed as horrified as he was.

"I am going with you," he stated.

There was no arguing with him, and, in the end, Guenlian and Guinevere insisted that they must go, too. Arthur and Merlin were already required to attend the council or trial, whichever it was to be. And, as the matter was serious and Mark refused to wait, they agreed to leave the next morning.

That night, Mark lay in his own bed for the first time in more than three years. He was clean and well fed. He was warm and no man's property. He was all the things he had never thought he would be again, but he could not sleep. Each time he drifted toward slumber, he felt again cool hands stroking his burning face.

CHAPTER SIXTEEN

$\mathcal{S}$idra met them in the courtyard.

"I'm glad you came so quickly," she told them, kissing her husband without missing a word. "Some of the men were for starting without you, not knowing if Guinevere could be recovered. They said that you would be too busy with her to bother about this and it wouldn't matter anyway whether she were safe or not, as the issue was the broken truce. Come in at once, never mind the horses. Your man can take care of them."

She gestured at Mark, who was again wrapped in his ragged cloak. He began gathering up the reins. Guenlian started to expostulate, but Leodegrance stopped her.

"Not now. We can explain later." His expression reminded her that it might be better if Mark were not present for the debate of the council.

"Guinevere, my dear," Sidra embraced her fondly. "I'm so glad that you are all right! I was worried until I heard of Gawain's plan and that Arthur was going to get you. Then I knew you would be back soon. Arthur hasn't failed at anything yet."

She led them all into the castle. It was late in the morning, two days after they had left the villa. Even with the spring sunshine outside it was dark within and chilly. The fire on the enormous hearth did little to dispel the gloom. It took some time for their eyes to adjust. First they only made out the forms of men, seated in a semicircle: the tribunal awaiting the prisoner. Then

216

Cador clenched his fists and strode to the man seated at the center.

"How is it, Colum, that you begin this meeting without us? And why are you seated in the place of honor? Are you the Dux Bellorum now, the leader of the armies of Britain? Under what authority do you convene this meeting without my permission?"

Cador was impressively angry, but Colum was too old and too powerful in his own right to be cowed, although he did relinquish the chair.

"This matter could not await your arrival, since we had no idea when that would be. It is a clear case of oath breaking, and the only question before us is how the girl should be punished so that her father and the other Saxon scum will not so trifle with us again. As the largest landholder present, I naturally presided. Now, however, I am happy to turn the matter over to you."

He moved to another chair with ponderous dignity.

Cador watched until he had settled himself. "Thank you, my Lord Colum. Normally, I would take the seat of honor in my own home, but today I feel that it is time to give it up to someone else, to a man who has earned it and who shall soon have the final decision in more cases than this. Arthur, the time is coming when this seat will be more familiar to you than the back of your warhorse is now. I would be honored if your rule of Britain would start here."

He stood behind the chair, waiting for Arthur to take his place.

Arthur swallowed hard. His eyes darted about the room in panic. He realized at once that the honor was barbed. He did not want to be the one to sentence Alswytha to death. Merlin moved within his range of sight and, almost imperceptibly, the older man nodded. With a sinking heart, Arthur sat in the seat of judgment.

Cador spoke again, in more normal tones. "My wife tells me that the girl has been sent for. Where is she?"

"I believe she wished to be formally dressed when she faced you," Sidra explained. "It seemed only fair. She should be down soon. Guinevere's maid, Risa, is with her."

Gawain sat at the other end of the hall in one of the many niches around the walls. It suddenly occurred to him that with everyone down here it would be a perfect time for him to slip upstairs with Risa. After all, no one had asked him to take part in this and for that he was grateful. It was not the sort of thing he enjoyed. So there was no reason why he shouldn't use the time for something better. He could almost feel Risa under him already. Then he saw them come into the hall. Risa was leading Alswytha gently, giving her an arm to lean on. When he caught the look of terror and despair on the Saxon girl's face, his desire for Risa crumpled.

Risa stayed next to Alswytha until they reached the center of the hall. A narrow strip of sunlight lay across the floor, having made its way through one of the lookout slits high overhead. Risa placed Alswytha so that the light shone directly on her. Then she gave the girl's hand a sympathetic squeeze and came over to the recess where Gawain watched. She sat next to him and took his hand. She gave him no other greeting.

Alswytha had dressed herself in her finest clothes. The swan cape came past her waist, and the light reflected off each of her golden ornaments. She made no attempt to soften her Saxon appearance, but faced her judges proudly.

"Merlin, speak to her," Arthur commanded. "Tell her what has happened and why she is before us now."

"I'm sure she already knows," Merlin answered, but he spoke a few words to her anyway. She nodded understanding.

Arthur sighed. He longed for a sword in his hands and a horde of bloodthirsty invaders to attack.

"The question before us is, what shall be done about this clear breach of faith and violation of an oath? This woman is bond for the good conduct of her father, Aelle. I have seen with my own eyes that Aelle has crossed into our territory, he has taken in Ecgfrith, who was also to be bond for him. And, worst of all, he kidnapped the Lady Guinevere, and, in doing so, has killed a number of good men who might one day have been leaders of our land. How can we ensure that this will not happen again?"

There was a silence. Then Leodegrance spoke up, his voice

sorrowful. "Her life is forfeit now. There is no other way. We can only do it as mercifully as possible."

"Here now," another lord interrupted. "What will that gain us? Aelle doesn't care what happens to her or he wouldn't have left her here. I say we send her back to him alive, but keep a few mementos for ourselves, her nose, say, or some fingers. Then he would know we mean business."

There was a murmur of approval for this. Guinevere listened in growing horror. Why didn't her father answer this? What was wrong with him?

Lord Stator of the south Welsh spoke now. "It seems more merciful to give her her life in exchange for a nose. And certainly, the knowledge that their children would be returned to them maimed would make those Saxons think again before turning them over to us on false promises. There would be no more broken vows if they knew their daughters would be returned to them in such a fashion."

How could they discuss this horrible thing so calmly, Guinevere wondered. Some of the lords were leaning back in their chairs, picking their teeth with their knives, and grinning at poor Alswytha. For a moment she forgot that Alswytha was Saxon, heathen and an enemy. She hated all those men with their ugly, leering faces. She almost hated her father for saying nothing to stop them. Only Arthur sat stiffly, his back not resting against his chair. His face showed nothing of his thoughts. Guinevere noticed that Merlin and her parents were not paying attention to Alswytha or to the other men. They were watching Arthur.

"You are too soft, Stator," Colum grunted. "Your lands haven't been overrun by these vermin. Your tenants haven't been killed and their daughters carried away by these . . ." he spat, not finding a word both strong enough for his feeling and speakable in the presence of ladies.

"That's true," another lord removed his knife from his mouth long enough to agree. "But I think she should be sent home alive. She should be able to tell them what happened to her. Why don't we just cut off her nose and little fingers and send her back to Aelle. But first," and he smiled as if well pleased with himself, "let the soldiers have her awhile."

The color left in Alswytha's face drained and her eyes rolled back in her head. As she fell, Guinevere screamed and rushed over to her. But Mark was there first. His cloak was off and he was dressed again as a nobleman. The scars across his face burned with fury. He caught the unconscious girl and wrapped her in his arms as he glared about the room. At first he was too angry to speak and all the lords just gaped at him. To their superstitious minds he might have just risen from the dead.

"You vile animals!" Mark finally whispered. The astonished silence was so complete that his hissed words sounded like shouting. "You will not touch her. Is this your city of reason, Arthur? Will you found your new world on innocent blood? Do you think anyone could make civilized men out of this base rabble? You are a dreamer and a fool and I want no part of anything you may try to do for them."

Alswytha moved in his arms and he lifted her face to his. Sidra was beside them now with a cup of wine which she held to the girl's lips. Her eyes flickered open and she gave a cry of joy as she saw Mark's face.

"Ceorl!" she sobbed, *"Me leofede Hlaford!"*

"Me leofede Wytha," Mark murmured, burying his face in her hair. He then rose and faced the assembly, but did not release her. She clung to him, unaware of the tears running down her face. Sidra gently took Guinevere back to her place.

"This is not for us to meddle in," she told her. "They must take care of it in their own way."

Guenlian gripped her husband's hand so tightly that her ring cut into his flesh.

"He is in love with her!" she whispered, her voice disbelieving and afraid.

Leodegrance nodded.

"But she . . . she's not even Christian!"

"Yes," he carefully disengaged her hand. "But Guenlian, we must not challenge him. We cannot lose him again."

Mark faced Arthur. His voice was still tight with anger. "What will you decide, Lord? I say that I have been more ill treated by the Saxon than any man here, and I claim this woman as retribution for my suffering. That is . . ."

He bent his face to Alswytha's and spoke so tenderly that Guenlian felt ashamed for listening.

"*Willest thu with me gerestan?*"

She smiled at him and answered in Latin, "I will stay with you or go with you anywhere, forever."

Arthur watched them. He felt a bitter pain at their obvious devotion to each other. He knew that it would be worse than murder to part them now. Why should he? It seemed such an easy and acceptable way out of his dilemma. But he feared that it would not satisfy all the lords, who wanted revenge. What could he do? He studied them. All of these men were for now secure upon their holdings. But they were in need of more wealth to rebuild what had been destroyed. Perhaps an appeal to their greed might induce them to relent.

"I agree that Lord Mark, son of Leodegrance, should have the right to purchase the hostage for his own use if he so wishes. I set the price of her release as the weight of my sword and my shield, in gold."

There was a burst of outrage from the men in the circle. Arthur raised his hand for silence. "I have not finished. It will be distributed among myself and the lords here for use in repairing damages caused by the invaders. Is that acceptable to you all?"

The lords were quiet, each one trying to compute his possible share. Arthur decided to take their silence as approval.

"Very well," he stated. "It is agreed. Mark, can you pay this amount for her?"

Leodegrance stood. "I will guarantee this sum of gold for my son. He shall have it from his share of my estate."

"No," Alswytha spoke for the first time to them all. "I can pay my own price. No one will say I had to be purchased. I come to him willingly."

She began fumbling with her brooches and the gold clasps on her braids. One by one, she pulled off her rings and bracelets, her arm bands and ankle clasps. She even laid her gold-leaf-covered shoes on the pile next to Arthur's shield. At last she stood barefoot, clad in her shift and cape, with a heavy heap of gold before her.

"I don't think that will be enough," Arthur said sadly. "You still have the weight of the sword to match."

Alswytha lifted the sword. It was steel and heavier than she thought. She thought a moment and then removed her cape, and placed it in Arthur's lap.

"This is worth more than all the gold before you," she said. "It was stitched from the feathers of a thousand swans for the marriage of my great-grandmother to the King of the Geats. There is not another one in the world."

Arthur stroked it. He had never felt anything so soft before. Before anyone could protest he consented. "Done. I take this for my share and the rest you may divide as you will. I suggest that you let Master Merlin help you make the division equal."

He dismissed the assembly simply by rising from his chair and turning his back on it. Merlin beamed approval of his protégé. Arthur was just glad that the whole thing was over. He wondered if Guinevere thought he had been too harsh or too lenient or if she had been watching him at all. He saw that she was with Alswytha and Mark. She was trying to wrap Alswytha in a spare blanket and Alswytha was explaining that she wasn't shivering from the cold. It was only the relief.

The formal meeting had dissolved into confusion. Everyone was talking at once. The lords were busy examining the gold and fighting over their shares and no longer paid any attention to Alswytha or Mark.

Leodegrance and Guenlian watched the commotion without interest. Their thoughts were on Mark and the bride he had apparently chosen.

"We have had him back only such a short time!" Guenlian protested.

"I am not sure we had him back at all, my love. Arthur has told me that Mark did not even wish to see us again, that he is so bitter that he hates everyone, not just those who hurt him. I have watched him constantly the little time he has been with us.

Arthur is right. He is disgusted with all men, with life itself. Who knows what it will take to make him want to join us again. We have seen men like that before, in the old days, when everything seemed to be crashing around us at once. That dinner when the Saxons invited all the great men of the realm and then slaughtered them. We were sick with grief and anger, but we didn't want to die, too. We fought back, even when our whole life was slipping away from us and all those of our elders whom we loved had been slain. But do you remember Lucius? He was a man of sanity and reason, one of the most brilliant scholars I have ever known. You remember what he did when he heard that Theodoric had taken Rome?"

Guenlian shuddered. "Poison in the wine glass. He couldn't bear to live with a barbarian in control of Rome. And dear, gentle Monica went mad when she heard her husband had died, and murdered her own children rather than let them grow up in such a world. Why do you remind me of this now? Mark would not do such a thing."

"I am not sure. I see them staring at me out of Mark's eyes. My poor son! He was always the dreamer, the one who believed. He was the only one who understood why he had to fight. Matthew was my grandfather again, never happy unless he was in some kind of conflict, and John—we named him well—was too loving to despair. But they died and Mark lived, and he has had all these years to ponder and brood on it. We must not oppose him in this, Guenlian, or he may leave us again, forever."

Guenlian knew that he was right. Leodegrance had always been a sure judge of their sons' minds. But to have this girl as her daughter-in-law! Always about, always reminding one of old wounds! Guenlian was not ready to cope with that, yet.

"But she is a heathen, Leodegrance. She must be baptized and instructed in the faith before they are married. You don't think Mark could object to that?"

"We must ask him, dearest. We might even ask her. She surprised everyone, I think, except Sidra, by knowing our language. Perhaps she will be more receptive to our way of life than we think."

"Perhaps," Guenlian sighed. "But whatever she does, she still cannot change her face."

Nevertheless, she resolved to be as kind to Alswytha as she could, and spoke hopefully that evening, when they were gathered in Guinevere's room, of returning soon to the villa and preparing a proper wedding.

Alswytha was upset by the suddenness with which her old family was taken from her forever and this new one supplied. At the council she had felt only relief and gratitude to Mark and joy at finding him again. She had had a confused idea of an idyllic life in a little wood hut, deep in the forest, just the two of them. It had never occurred to her that he might have a family, too. Now it seemed that they must be considered before she did anything. Mark was apparently related to every British family on the island. And this woman beside her, who rather frightened her, was proposing to invite all of them to see her married. Guinevere sat at her other side, listening and nodding as if it were all quite natural. Alswytha smiled and nodded and agreed with everything that was said, but she felt as if a giant cage were slowly being lowered over her head.

Her nervousness continued to grow over the next few days as she became more fully aware of Mark's place in his society. She had not paid much attention to the customs at the castle. There had not been much difference between the table manners of Cador and the ones of her own hall. She had not had much conversation with anyone except Guinevere and Geraldus. Now everyone wanted to speak with her. She found she was being treated with patronizing condescension by the women who had sneered at her before. She was touted as a heroine who was giving up heathen ways for the true religion. But from the way they carried on, she wasn't sure if the true religion was something one believed or something one did. Mark saw her panic but felt helpless. He longed simply to sweep her up and carry her away to that little hut in the woods, but logic told him that food and clothing must somehow be provided also, and that huts were very cold in the winter. In his life and hers, someone else had always done the providing. He needed a plan. And until he worked one out they would have to remain.

Arthur certainly sympathized with Mark's wish to be able to carry off his love and court her in some remote place, far from prying eyes and listening ears. Every sight he had of Guinevere convinced him that she was the only woman he wanted, that she would make a far better queen than he would a king, and that all he wanted was to tell her so and be married as soon as possible. But how could he do this when she was always surrounded by people? If she wasn't with her mother or the other women, then she was off somewhere laughing with Gawain or Geraldus. He realized now that neither one of them had any romantic notions about her, although how any man could keep from falling in love with her was beyond his understanding. He glumly forced himself to admit that he hadn't made the most of his chances, either. So much had happened since he had rescued her that he was almost afraid she had forgotten it. She hadn't mentioned the matter and he didn't see any way of bringing it up. The few times he had been close enough to her for speech, he had fumbled and stuttered like a schoolboy. In consequence, he was even more brusque and short with the lords and the soldiers who had come with him. He even fought with Cei, who was his closest companion and who never had an idea of his own without checking it with Arthur first.

Cei just gaped when Arthur berated him. Then he shook his head worriedly and left. This had gone on long enough. Soon afterwards, Cei ran into Merlin and demanded that he do something about the matter.

"What are you babbling about?" Merlin asked sharply.

"You know very well," Cei replied, flicking his fingers behind his back to ward off the curse in case Merlin was planning to strike him down for his impudence. "Arthur is in love with the daughter of Leodegrance. We can't see why it has gotten no further. There is nothing wrong with the match. Why don't you help him? Talk to her parents or something. Maybe you could have him save her from a dragon?"

Merlin gave him a glance of contempt. "I already did that,

if you recall, or as close as makes no difference. What makes you think it is such a good match?"

"Everyone says so," retorted Cei.

"Everyone? Just who has been discussing it?"

"There isn't a man of his lieutenants who doesn't know how he feels and doesn't wish him well. But he is acting like a fool and someone has to stop it before he loses their respect. So can't you just get him married so he can get his mind back on important matters?"

Merlin swore something that Cei didn't catch, but Cei's fingers moved even more frantically than before. He tried to edge away. Merlin did not seem to be paying him any attention now. He was lost in thought.

"Wait a minute!" Merlin's voice startled Cei, who sprang up about three feet. "You say that Arthur's men all know about this and approve of it? All right. I don't approve. I think it is an idiotic venture and that we all will live to regret it. But it seems that everyone, including Fate, is fighting me in this. I will do what I can to speed matters since it seems that this will happen anyway. From now on, however, you will keep your mouth shut about this."

"Yes, sir," Cei gulped, glad to find that he could open his mouth at all. He quickly made his escape, but not without a feeling of having fought a dragon himself, and won. He vented his excitement by running up and down all the steps in the castle, twice. It was only then that he could calmly go on with his work.

That night Merlin had a long talk with Leodegrance, after which Leodegrance had a long talk with Guenlian. The consequence was that they sent for Arthur to confer with them as they sat in the courtyard the following afternoon.

Spring had blown in gustily that week. The air was still chilly, but inciting, and something about the day was conducive to rash acts. Arthur tried to gain courage from deep breaths of the moist air as he hurried to the meeting. He had seen Guinevere that morning at breakfast, and she had smiled at him and inquired about his health in a tone that had set his heart pounding. He wondered if she had been told yet of his intentions. He was trying to consider what impression he should try to convey about himself to Leodegrance and Guenlian. He wanted desperately to be as elegant and assured as they, but had given that up as hopeless. He must somehow convince them that Guinevere would give up nothing in the way of comfort or care by marrying him. He wondered if he could make them believe how much and how truly he adored her.

He would have been deeply embarrassed to know how unnecessary the last worry was. His love for Guinevere was so obvious that the only person who hadn't noticed it was Guinevere herself.

"Well, young man," Leodegrance began in the tone used by all prospective fathers-in-law, "I understand that you wish to marry my daughter?"

"Yes, Sir," said Arthur, looking miserably at his hands.

"Can you tell us why we should approve of such an alliance?"

Arthur didn't look up and see the softening amusement of Leodegrance's expression. He only heard the question, and suddenly all the reasons why he shouldn't marry her came into his head.

"I know I'm only a crude soldier," he blurted. "I have little education, save what Merlin has given me. I don't know how to talk to fine people or to use a napkin. I am only really comfortable and at ease in a camp, preparing for battle and surrounded by those like myself. I am clumsy and my foster brother, Cei, says that I snore. I don't even have a family name to give her. I have come from nowhere and am no one."

He sank ever lower in his seat as he recited his defects. The hopelessness of it crushed him.

When he finished, Guenlian turned to Merlin. There were sparks of anger in her eyes.

"You haven't even told him about his family yet?" she complained. "When is this perfect time you said you were waiting for, your deathbed?"

"What do you mean?" Arthur sat up again.

"My dear Arthur," she said forcefully. "I really don't think that any of your dreadful flaws are an impediment to marriage.

If Guinevere is upset, she can show you how to use a napkin. This business of your family, however, is another matter. My cousin apparently doesn't think the time is right to tell you the names of your parents. I can't imagine why. You have certainly proved yourself in every way a successor worthy of your father and far more able to mold this poor battered island into a civilized country again. It is cruel for you to be allowed to think you are worthless. Your family is certainly as old and as respected as Guinevere's. You need not worry about that. What I want to know is, one: do you love her enough to take care of her and protect her no matter what happens? and two: how does she feel about you?"

Arthur tried to stammer an answer to her questions but he felt as if someone had just picked him up by the heels and thrown him into a whirlwind.

"Merlin, what is she saying? Who was my father?"

Merlin gritted his teeth. What *this* would lead to, he couldn't guess. Was nothing to be left in his hands?

"Arthur, I said I would tell you someday. You may as well know it all now. You are the son of Uther Pendragon and his queen, Igraine. If you feel that you need a legitimate right of inheritance to rule the Britons, there it is. But I wanted you to take the crown on your own merit, without resting on anyone's name or earlier conquests. Uther was obeyed but not loved. Guenlian is right when she says that you will do a far better job than he did. The matter at hand, however, is Guinevere. Do you still want to marry her, now that you do not need the grandeur of her name to bolster your authority?"

"What an insane question! Of course I want her. It is I who was not worthy of her. I love her so much I am afraid even to speak to her lest I frighten her by shouting out my feelings too soon."

Leodegrance gave the boy a look almost of pity. "That is something you must overcome soon. I take it, then, that you haven't told her anything. No? Well, we will do that for you now. If she is willing, I can see no objection. Can you, my dear?"

Guenlian's smile almost blinded him. "I can think of nothing to keep this man from joining our family, if that is what he wishes. I do think that you gentlemen should discuss her dowry, in case Arthur is not satisfied with the little we can offer. I'll not have it said that our daughter could not bring something to her marriage appropriate to her husband's position. Now, if you like, I will go and speak to Guinevere. If you will excuse me?"

Arthur was fast losing his capacity for clear and decisive thinking. His head seemed to be stuffed with some foggy, blue substance, and stars and comets were flashing through his brain. He vaguely knew that Merlin and Leodegrance were haggling over certain parcels of land and an amount of coins but it was some time before he bothered to attend to them.

"I don't want any land. I have the site for my city already chosen. It's a fine hill near Glastonbury Tor. Guinevere doesn't need a dowry. There is nothing you have more precious than she is. But, if we must have something, all she need bring is the table you have hidden in the cave under your home."

"What!" Leodegrance tensed his jaw. "How do you know about that? No one is supposed to know anything about it!"

"Matthew told me, long ago. He didn't know much. It is perfectly round and will seat a hundred men or more. There are words carved on it but Matthew never had enough light to decipher them. There is supposed to be some sort of magic connected with it. It is very old and no one knows how it was put there or where it came from."

"I put it in there," Merlin said in a tired voice, "and it came from Uther, at least most recently. The last time he ever took my advice was when I told him it was too dangerous to have it about."

"What do you want it for?" Leodegrance waved off Merlin's protestations.

"I want a symbol for my new society, something exclusive and yet open to all equally, if they can earn a place. Ever since I heard of this table, it has drawn me. I think it is what I was looking for."

"I see," Leodegrance rubbed his chin thoughtfully. "It may be that you are indeed the one that I was to save it for. I must consider this."

And, without further conversation, he strode off into the darkness of the castle. Arthur looked at Merlin.

"I suppose you are angry with me?" he sighed.

"No, I am resigned to anything now. But it does appear that I have a great deal to tell you. Come with me."

And they wandered down the narrow path to the beach and were not seen again until evening.

CHAPTER SEVENTEEN

uenlian found her daughter alone in her room. She was sitting balanced in the narrow casement, staring out to sea. Guenlian came up to Guinevere gently and touched her shoulder. Guinevere started and slipped from her perch back to the floor.

"You startled me, Mother. I didn't hear you come in."

"I could see that. Lost in daydreams?"

Guinevere shrugged evasively. "Not exactly," she hedged.

"She's slipping away again," Guenlian worried to herself. "Marriage would be a good thing for her. She lives too much in another world."

"Come sit with me, darling. I want to speak with you about something important."

Guinevere felt a thrill of apprehension. She couldn't remember anything terrible that she had done lately, but her mother's tone was so serious that she felt sure she was about to be reprimanded for something and braced to explain herself for whatever it was. So she was a little bewildered by Guenlian's question.

"What do you think of Arthur, dear?"

"Arthur?"

"Yes. You wanted to meet him for years and now you have. What do you think of him?"

Guinevere mused for a moment.

"He's different," she said at last. "He always moves as if he knows just where he is going and the best way to get there. He got Mark to come with us, when I couldn't even make him talk to me. I think I like him. But he doesn't seem to care for me very much."

"He doesn't? Why ever do you think that?"

"He won't talk with me. Every time I see him, he just mumbles and slides away. Do you think I offended him? Perhaps I didn't thank him properly for saving my life. Or maybe he just doesn't feel I would be very interesting to discuss things with. I'm not very well informed on what is happening, the way Sidra is."

"You may be correct, Guinevere. But that isn't the impression I got from him this afternoon. Far from being offended by you, this man appears to be very much in love with you. He has asked your father and me to arrange a marriage between you, if it pleases you."

"A what?"

"He wants to marry you, my dearest child. How do you feel about that?" Guenlian watched her carefully. It suddenly occurred to her that, unlike other girls her age, Guinevere had never considered marrying anyone.

Guinevere was quiet. At first she only felt numb and then cold and a little frightened. She tried to imagine marriage. Her parents liked it well enough. It would be nice to have someone to share things with, to talk to every day, someone who loved her. Then she remembered Gawain and Risa. Her stomach turned. Could she do that? She didn't see how. Yet Risa liked it very well. It was clear that it didn't worry Alswytha. You could see that every time she and Mark were together. One almost felt embarrassed watching them look at each other. It was so totally private. She wondered if she could feel that strongly about Arthur.

"I don't know him, Mother!" she blurted. She tried to picture Arthur again in her mind and only got a vague impression of strength and excitement.

"Do you want to know him?"

"Yes, I think I do." Guinevere's answer surprised herself.

"Then you must make him speak to you. He is only shy of you because he cares for you so much. Let him tell you about himself and his plans. He has many grand dreams, not only for you and for himself but for all of Britain. If you married him, you know, you would likely become queen."

If she had hoped that would impress Guinevere, she was mistaken. The information seemed to surprise her and then she laughed.

"How very odd!"

"Shall I tell him that you wish to see him?"

"If I am going to marry him, I would like to do that first," she replied, without a trace of humor.

Within an hour everyone at the castle had heard the news that Guinevere was engaged to Arthur. Her room was crowded with people fluttering around her with good wishes and obsequious comments that she didn't understand. Although she had not made up her mind at all, so many people told her the matter was settled that she began to believe it was.

It was not until after dinner that she finally had the chance to talk with Arthur.

For the first time, she really studied him. He was tall and strong and handsome in the clean, chiseled Roman fashion. His normally pale skin had been tanned and roughened by weather and years of campaigning. His tousled red hair had probably once also been lighter, but the same forces had deepened it to a rich auburn. His hands, she noticed with satisfaction, were large and yet finely made, with long, tapering fingers. She thought of her own stubby fingers and wondered, inconsequentially, if their children could hope to inherit his.

She stood watching him so long that he flushed with embarrassment and gave her a look of such pure devotion that she smiled at him tenderly.

"If I am going to be your wife, Arthur, you really must stand closer to me," she admonished him.

"Are you?" Arthur stuttered, "I m—mean, will you?"

"Everyone says so," she answered. "Are you certain you want me?"

"Am I certain!" he shouted and then made an effort to modulate his voice. "I've wanted nothing else since I first saw you. I will be so good to you, I promise. There is so much we can do together. We can make Britain a real country again. We will build a beautiful palace and everyone in the land will flock to our court just to gaze at you."

"What a strange thing for them to do. I'm sure I could arrange some better entertainment."

"Of course, anything you like," Arthur responded. If she had suggested that he travel to Africa for a performing elephant, he would have picked up his sword and gone without a word.

Timidly, he reached out his hand and touched her cheek. His fingers were rough, like fresh leather, but curiously gentle. She smiled again and whispered, "I think I will enjoy being married to you."

Arthur suddenly felt as if the whole world had been laid out before him. He knew without doubt that he could create a civilization grander than any the world had ever known. He could build cities more glorious than Rome or Jerusalem. He could defeat any foe and then convert them so thoroughly that they would serve him with devotion. The lightness in his head almost convinced him that he could fly.

Guinevere thought only, "There is something very nice about him. He makes me want to do something for him, like remind him to wear his cloak when it rains."

Since there were no clouds in the sky, Guinevere settled for reminding him that it was time to eat and suggested that they join the others in the dining hall.

Arthur thought it the most wonderful idea he had ever heard, and they went happily in to be greeted by cheers and congratulations from everyone there.

The next day Mark drew her aside and surprised her by giving her a hearty kiss.

"Thank you, Guinevere. I know you will be very happy and now, maybe, I will be, too," he grinned, the unscarred side of his face looking almost like himself again.

"Mark, what are you talking about?"

"Little sister, I could kiss you!"

"You already did. Please explain what is going on."

"Don't you see? Your nuptials are far more important and

welcome than mine. Mother and Father and all those people will stop tormenting us and concentrate on their plans for you. Poor Alswytha has been worn out by all this nonsense, especially about her being baptized and our living back at the villa and all that. She never wanted it and neither do I."

"Mark! Do you mean you would marry her without her becoming a Christian? That's dreadful!"

"Oh it is? Being a Christian wouldn't make her one iota different than she is now. It wouldn't make her kinder or more gentle or more loving. Why should I care which god she believes in?"

"But what about eternity?"

"We have already lived through eternity. Alswytha and I have each done our time in hell. I have no fears about that."

"I don't understand all you are saying, but perhaps you are right. But if you don't plan to marry and live with Father and Mother, what will you do?"

Mark took her face between his hands. "If everyone in the world were like you, my precious, I might stay here and live contentedly. But since that is not the case, I am taking Alswytha away, to the most remote haven I can find. Somewhere quiet and peaceful and empty where I need never see another weapon or hear another scream of pain."

Guinevere pulled from his grasp. He had unconsciously tightened his hands on her jaw and pressed until he hurt her. He dropped his arms with a guilty start. "There. I could even hurt you. That is yet another reason why I must remove myself from this place. There is still so much anger and hatred within me. I could not stay, as Arthur does, and deal with fools. He is a good man, Guinevere. He would never hurt you as I just did."

"Of course not!" Guinevere was shocked at the thought.

"That is why he is the one to continue this governance. He has the patience to rebuild, brick upon brick, until he achieves his purpose. I do not. If I stay here another day, I may just go mad."

His voice was so quiet that she almost missed the last word, but the ferocity was obvious. She had thought that she might find her brother again, but now she knew that if he still existed it would take years to find him beneath the layers of bitterness and pain.

"But how will you live, Mark? You know nothing of planting or building. You can't just wander away to some cave to live. Even the hermits and saints keep bees or gather whelks or something to survive."

"I know that. But I will learn. I know an excellent teacher. It just amazes me that I didn't think of it sooner. We could have been away days ago."

"All right," Guinevere gave in. "If you must go, then do. But couldn't you and Alswytha wait until after I am married. I want you to be there. Please!"

He chewed the corner of his lip, considering. "I heard someone say that it wouldn't be until winter."

She nodded. "The calends of January, Mother thinks. There is so much to be done first. People to contact, provisions to order, the ceremony to arrange. It's really very exciting."

He shuddered. "I can't stay here until then. Wait! This is what we will do. We can go find the teacher I told you of and stay there until the time comes. Guinevere, I want to leave as soon as possible, without questions or explanations. Will you help? Can you tell Alswytha to make a bundle of her things and then tomorrow morning will you lower them down to us? We will be in the courtyard, below your window."

"Yes, if you wish. But won't you tell me where you are going?"

"Don't worry. I promise we will be back to see you wed. If you must contact me, ask Geraldus to send a message. He will know how."

So, early the next morning, a bleary-eyed Guinevere let down a small bundle of clothes and combs, mostly her own, for Alswytha. Below, in the courtyard, the couple waited. Mark carefully untied the bundle, hitched Alswytha on his horse, and prepared to go.

"Tell Father I will leave the horse at the farm of Risa's family. I want nothing that is not my own," Mark hissed up at her. "Thank you, my dearest sister. We promise to return. Don't worry."

They both waved up at her with such radiant smiles that she felt certain that they were doing the right thing. She absently wondered where they were going that they wouldn't need a horse, but she was really too sleepy to care. She stumbled back to her own warm bed and burrowed down into the covers.

She was not so sure about what she had done later that morning when Geraldus told her that her parents wanted to see them both immediately.

"Guinevere, how could you let them go like this?" Guenlian protested. "And you, Geraldus. You tell us that you knew about Mark's plans. What were you thinking of not to tell us, then? Are we monsters that we would try to keep our son prisoner?"

She wept angrily as she tried to chastise them.

Leodegrance intervened. "Never mind, my dear. We just want to know why they felt they needed to sneak away from us. We thought we had done everything possible to make Mark happy. We accepted the girl, difficult though it was. We asked nothing of him."

"We were going to give them such lovely things at their wedding." Guenlian sniffed. She was still fighting tears. She felt such a fool.

Geraldus didn't know how to begin. He loved Leodegrance and Guenlian almost as if he were one of their own. He understood how they felt. But he understood even more how Mark felt. It was peculiar how the most astute people could be so blind regarding their own children. He remembered his own parents. They still didn't understand why he roamed about the country instead of settling in with some pleasant religious community.

"Mark is not the same man he was even a few years ago," he began gently. "He can't forget any of his scars. Every time he blinks his eyes, every time he moves his mouth, he feels the pulling of the twisted skin. Each time it reminds him of the deeper wounds, which will not heal. Even before he was captured, Mark was near to breaking. And then, it was all too much for him.

You are lucky that he found Alswytha. She is all that is keeping him from madness."

"We know that," Leodegrance said. "That is why we tried to be so careful with him, to agree with his wishes, even to take his Saxon bride into our home. No matter what it cost us."

Guinevere put her arms around her mother. "But he didn't want that. He told me. He only wanted peace and solitude and no memories. Alswytha wanted that, also, not just for him, but for herself, I think," she added, with one of her rare perceptions. "I think she is as beaten as he. Mother, they did promise to come back to see me wed."

Guenlian twisted her hands uncontrollably. "I don't understand. I was so close to him. I love him so. How could he have changed like this?"

There was no answer to give her, but Guinevere tried to be reassuring. "He still loves us, Mother. Please don't cry. Perhaps when he returns, things will be better."

Guinevere fought a kind of panic, much as she had felt on that horrible night when she had known that her brothers were dead. Her mother was her source of strength, a firm, cool, calm center in spite of all chaos whirling about them. Guinevere could not bear to see her trembling so, fighting tears and anger. When Guenlian spoke again, there was a bitterness in her voice that no one had ever heard before.

"Never mind, Guinevere. We will continue with our plans for your wedding, if you do not object. You might care to remember, in your extreme sympathy, Geraldus, that Mark is not the only person who has had much to withstand. I will talk of this no more."

She stalked away from them. Leodegrance watched her go and then, with a strangled cry, buried his face in his hands.

Guinevere gently patted his shoulder, but he pushed her away. "Not now, daughter. Leave me alone!"

She turned to Geraldus, for some clue as to what to do next, but he only raised his hands in defeat. Finally, as Leodegrance did not lift his head or give any indication that he knew they were there, Geraldus gently led Guinevere away.

Out in the courtyard, they came upon Gawain, practicing his standing spear thrusts. He was tearing a pile of leather and pillows to ribbons. He stopped when he saw them and hurried over.

"Is it true that you are to marry Arthur?" he panted.

"Everyone tells me so," she assented.

"Then you must speak to him about my joining him. He said something before, but I think he has forgotten. Then I could see you all the time. We could still play chess and sing and . . . go riding together. Tell me you will speak with him, please?"

"If you want me to, Gawain, but why can't you do it yourself? You're the one who knows all the reasons why you are so wonderful. I can never remember the technical terms for all that swordplay and your other maneuvers."

"Guinevere, I can't just go up to him and say, 'Here I am, the greatest fighter in the world.'"

"Why not? You say it to everyone else." Guinevere asked this in honest surprise, but Gawain thought it a very funny riposte. So did Geraldus. Guinevere tried to divert Geraldus to another topic.

"Have you heard that Arthur has finally learned of his parentage? Merlin has told him that he is the son of Uther Pendragon and Igraine, his wife. Isn't that strange? Everyone thought they had no children."

Gawain was certainly diverted. He grabbed her arm roughly. "Are you sure about that?" he demanded.

"Of course, let me go! Arthur told me himself. He wanted me to know, for some reason, that his ancestry was as good as mine."

"But Guinevere, don't you remember? Igraine was my grandmother! If Arthur is her son, then we are relations. Let me see. Good Lord! He would be my uncle. Guinevere, you are going to be my aunt!"

"That's not funny, Gawain. It's ridiculous. You are a year older than I am. How could I be your aunt?"

"You don't know my family. Arthur is only eight or nine years older than I am. So what?" Gawain chortled. "Now he must let me join him. I have bloodright."

He pranced around in delight, waving his spear at a dangerous angle.

"This can't be true!" Guinevere insisted to Geraldus.

"It seems logical to me," Geraldus replied. "Igraine's daughters from her first marriage were almost grown when she married Uther."

"Gawain, stop that! You nearly hit my ear. All right. I believe you and I will speak to Arthur. But if you ever call me 'Auntie Guin,' I will personally expel you from the court. Do you understand?"

Gawain dropped the weapon and swung Guinevere around a few times instead.

"I promise, oh, aunt-to-be. But you must see Arthur at once, today, now. I will not wait any longer."

Guinevere sighed. "Yes, if it will appease you. I think he is in a conference with Merlin and Cador now, but as soon as I see him, I will tell him all about you."

Gawain gave her a loud kiss on the cheek and, retrieving his spear, danced off again to further damage his practice target.

Guinevere found Arthur a little later. He greeted her with shy friendliness, as if he were still not sure that she would like him. She told him first of what Mark had done and was relieved that he agreed with her that it was right to let them go.

"Old Aelle must have been demented to send someone like Alswytha as hostage. I knew from the moment I took charge of her that she was too delicate to be treated so. They may never be able to live with other people again. I'm sorry, though; I needed him."

This reminded Guinevere of Gawain's request, and she explained it to Arthur along with the relationship, which she thought would amuse him. She was startled, though, when Arthur rudely interrupted her.

"What is Gawain's mother's name?"

"Morgan, wife of King Lot. She is the daughter of your mother from her first marriage. Isn't that correct? She would be your half-sister and Gawain your nephew." She stopped. His face had gone white. "Arthur, what is the matter? Where are you going?"

"Merlin!" he called over his shoulder. "I must find Merlin!"

Guinevere sat for a time, trying to understand what had just happened. But she could find no answer. She hoped he didn't do this often. It could be very disconcerting in a husband.

Arthur found Merlin easily. He was relaxing by the hearth and chatting with Sidra and Cador. He had a cup of wine and was beginning to think that things might, after all, turn out nearly as he had planned when Arthur descended upon him and dragged him away without even greeting Cador. Merlin was about to scold, but Arthur gave him no chance.

"Why didn't you tell me Morgan Le Fay was my sister?" he whispered fiercely.

"Morgan. Yes she is. What of it? You need not have anything to do with her, although I suppose we must invite her to this wedding of yours. I will put her on the list."

"What of it? I don't want to have anything more to do with her. Why did you have to keep me so ignorant? Do you remember the year we wintered in Cornwall and you left me with those hermits?"

"Yes, of course. You were about sixteen then."

"Morgan fancied herself as patroness of the group. She often visited us in the afternoon when most of the holy men were at prayers or meditation."

"Oh, my God!" Merlin seemed to shrink inside his robes. "Don't tell me any more. I've known her far too long. No, don't make excuses. Everyone knows Morgan. If anyone is to blame, I am, for not taking her into consideration. That woman! She was almost twice your age then. She is disgusting. No sense of propriety!"

"But Merlin, it was incest!"

"Yes, I know. An old Roman custom also, but not one likely to be revived today. Have you seen her since then?"

Arthur shook his head emphatically.

"Then try to forget it. You acted in ignorance and certainly no one who has ever dealt with Morgan would censure you. She may have forgotten the incident, herself. You were nothing to her then. It may have been a dull winter. Now calm yourself and return to your betrothed. You seem to have left her rather abruptly."

Arthur was somewhat reassured and hurried back to excuse himself to Guinevere, but Merlin's peace of mind was shattered. He knew Morgan Le Fay too well to think she would fail to remember Arthur. He also knew the twisted bitterness she felt against Uther and himself. This wasn't the end of the matter, he was sure. He returned to the fire and automatically poured some more wine.

"Dear Lord," he prayed, although to whom he wasn't sure. "Can't you make something happen between now and the calends of January?"

Spring was in radiant form two weeks later as a man and a woman slowly climbed the narrow path through the forest. They did not seem fatigued by the walk, only not very interested in quickly getting to their destination. To them the world was a rainbow of green, gold, brown, and blue. A delicate mist seemed to float around them. The natural elements were doing their best to measure up to the high opinion the couple had of them, but at the stage they had reached, raging winds and hail wouldn't have worried them greatly. Alswytha and Mark had found their haven in each other and knew that nothing could ever harm them again.

"Would you rather have waited for a proper marriage?" Mark asked.

"Would the words of any man make me more or less your wife than I am now?" Alswytha replied smiling.

"I can think of no ceremony that would not seem a sacrilege to my love for you. It is so far beyond anything mortal man could hope to know."

Alswytha knew that, but she enjoyed listening to him say so.

"Would you like me to learn to read?" she asked.

"If you wish it. Would you like me to learn to fly?"

"It might entertain our children."

"Very well. I will start crafting wings tomorrow."

They were so intent upon each other that they almost missed the clearing altogether, and only the deep sound of laughter caused them to stop and notice that they had reached their destination.

"Do you intend to pass your old friend by, Mark, simply because you have something better to look at?" Timon's voice boomed. "Or will you stay a while and introduce me to your wife?"

Mark was pleased to see that Alswytha was not intimidated by Timon's size. Her slender hand was so pale and fragile in his rough brown paw. But she held it tightly and greeted him with soft pleasure.

"You must be Alswytha," Timon grinned. "A lovely name. I've often heard the trees sing it in the evening. So, you have come to visit us. Wonderful! We always have room for guests. I haven't had help with the planting since Guinevere stayed with us. Will you stay that long? Perhaps you could even stay with us through the fall and help me brew the mead?"

"If you will have us," Alswytha answered, not at all surprised that he knew her name. A man like this must know the secret names of the stars.

"Since you are so well informed," Mark added, "you must already have heard of my sister's betrothal to Arthur."

"I have," Timon grinned tauntingly. "And Gaia and I are even considering attending this event. There has been nothing interesting enough to get me from this mountain for over twenty years, but that may be something worth seeing. But now, I have kept you standing here talking after your long walk. You must have a wash and some food. Gaia is out gathering mushrooms now for our dinner. She will be happy to see you both."

He lowered his voice, as if she were near enough to overhear.

"Try not to notice how she has aged. We have not seen Nennius for two years now, and word has come that he may have been lost at sea. Another wanderer told us that Nennius had some very rare old manuscript from Egypt that he wanted copied by some Irish scribes. There is such turmoil in Gaul now, what with the Franks practically controlling the entire country, that he decided to sail through the pillars of Hercules and return by the Atlantic. There has been no word of him since."

"But I always thought Gaia hated him!" Mark said.

Timon looked at him in wry amusement. "If she had hated him," he replied, "she probably would have married him years ago. But then I would have had to find something else to do with my life not nearly so pleasant as living up here. Please don't mention this. I only told you so that you will be prepared for her and not mind her so much."

They promised to be considerate of Gaia and, having gotten that off his mind, Timon proceeded to make them comfortable. It was well that they had been warned, for on Gaia's return the gaunt sorrow on her face would have shocked them otherwise. As it was, they showed no surprise and spent the evening conversing politely about other matters and making plans for their visit. Timon offered them a corner of the hut to sleep in but Mark said they would rather lie under the stars since the night was so mild. He did not wish to inconvenience them. Timon smiled with understanding and gave them several thick woolen coverlets and a sort of mattress stuffed with wild herbs and grasses. They took these a little distance from the hut and made up their bed.

Much later, Alswytha lay watching the moon rise through the trees. She assumed that Mark was asleep, but he rose on one elbow and put his other arm around her.

"What are you thinking of?" he murmured tenderly.

She turned in his arm to embrace him but then playfully pushed him away. "For the moment, not of you. I was worrying about that poor woman in there. I cannot understand how she could purposely destroy her own happiness."

"I have known her all my life, but it has never been clear to me either."

"She wants me to be baptized in your religion. But I do not see how I could accept a faith that could cause such sorrow."

"The sorrow is of her own making, Wytha, my love. God

had nothing to do with it. But you do not need to become a Christian. I have told you that before. There is nothing in you that would deny you entrance to heaven, I am certain. And I want nothing greater to believe in than what I have before me now."

She drew him back close to her and felt the warmth of his breath upon her neck. All her life she had heard that the forest night was full of wild beasts and horrible ghouls. The earth itself was a constant battle between forces, none of them caring about the humans involved. But at last she knew that these stories were lies, only fireside tales for children and fools. There would be no more battles for her. Even death could not frighten her. Alswytha had found her place in the universe and there was a still, clear feeling inside her which assured her that she would never be an exile again.

Chapter Eighteen

$\mathbf{A}$s the months passed and January approached, it became clear to everyone that this was not simply to be a marriage ceremony, or even a union of two houses. It was a political event; a social phenomenon; a rebirth of society. Guinevere, fortunately, had no private plans or wishes about the matter, and so all arrangements were handled by her elders. Only occasionally was she told about the progress of events, when it was necessary to remind her of what she was to say or do. She didn't care. She had no idea of exactly how much preparation and fuss was going on.

The family remained at Cador for a time. The spot on the Saxon shore was better for sending messages and organizing a wide variety of people. Guenlian threw herself into the planning with a grim intensity, hoping to forget her disappointment in Mark. It had been agreed that the best place for the nuptials was London. It had not been damaged by Saxon raids. There was a small but thriving community and a church. It was accessible not only to those coming from all over Britain but to those returning from Armorica.

This last group delighted Arthur so much that he was reconciled to his wedding becoming a national event. Leodegrance had sent messengers to various families who had emigrated long before, telling them of the new order and requesting them to return for the festivities and to help rebuild Britain into what it once had been. The news came at exactly the right moment for the homesick Britons. The tribes of the Franks had, in the past few years, overrun all of the northern part of Gaul. Trade had fallen off and many of the younger members of the families were becoming disenchanted with their self-imposed exile. Each day brought word that another group was returning, at least to survey their old estates and decide if it would be feasible to settle there again. Those who didn't wish to see Britain again were eagerly sending younger sons and nephews who had no land of their own and were willing to start again in the abandoned homesteads. Here was the sort of manpower Arthur had dreamed of; educated people who knew the old ways and would accept the old authority. He could hardly wait. His head was so full of plans that he took to wandering about the countryside, talking to anyone who would listen about the new society he would give them. He couldn't stand being kept in the castle, doing nothing. When he was back there, he paced the floors like a caged lion.

Only Guinevere could calm him. Just looking at her made him feel peaceful and comforted. She radiated serenity and he bathed in the quiet of it. Each evening he was there he sat with her and told her, again and again, of every intricate detail. First the roads would be rebuilt, then the towns could be linked and trade would grow and then government could be established, all of it answerable to and centered at Camelot.

"Camelot? Where is that? What a strange name. Isn't it a kind of cloth?"

"No, that's what I mean to call my new city. It isn't built yet, but we will do it together, you and I. I want you to advise me on everything. I've found just where it should be, near Glastonbury. There is a high, level hill. There is plenty of room for buildings and shops there but the whole thing will rise above the plain."

"Glastonbury? Isn't it rather marshy there? The damp air is not good for the chest, you know."

"A bit," he admitted. "But Merlin has a plan of draining some of the swampy areas and planting grain. Also, it's a very defensible place. Of course, I don't want it ever to need defending, but I still tend to see things from a military viewpoint."

"That's very sensible of you," she assured him. "I shall feel quite safe there."

One day he surprised her with a large package. It was a wooden box wrapped in oilcloth and leather to keep it dry. On the cover were strange designs that she couldn't decipher. With difficulty she pried the lid off. There was more oilcloth inside. She carefully unwrapped it and then stared in wonder at what she had revealed.

"Oh, Arthur," she breathed.

"Is it all right?" he asked worriedly. "I sent for it myself, months ago. I didn't tell anyone for I was afraid it wouldn't arrive. If it's not what you want, I will send it back. I just wanted so much to have something to give you myself."

"I have never seen anything so beautiful," she said. She slipped her hands under the rich material and held it up to catch the light. It was a thick silk of midnight blue, threaded with strands of pure gold. Beneath it in the box was another bolt of white silk, thinner and stronger than anything she had ever worn.

She just held it for a moment in wonder. Then she threw her arms around him. It was the first time she had done so of her own accord.

"How did you ever think of it? Not a woman in Britain will have a dress so fine! I was so afraid I would shame you by having to be married in rough, faded robes. Thank you, Arthur! You are so good to me!"

She scooped up the box and ran to show her mother, leaving Arthur groping in the air for her. But in his life he had learned patience and he reminded himself that after the calends of January he would be able to hold her all he wished.

A few days later, another messenger came to the castle. He told Sidra that he had come all the way from Gaul with a present for the Lady Guinevere and had been charged with powerful oaths to deliver it to no one else.

When Guinevere arrived, the man studied her closely before he would give over his package.

"Yes, you must be the one. His description couldn't fit another woman," he finally decided.

Guinevere laughed. "Who was this person who can picture me so well?"

She held out her hand for the gift.

The man drew forth a small packet from a hidden pocket in his cloak.

"He wouldn't tell me his name," he explained. "It was at a court in the east of Armorica that I met him. He was some sort of man at arms for the household of this lord, although his rank may have been higher. He seemed to have some reputation as a horseman. I delivered my invitation to the lord of the place, as was my mission. They were not interested. They have a good life there. But as I was preparing to leave, this man came up to me and gave me this, charging me to deliver it to the Lady Guinevere and no other. I have kept my word."

Guinevere took the small package. She couldn't imagine who could send her a gift from so far away. "What did this man look like?"

"Oh, I thought I told you. Well, if I had been home, I'd have said that he was one of the oldest people. Small and dark but very strong, and with that glow in their eyes that they've got, sort of like a cat."

Guinevere quickly ripped off the outer layers of cloth and found a small hard object, wrapped in parchment. She unrolled it and out dropped a pearl, perfectly pear-shaped and of the most lustrous sheen. She held it in her palm, fearing it might magically vanish. She knew who must have sent it, but couldn't believe it was possible. Then she noticed that there was writing on the parchment. Still carefully cradling the pearl in her hand she smoothed the parchment out on her lap. There, in large, painstaking letters were the words "Caet Pretani." How could it be? How did Caet get so far from home, and who had taught him to write his name? Even more, how could he have come by such a rare and beautiful gift? Yet there it lay, like a frozen tear. Guinevere finally remembered the messenger.

"Do you remember the place where this man lived?" she asked.

"Of course," he replied scornfully. "Would you like me to return there for you?"

"Yes. Don't worry, I will pay you well. He must know that I have received this. You must take this to him." She pulled a few strands from her hair, bound them with thread and wrapped them again in the cloth. "There. Now he will know that it came to me. Tell him that I have no other way to thank him for this treasure, but if he should ever return, I would be terribly hurt if he did not come to see me."

Guinevere had the pearl set on a gold chain to wear with the robes sewn from Arthur's gift. Sidra disapproved.

"There is something strange about this. Even if he was raised in your house, he was only a stable boy, hardly a companion of yours. And they say that the old ones have never given up their struggle to drive us from this land. Perhaps there is some spell attached to it. Pearls are for grief, they say."

"I don't believe you," Guinevere insisted. "Caet only sent me this to remember him by. It is beautiful and I will wear it, if Arthur agrees."

"Arthur would agree to anything you say just now," Sidra sniffed.

"I don't remember Caet well," Arthur said when she showed him her present. "I only was with him on the trip we took with Mark. He didn't say much then. But he was with us when we saw the vision of the Holy Mother. She wouldn't reveal herself to anyone evil. I see no reason why Guinevere should not wear it."

The day finally came when they set out for London. It was late autumn again, with bone-chilling rains and thick mud. But everyone was well wrapped, and the route had been planned to require only a few hours' travel every day, with stops at various villas and small towns. The company would be excellent, for people from all over the entire country were slowly converging upon London. As Arthur and Guinevere's caravan approached the town, the roads became crowded with people of all classes. This marriage was an event to tell one's grandchildren about and no one was going to miss it.

Geraldus and old Plotinus lumbered along, both draped in dozens of blankets. The singers flitted beside them, still clad only in their thin robes despite the raw weather. He confided to Guinevere that they had been practicing an epithalamium in her honor, and he only hoped it would be better by the day of the wedding.

"I simply can't manage the tenors," he mourned. "They never would listen to me."

Gawain was so muffled up that only his nose was visible, but he was cheerful, too.

"Arthur has promised me that on the day of your marriage, he will make me a knight of the Round Table," he gloated.

"What is that?" Geraldus wanted to know.

"Oh, something he has invented. I'm not too sure of it, myself, but he assures me it is something very important. He was most impressive when he told me about it. I am greatly honored. Are you sure we will only be traveling until early afternoon? I'm freezing."

"Probably not even that long, if this weather continues." Geraldus shivered.

Before they left Cador, Guinevere had gone down to the beach for one last meeting with her unicorn.

"You have neglected me recently," he chided her.

"I know. I am sorry. There was so much to do, so many people demanding my time that I couldn't get away to you. But after this wedding is over, I will have time again. Won't you come with me to London? Then, as soon as all the people are gone, we can have a lovely walk."

"A wedding?" his eyes whirled in thought. "I do not know this word, but it frightens me. What is it?"

"It is nothing bad. It only means that I will have a husband. It doesn't matter, though. I will still love you as I always have."

He shook his mane and salt water splashed across her face. "I do not know what is wrong. I am very tired and I feel that something important is about to happen to me. I cannot understand it, but I see myself in a small garden surrounded by walls. It is very cold and everything in the garden has died. Do you think that it is London?"

"I don't know. I have never been there. You are very cold now." She drew away from him, puzzled.

They were silent while the world spun them closer to their fate. At last the unicorn spoke again.

"I think I will see you in London."

She didn't notice the grief and exhaustion in his words, and so she left him with a light heart, certain that she would soon be with him again.

The last few days before the ceremony were a blur to Guinevere. Much later, she was to remember a bewildering crush of people everywhere she went, all trying to say something to her. Some of them had such strange accents that she could barely understand them. Guenlian seemed to know everyone and was always greeting someone with a cry of joy and insisting that they be introduced to Guinevere. Arthur was always busy with these strange people too, and barely saw her. Even at dinner, he was kept busy talking to someone far down the table from them. He was aware of it, at least, and promised her in a husky whisper that it would soon be over and he would never leave her again. She smiled and told him that would be nice.

The day itself was awesome in its pageantry. The only thing that stood out in her mind before the actual ceremony was Gawain wishing her happiness and in the next breath crying out: "Oh no! Mother has come. I never thought she would be here."

Guinevere followed his pointing finger and saw a middle-aged lady, rather plump and dressed much too gaudily. She was not the siren Guinevere had expected. With her was a boy of twelve or so. He was very striking. His skin was so pale that it was almost a translucent blue and his hair was a mop of red as bright as Arthur's once must have been.

"Gracious," she commented. "Is that one of your brothers?"

"Oh yes, that's Modred. He's the youngest. I haven't seen the others but they must be about. I've often wondered about his father. He's as odd-looking as I am."

But Guinevere at that moment passed on to other wellwishers and soon forgot about her sister-in-law to be.

In order to provide as much entertainment as possible, a long processional started the proceedings, and then various speeches and sermons ensued. But at the heart of it there was a brief moment when Arthur and Guinevere stood alone upon the dais, and suddenly the crowded church was soundless. The candles sparkled in the winter mist around their heads and more than one person wondered if he ought to kneel before them.

Guenlian had a sharp pang as she watched. She felt as if Guinevere were about to go through a door into a world where she couldn't follow. She wanted to call her baby back, to stop everything and rush her home in her arms, safe and protected forever. She was ashamed to find that she was crying.

Guinevere gazed down into the hundreds of faces. Each one held an individual secret for her and she wondered what they were thinking about all this. Far on the edge she noticed one man towering over the others. She caught his eye and he smiled encouragingly, gesturing to show that he had brought Mark and Alswytha with him, as promised. Then the priest muttered something and Guinevere faced Arthur. He slid a ring on her finger and repeated the priest's words, and then she recited what she had been taught. Then she was looking into Arthur's eyes and he was kissing her. There was wild cheering, which was ineffectually hushed by the priest, and she was somehow conveyed out into the streets where even more people cheered and called out blessings on her. Through all the tumult, Guinevere suddenly heard singing. It was the most beautiful music she had ever heard, full of hope and joy and certainty. She looked around and around for the source and finally saw that it was Geraldus. He was directing his chorus, which was floating above his head. He had a seraphic smile on his face, and for once the whole chorus was standing together and singing in tune, for her. Nothing that had happened so far had affected Guinevere so much.

"Thank you all," she whispered, sure that they would hear her. "The angels must envy such music." At this they all smiled from ear to ear without missing a note. Their voices remained with her until the procession reached the home where she and Arthur would spend the night.

They were left at the door, with speeches and laughter. Then everyone went away to leave them to themselves, and to finish their own celebrating.

Arthur led Guinevere up a narrow staircase to a beautiful room. The floors and walls were covered with warm hangings and carpets. There was a small fire in the brazier and a supper had been left for them. The bed was covered with fine linen and furs and her night dress lay on top.

Guinevere took her husband's hand and smiled at him. They

were both suddenly very shy. It occurred to Arthur that this was the first time since he had met her that he and Guinevere had really been alone. He was seized by sudden panic. What if he held her too tightly and she broke in his arms? She was like a clear porcelain to his touch. It would be so easy to harm her.

"Shall we eat?" she asked politely.

She seated herself at the small table and began dishing out the meat and gravy. "I don't know what the custom is for men, but they wouldn't let me have anything to eat or drink today and I'm starving. Do you want some?"

He forced himself to sit across from her and choke down some food. It had grown dark by the time they had finished. Guinevere was looking nervously at her nightdress. For a few minutes she drew designs in the gravy remaining in her bowl. Finally, she set down her spoon, stood, and walked around the table to Arthur. She gulped once or twice and fumbled with the catch on her belt as he watched stupidly.

"It's not that I don't know about this," she explained, twisting a lock of her hair around her finger. "Mother finally told me yesterday and of course, Risa . . . It's just that I'm rather unsure about it. Don't you think we could just talk for a few days until we feel more comfortable?"

Understanding was dawning in Arthur's eyes. "Oh, Guinevere! I'm sorry. I didn't think of how you might feel. I wouldn't hurt you, truly. You know how much I love you."

"Oh yes," she answered eagerly. "And I do want to be your wife. It's only . . . not quite so. . . . I'm just . . ."

She trailed off.

"My beautiful, precious Guinevere. I promise that after to-night I won't even touch your hand until you tell me I may . . . but, tonight. . . . The marriage must be consummated tonight or everyone will know it wasn't, or worse yet, believe you are . . ."

"Must!" she cried, "But why? What difference does it make? I thought you understood!"

"I do!" He felt horrible, almost sick. "But we have to. They will come for the sheets in the morning."

"They will what? But that's barbaric!"

"No, it isn't. It's an old Roman custom. I thought you knew."

Guinevere sat back down. "No, no one told me about that. Are you sure?"

He nodded. "I'm so sorry."

"I know you are. Well," she took a deep breath. "If there is nothing else to be done, I might as well start learning how to be your wife now."

With a swift, determined movement, she unpinned her blue surcoat and laid it carefully across the clothes chest. She then took off her shoes and began unpinning her shift. She paused as Arthur watched, dumbfounded, and then she blew out the lamp. By the light of the brazier, she finished undressing.

When he realized what she was doing, Arthur quickly removed his formal garments, too. He was glad that she couldn't see him clearly in the dark. He was terrified that she would find him repulsive.

When he had finished, he stood still in the middle of the room, not sure what to do. Then a voice called from the bed.

"Arthur, you will freeze out there. Don't you want to lie here with me?" said a pathetic little voice. "I'm rather nervous, Arthur. Please be careful."

"Oh, I will be," he vowed. "I could never hurt you."

He slid into the bed beside her and tried to touch her gently. But she was so frightened and his desire and inexperience were so great that he hurt her very much. She screamed once and then bit her lip, horrified that someone might have overheard.

In the end, though, it was he who cried in shame and sorrow and she who comforted him with caresses.

"It's not your fault. I didn't know what to do. Never mind. I will learn. We have time. I intend to be your wife for many years."

But he could not be comforted and only clung to her, murmuring apologies until he fell asleep.

When she was sure that he was not going to waken, she slipped from his grasp and got up. She washed herself carefully and put on the nightdress, which had fallen to the floor. She didn't want to return to bed immediately. Quietly, she wandered about the room, stopping at last at the tiny window. It had no glass, but wooden shutters. She opened them a crack.

The moon shone down on a small walled garden. The plants were all brown and bedraggled from the winter rains and the tiny fruit trees were bare. In the middle of it stood her unicorn.

"I didn't feel you there!" she said in surprise.

"I know," he replied, his voice thick with resignation. "The time has come."

"What do you mean?" A chill swept over her as she remembered Rhianna's bitter cry, "He won't stay for me. Only a virgin can tame a unicorn!"

"But you are my unicorn!" she sobbed. "It can't matter that I am no longer a maid."

He gazed up at her with pleading eyes. "I am your unicorn. That will always be. But I have lived too long already. The time has come for a new unicorn to be born."

"Then take me with you!" she pleaded. She stretched her arms down to him.

"That is not the way. I have told you this before. I have only come to say farewell to you and to let you know that the memory of you will be forever in the mind of the unicorn kind. All who come after me will dream of finding someone like you. Please do not cry for me. We could not be together now as we were before and I would be so lonely without you. This is not the world I was meant to stay in. Let me go now to search for my place."

She could not answer but she held out her hands to him. He reached his head up and she felt his hot breath against her fingers. Then she turned away and knew he was leaving. She felt a vibration within her body as of music played so high that it cannot be heard by human ears. It grew until she could no longer bear it and then she felt a shattering of something in her heart, like crystal smashing on a stone.

She must have wept for a long time, for the moon had moved when she looked up again. She felt drained of more than tears. Something in her life was gone and she blindly groped for something to replace it. Her eyes fell on Arthur.

Asleep, he was much younger-looking than his twenty-eight

years. His hair fell over his forehead and he was snoring gently. Guinevere studied him for some time.

"There is something very dear about him," she decided at last. "I think I could learn to love him. At least, I will try."

She shivered in the chill air and closed the shutter. There was nothing outside any longer to interest her. Slowly she crossed the room and climbed back into bed beside her husband.